MW00560947

SUMMER OF HATE

SEMIOTEXT(E) NATIVE AGENTS SERIES

Copyright © 2012 Chris Kraus

Published by Semiotext(e)
2007 Wilshire Blvd., Suite 427, Los Angeles, CA 90057
www.semiotexte.com

Special thanks to Amanda Atkins, Kim Dower, Marc Lowenthal and Sarah Wang.

Cover Photography by Marcela Rico, *The way I remember the sea*, 2009.
Back Cover Photography by Daniel Marlos
Design by Hedi El Kholti

ISBN: 978-1-58435-113-9
Distributed by The MIT Press, Cambridge, Mass. and London, England
Printed in the United States of America
10 9 8 7 6 5 4 3 2

SUMMER OF HATE

Chris Kraus

How can a poor person matter in this world? Rising, out of an uneducated environment, bearing the resentment of his parents toward all he meets and resting upon a religion that fosters guilt and repression, where in what hope may he escape?

— John Wieners
After Dinner on Pinckney Street

1

CATT: HER KILLER

THERE ARE SOME PEOPLE who seek out the illusion they've arrived at the end of the earth. The opacity of an alien place: an open and desolate feeling.

Catt Dunlop stands outside her room at the Villa Vitta motel. A slight western breeze off the Gulf flavors the morning with promise—a promise Catt knows will seem like a distant memory in the harsh glare of 11 a.m. She's wearing the same clothes she dropped on the floor after arriving last night—an old pair of jeans and a cardigan sweater—her "Mexico" clothes, not that these clothes are especially ethnic. When she's in Mexico she puts on whatever clothing she pulls first out of her bag. Her childless middle-aged body is still lank, which has so far spared her the effort of devising a "look." Catt left LA in a rush. Her long, tangled brown hair is pulled off her face with a sweatband she found in the gym bag she forgot to unload from the back of her new Subaru Outback.

The rooms at the Villa Vitta are set behind stucco arches under an awning that offers two feet of shade. In front of the parking lot, there's a badly paved two-lane road and beyond that, a blue strip of ocean.

Looking down the cement colonnade, Catt sees she isn't alone. Outside number 10 there's a plastic lawn chair and a cooler of beer in front of a new Ford F-150 truck with Oregon plates. She and her small spaniel mutt Stretch are in room number 8. Otherwise, the motel is empty. It's a Tuesday morning in March, 2005, and she finds it unlikely this neighbor is here on vacation. He must be working. Even though the town doesn't exactly look ripe for development, he could be some kind of construction surveyor, which means he'll be gone most of the day.

Catt feels somewhat safe and relieved. Since throwing her gym bag into the car yesterday morning, she's put more than six hundred miles between herself and the person who, she believes, has threatened to kill her. The person is male, but even now, after spending nearly a decade revising her default androgyny through the pursuit of recreational sex, Catt rarely focused on gender. Her killer identified this as one of her problems. The killer, "my killer," as she'd begun saying, would be driving an older black BMW sedan that luckily seemed not very well suited to Baja's back roads.

"Is that a threat or a promise?" Catt vaguely remembers this comeback used by neighborhood kids in the blue-collar Connecticut town she partly grew up in. She doesn't remember much of this culture, having spent most of her life trying to flee it. But sometimes, when she's in trouble, odd phrases drift back. There was also "Tom Tit," a description of her twelve-year old chest that followed her down the seventh grade hallways, and "My ass your face," the boys' rejoinder whenever she took out a Kool cigarette and asked one of them for a match.

Three and a half decades and several continents later, Catt no longer smokes on a regular basis but she still has small tits, "the kind of tits that will hold up 'til she's sixty," as a colleague of hers once appreciatively wrote in *Details* or *Index* or *Nylon* about Charlotte Rampling. But yes: Catt's problem, she knew, was that she'd seen her killer's threat as a welcoming promise. She was tired of running the show, she didn't know how else to stop. The death she imagined was preceded by pleasure, a dreamy trance ending in blackness. It hadn't occurred to her that the moments preceding this death—which, had she not fled, would be happening this week at an off-season Acapulco resort—would involve any actual pain, any stabbing or gunfire. The hotel would be pretty. She and her killer would check into a one-bedroom suite with sliding glass doors opening onto a balcony. She pictured herself at the fake Regency desk, feet sunk deep into white carpet, her hand invisibly led by his gaze, signing papers transferring her real estate holdings into the name of her killer.

Within a week of their first meeting, which took place at Chateau Marmont, her killer had said, "I want you to surrender control of your finances to me." The idea had shocked her at first, but in a good way. As an action, it seemed liberating. Who would say such a thing, and who would agree?

After leaving Michel, her two-decades older, not-quite-ex husband, in New York to start a new life in LA, Catt had begun a career as a cultural critic. Given her wide range of tastes and lack of any degrees, the idea of supporting herself that way was a joke. So in her spare time, she'd turned her shrewdness and charm towards investing in real estate. It was the late 1990s and the city was full of foreclosures. Walking the desolate streets near downtown LA, she found it hard to believe that nobody wanted these stately old buildings, with their cavernous bed-rooms and endless oak floors. In New York she would have traded her soul to live in such an apartment. Presenting herself as an affable amateur while part of her brain ran the numbers, she coaxed the bank's brokers into accepting her low-ball cash bids. *It was a game.* The money meant nothing. Money was an abstraction. A child of the deconstructionist '80s, Catt's guiding belief was in chance, process, and flux. Once set into motion, the game played itself. And it worked. Setting her sights on achievable goals and living modestly, she no longer had to beg and compete for adjunct teaching jobs. She could do as she pleased. So why, in the dead of night, when her brain finally slowed down, was she so troubled? "The bill always comes due," a rock & roll colleague once cautioned when she explained her penchant for recreational sex. And she'd never believed this, because really what was the debt?

Before their first meeting, her killer—whose real name was Nicholas Cohen—established some rules: a classic BDSM pro-tocol. She was not to ask questions. She was not to cover her legs with stockings or tights in His presence. She would give a truthful account of her response to all His commands after obeying. She'd assented with glee, because how can you play a game without rules? But it was cold that night and walking into the Chateau Marmont lounge bar, the long skirt and boots she'd worn to comply with his No Tights demand made her feel woefully overdressed. Bright boys and girls wearing gym shorts and pajamas—the hotel's actual guests—were draped on sofas and cushions in front of the Spanish Colonial fireplace.

Wearing a black Nehru-collared Armani jacket over a pair of pleated brown slacks, her killer was overdressed, also. Clearly the

Chateau had changed, her killer remarked, since he'd "inked deals" in these rooms in the '80s. The air-quotes he placed around these dated expressions led Catt to surmise that his inspired purchase of rights to *Bewitched* and *Gilligan's Island*— actually, half the *Nick at Night* playlist—during the first years of cable TV was merely a stop on a longer entrepreneurial highway. Deprived of the right to ask questions, Catt's mind leapt into motion. And that was nice. But the jacket: When was the last Return of the Nehru? Did his jacket date all the way back to the early '90s?

Her killer was tall, trim, and well preserved in that LA way for his age, which she guessed to be in his mid-fifties. The child of two Polish Jews, he told her his name was Nicholas Cohen. But what struck her most was his face: too fluid for someone his age, it was "unformed," as Michel might say. After ordering drinks, there was nowhere to sit except the freezing, unheated terrace. The restaurant was jammed and her killer had not thought to make reservations. He decided they'd leave. Catt's car was in the garage. She'd grudgingly given the valet a twenty—fifteen dollars for parking, and a five-dollar tip. "Wait here," her killer instructed. Muttering something about dings, not trusting valets to park his rare BMW, he disappeared up the hill where he'd parked on a side street for free. When her killer's black car finally appeared, she tailed him half a mile east to a strip mall café where he ordered two glasses of cheap Pinot Grigio.

Legs crossed under her ugly, long skirt, Catt held her breath when he paid the check with his Amex. Would it come back declined? She was already frightened for him. Because over the drinks, a strange psychic transference took place. While her killer recited the highlights of his entrepreneurial life, she saw him see her unhappiness. She felt it leaving her body and entering his, through his eyes. After flipping the cable TV rights for a fortune, he'd devoted himself to scientific research and invention. Soon after that, he filed original patents for the remote keyless car entry device and purchased a house in Benedict Canyon. Secluded in Beverly Hills, he'd trained himself as a neurobiologist. Further genetic research had led to his invention of Novanex, a miracle cure for the symptoms of aging. *Not a drug but a compound*, the substance was now in its first round of clinical trials in Beverly Hills and Long Island. Trained as a classical pianist, in his spare time he'd composed, performed and recorded a three-disc album of electronic music, which would soon be released on his Halcyon label. Buzzed with excitement, Catt's imagination circled the room while she held onto her wine glass. Free of the hard grip of ambition, her killer's voice was at once aloof and intensely present, as if he'd entered a realm where abstraction was painfully visceral. He was *all mind*. Catt didn't share this condition, but as she sensed it, the air between them grew heavy. He saw her seeing. They were joined in a double helix. Minutes after this recognition took place, her killer's right eye started to twitch. The twitch was a dance that went on too long. Overloaded with content, his face was a physical mirror for her psychic malaise, and this was painful. She didn't know where to look.

She'd seen him several more times after this. She knew then she had to protect him. Each time he wore the same clothes and his right eye twitched.

Still. Whenever she thought about signing her deeds over to him, she pictured her corpse on the floor of the Acapulco resort suite. At first, Michel and her friends would reject the bland, noncommittal report filed on the scene by the Mexican coroner. She imagined the private investigator they'd hire, the clues leading nowhere, the judicial gray zones of crimes committed on foreign soil, not prosecutable, anomalies wherever they turned. Enterprise thrived on anomalies. Eventually these efforts would fizzle. Michel and her friends were artists and college professors. Rationalists all, they were not the type to seek closure. After one or two trips they'd conclude that none of these costly efforts would succeed in bringing her back. The investigator's retainer would not be replenished; he'd return to New York or LA and her case would grow cold. Doubt, the existential disease of the twentieth century, would trump narrative.

But since Catt was more realist than fabulist, she knew that her actual death at the hands of her killer would be something much slower. It would be a classical feminine death, like a marriage. But the process would be highly compressed, her disintegration achieved in one or two months. She saw her descent: money rapidly spent and as it dwindled, her killer growing bored of her submission. Her dumb animal state would become oppressive to him. She would end up on the floor, not as a corpse but on her hands and knees, hollowed out, begging and lost. What frightened her most was that even this realist death held a certain appeal. There was nothing petty about it. It was a *grand mal*. It offered a knowledge she would not otherwise have, which at the time, seemed like the same thing as pleasure.

Raised by meek, working-class parents, Catt despised all forms of groveling. Since leaving Michel, she'd built an artistic career based mostly on nerve. Having no talent for making shit up, she simply reported her thoughts—an enterprise that seemed, to her, squarely within a tradition espoused by Michel and his friends, philosophers who held endowed chairs at elite universities, and traveled the world. And to a certain extent she'd succeeded, but as a female whose thoughts arrived mostly through the delirium of daily life. She saw no boundaries between feeling and thought, sex and philosophy. Hence, her writing was read almost exclusively in the art world, where she attracted a small core of devoted fans: Asperger's boys, girls who'd been hospitalized for mental illness, assistant professors who would not be receiving their tenure, lap dancers, cutters, and whores.

With the small fortune she'd made buying buildings, Catt no longer depended on institutions for her support. She came to see herself as Moll Flanders, outsourcing her visiting professorships and writing commissions to younger artists and fans. Since her work was mostly perceived as a novelty act or dirty joke, the only value she saw in her name was how it might be used to help younger people whose work she believed in. But lately she'd reached a point where these same young people were blogging against her, exposing the cottage industry she ran out of her Los Angeles compound ... the compound they'd stayed in rent-free after arriving from Iowa City, Toronto, and Auckland. Loathing all institutions, Catt had become one herself. Even her dentist asked her for money.

When Catt met her killer, she was beginning to wonder whether her shrewdness and charm had, in fact, served her. She was a rock being used as a whetstone for vultures: people who took and gave nothing. So her killer's idea that she "surrender control of her finances" struck Catt as brilliantly Zen and profound. Even a slow death at his hands would be better than the death she'd inflicted herself. At least, he was putting himself on the line.

Since giving her killer the twitch, she'd spent several weeks within this delirium. But when he asked her to travel with him to Acapulco, she came to her senses, woke up and fled. Once on the road, to her horror, her left eye—the one that had been opposite his—started twitching.

She didn't realize it then, but she'll spend the next several years trying to decode what she has come to define as her death wish. In search of a structure, she'll enter psychoanalysis, as if retracing events in the past leading up to the day she met her killer might show her where this death wish began. *There is a recurring belief that certain decisions were made while we were still lost in the womb of our childhoods,* Catt wrote in her notebook while she was still on the road. *Transactions were brokered in windowless rooms. Armies of people speaking in bland west coast American accents. Audiotapes washed up at a yard sale. Always, the real story was elsewhere. Las Vegas, Nevada. Phoenix and Tempe. What were the voices describing? A box of instructional manuals found, water-stained, in an old man's garage. Proliferation of data surpassed proliferation of nuclear warheads. Old metal, junked electronics. Dictation equipment. Deposing as testament. The sloppiness of all this. Political porn.* This is the kind of thing Catt gets paid to write about visual art. She does her "best" work zoning out and writing down words that seem to be draped on the surface of things. She has no idea what they mean. She is trying to place more faith in narrative.

Arriving well after dark, Catt chose the Villa Vitta over the town's other motel, the Casa del Sol, because it was familiar … she'd stayed there a decade before with Michel. Not much has changed since then except for the manager: an ex-San Diegan with Baywatch looks who introduced himself as Raoul. While she exchanged her thirty-five dollars cash for the number 8 room key, Raoul explained he was "new to the hospitality industry." In his late twenties, he also mentioned he was single. It was his first week on the job but he already had plans to upgrade the motel, maybe add a spa and turn the grotto-like restaurant into a disco. Before coming down, he had a tech job installing phones.

A single, bare, low-wattage bulb hung over the desk. The town generator up on the hill wouldn't shut down until ten. Catt wondered what misdemeanor or felony had brought Raoul here. INS problems, custody, drugs, failure to pay child support? She wondered what group of investors owned the motel and how Raoul found them. The movement of money being the most obvious forensic trace in any psycho-geography.

Trained as a journalist, she'd rather know things than not and could not stop herself—even while fleeing her probable death— from finding Raoul's story *interesting*, less for what he said than for what she surmised he left out. And so she remained alert, asking appropriate questions and feigning an interest until some item of real interest took hold. This alertness, she knew, was precisely the thing her killer had promised to help her renounce. If she'd followed her killer, if she'd signed over the money to him instead of *moving* the money to the under-tapped market in Albuquerque where it would double within sixty days, he would have spared her the effort of summoning up this bright curiosity over and over again, which carries her, ever more tired, through most of her days.

Around nine a.m. the morning sun still hangs over the Sea of Cortez. Catt has a Mexican cell phone but it doesn't work in this town, halfway down Baja at the end of an unpaved desert road.

The timing couldn't be worse: With four deals set to close, this is precisely the week she needs to be on the phone. After the giddy conceit that she would "surrender control of her assets" turned into an actual *plan* in which she would purchase a disused resort for her killer to use as a medical spa, she woke up and turned things around.

"When I decided not to give my money away, I figured I might as well make more," she'll say two years later to her psychoanalyst in what her not-quite-ex husband Michel calls her money-voice. By then it would be the height of the SoCal real estate boom, and the dumpy Victorville twelve-plex she'd picked up in '03 for $300K would be worth almost $2 million dollars. Anyone with any sense knew this boom wouldn't last. There was nothing there to sustain it.

The analyst, who uses only *one* voice on the rare occasions she speaks, will look at Catt blankly, her silence a challenge. The analyst's Mar Vista home office, shared with her husband and eight-year-old son was purchased exclusively through forty-five minute, $200 sessions like this. "But," Catt would continue, "there's no point trading apples for apples. You've gotta sell at the peak and then pick a market that hasn't maxed out."

Cranked up on profits, investors were unloading their assets without a plan. Forced by the tax code to reinvest profits within forty-five days, they were desperate to buy, but too lazy to get on a plane. Catt's broker suggested she try Las Vegas or Phoenix. But these were abhorrent Republican strongholds. Instead she picked Albuquerque, because she knew some kids there who published a 'zine about underground film.

And now, just several weeks later, the deals on three buildings she'd found there were almost ready to close. She needs to find a way to reach the brokers. She also needs coffee, and maybe something to eat. Calling Stretch back in the room, she leaves it unlocked and walks into town.

At first glance, the town hasn't changed much since she came here with Michel. The same wrought-iron gazebo benches in the *zocalo*, the fence around the primary school made from brightly painted old tires dug into the ground. As well-meaning travelers and veterans of leftist youth groups, they'd been charmed by the well-tended park and the freshly built, sturdy school in the midst of the town's otherwise pervasive poverty. While Mexico was by no means a socialist state, they felt more affinity to the cultural values of practically any third-world place than their own. They'd driven down to the town on a whim at the advice of two goat-hippies they'd met camping near their getaway place in Campo La Jolla, a glorified trailer park on the bay just south of Ensenada. Catt and Michel hadn't been camping. They were merely exploring, the thing they did best. Every so often they'd rally themselves out of their conjugal misery and take little trips. At these times, their hopelessness faded—things became newly vivid and they saw the world through fresh eyes. It was a gentle delirium.

Alone, Catt can't seem to access the town's former charm. She needs a strong cup of coffee. She can't find a phone. The pharmacy's old-fashioned, long-distance phone cubicles have been replaced by calling-card phones in the street, but these are all trashed. Walking back to the Villa Vitta to pick up her car, she meets the Oregon neighbor from room number 10 pulling something out of his truck bed.

The guy's name is Dino. White, with a broad chest, he's roughly Catt's age and looks like an old hippie but with a slight scheming edge. He's wearing a short-sleeved button-down shirt instead of a t-shirt, leading Catt to conclude he's here on some kind of business.

"Well," Dino says, "so you're the new neighbor," and offers her something to drink. "I heard you come in last night before lights-out." There's an ice chest of beer and a thermos of coffee beside the lawn chair outside his door. Catt takes the coffee, which is delicious and sweet. "Lourdes, the day girl at the desk, fixes me up when she comes in at eight," he says. Evidently he's been here long enough to establish routines.

Reaching into the shadows behind his screen door, he pulls out a second lawn chair. Sitting under the awning, Catt gratefully ingests the coffee while her eyes adjust to the shade. As Dino recounts the recent events of his life, they check out each other's vehicles, surveying the sexual possibilities of the situation. He's in town to set up a clam-farming operation offshore, but there have been problems. Six weeks ago he hired a team of unemployed local fishermen-divers to survey where to sink pylons. He's paying them by the week but this morning one of the three district police came by and shut down the operation. Something about documentation, heavy equipment, importation. There's a vaguely ecological, community-based cast to this aqua-cultural project, involving the creation of jobs, although he stops short of using the word *sustainable*. He speaks no Spanish, which seems, somewhat, odd?

Given the soft boastful way Dino proffers these facts, Catt concludes he'd rather fuck her than not, for lack of anything better to do. He mentions something about an ex-wife, as if marital status would be a factor. Thinking ahead, Catt pictures them sweating on the room number 10 bed. A peripheral image within the circle of wide possibility, the idea is not very appealing. Meanwhile his Seattle partner has stopped taking his calls after learning the Ensenada factory they purchased for practically nothing last month may not have been legally owned by its Japanese sellers. Bank trusts, attorneys. Catt recalls a cartoon from her childhood. Was it Mr. Magoo? A little man talking about clams when he really meant dollars. "That'll be one hundred clams." But then again, wasn't clam also a slang word for pussy? "Ah yes," Catt intones. "There's a large Japanese community in Ensenada, they say the migration dates back to the Great Abalone Shortage of the 1920s." Sensing the sexual case has already closed in her mind, Dino starts talking about his fifteen-year-old son who lives with his mom. "Great kid," he says. "Just made the high school varsity team." Etcetera.

Dino's not very smart. Catt wonders where he got his money. Later, she'll walk back into town and when she returns, Dino will be drinking beers on the porch with another American who looks like his twin. For the rest of the time Catt stays in the town Dino will be hanging around. They won't speak again. Whatever his business here might be, it doesn't concern her.

Did Catt Dunlop really believe that Nicholas Cohen was trying to kill her?

Novanex: Age management therapeutics for a new generation of health care. "It isn't a drug," he'd insisted gravely to her. "It's a compound."

But reversing the symptoms of aging was never the interest they shared. What each of them sought was delirium. In

November (or was it December?) guiltily trawling a BDSM dating site, Catt typed "Delirious" as her username. Elsewhere on the site, Nicholas Cohen (aka "Dominant Realm") was using that word to describe his soon-to-be-released electronic music CDs on Halcyon Records.

And now, hiding out at the Villa Vitta motel, Catt *is* delirious. The game is no longer a fantasy. Events have no more substance than clouds. She can't remember which ones transpired between them telepathically, which ones in the world, or if there was a difference. But somehow they'd led to the phone call last week, when her killer proposed driving down to her getaway place in Campo La Jolla—where she was hard at work on an art catalogue essay—to seal their Master/slave pact. From there, they'd drive up to the Tijuana airport and catch a plane to Acapulco, where she'd advise him on a real estate purchase. At some point she'd come close to agreeing to everything. At some other point—after researching her killer online—she'd changed her mind and started working on deals without saying a word. By then, she was terrified.

In her delirium, Catt is convinced that Nicholas Cohen may have surveilled her online investigation of him. Not to track her location—he'd already been to her house in LA, they'd had several dates there—but to know what she knew: to gauge, keystroke by keystroke, the depth of her suspicion, the way she'd cross-referenced each of the facts of his life that turned out to be lies. Her biggest mistake had been to access his Novanex site at the internet café two miles from Campo La Jolla. Was the site monitoring every hit, tracking the IP address to the local server? Probably. How long would it take him to hack into Prodigy Mexico? She'd emailed him on the dial up at

Campo La Jolla, keeping things vague, saying she'd be in touch later on. And then when he'd called—did she really give him her number?—with the Acapulco proposal, she'd said, *Let me think about this*, because she'd been too frightened by then to decline.

The public records she'd found online revealed two charges of spousal battery filed and then abruptly withdrawn by a woman named Daniella Koreli. This entry appeared *after* the numerous entries concerning fraud litigation in which he appeared as the plaintiff, but *before* the civil suits filed against him by his own attorneys for non-payment of fees.

Knowing she was out of her league, Catt enlisted the help of her friend Bettina, a former investigative reporter who now worked for a business espionage bureau. After combing through several classified databases, Bettina concluded, "This is a really bad guy." Liens on the Benedict Canyon house, which he'd sold for $3.6 million dollars ten months ago, suggested bad debts. Because after the sale, these proceeds had been swiftly disbursed through a chain of now-defunct LLCs whose Israeli principals, Bettina found out, were active in organized crime. Six weeks after that, Daniella Koreli had "sold" him her Verdugo Hills house for one dollar, which he'd proceeded to flip, but since it was heavily mortgaged, he made only $150,000 on that sale. Deploying all of her bureau's resources, Bettina could not find a trace of where this money had gone.

Catt imagined her killer hunted and angry. Even though she'd never given him directions to the La Jolla getaway place, she imagined her killer's black BMW gliding past the old drunk asleep in the guard shack under his poncho in the light of a black and white transistor TV. The car would come to a smooth quiet stop outside her house, #53D, it would be around ten thirty at night and this time she pictured actual violence, physical pain, maybe a knife.

Midday heat drives Catt out of the room. With Stretch curled up by her side, she cruises the town's only paved street. Finally she stops at a fish taco stand under a giant palapa. It's a nice place: A tall bamboo bar, square tables covered with the same retro-Mexican oilskin cloths patterned with tropical fruits they sell by the yard in Los Feliz gift stores. A young girl takes her order and a woman—her mother?—prepares a fish taco. Suddenly Catt is no longer hungry, but she doesn't want to be rude. Forcing down bites, she wonders if the woman has modeled her restaurant on the third-world themed cafes that have sprung up in hip neighborhoods throughout the US. There's a TV over the counter, the daughter keeps flipping the channels—the same four hundred twenty-six channels Catt subscribes to at home in a half-hearted effort to "keep up with the culture." It's a real blood-drenched carnival up there on SKY Cable. People outside a federal courthouse protesting a judge's decision not to sentence a killer to death, and then Luxury Life and QVC Shopping. On Fox, Bill O'Reilly refers to a politician as "that frigid pear-shaped bitch," oh right, he's talking about Hillary Clinton. And then a reality show about dating.

Catt's at a loss trying to figure out where her death wish began. A literal-minded observer might link it to her history of kinky sex play, but that wasn't right. The adventures she sought out with strangers were a high form of theater, a tiny escape from the ambivalence that surrounded the rest of her life. She was an actress before she met Michel and had spent her first years in New York studying *commedia del arte*. "Think of each character you play as a color," the teacher used to say. The binary roles of BDSM were as primary as the deep reds and blues on the tropical tablecloths. Before taking up with her killer, she was the long-distance submissive to a Canadian Dom who made her wear a studded dog color somewhere on her body throughout her last North American book tour. It was simultaneously erotic and deeply hilarious. The feel of the leather evoked acts he'd make her perform when they met in Toronto, but its provenance—the Pasadena Petco—seemed like a great private joke about the art critic's role in contemporary art. She'd been mildly blissed out on the road, but when she finally met 'Master Shade' in Toronto and he behaved like a jerk, she'd thrown the collar in the trash and departed.

The real death, she'll tell herself later, was the champagne surprise staged by her assistant and two interns for her forty-fifth birthday. The assistant, a beautiful, brilliant, and tormented girl, was doing a terrible job, but she wept each time Catt tried to fire her. Tommy, the business manager she'd hired so she could "practice her craft," had stopped by with a gift, a pair of tourist-shop abalone earrings. Tommy adored Catt. To him, their business was "all about heart." Debarred as a certified public accountant, Tommy had left a Westwood administrative job and moved to Crestline, a mountain community near San Bernadino, about seventy miles northeast of LA. Dressed in Dockers and sports-shirts, he was overweight and effusively feminine, as if he'd learned how to be gay by watching decades of daytime TV. Catt was fully aware that Tommy was stealing. He'd taken so many unpaid loans from her account that the gas in her house was shut off when she returned from Toronto. How much had these ten-dollar earrings actually cost? Catt guessed $25,000, maybe $35,000, but in order to calculate just how much he'd grabbed on the curve over the last couple of years she'd have to stop everything dead, fire, and then replace him; and how much time and expense would *that* cost? She'd been punk mom for so long she felt like punk grandma.

As Catt raised a plastic champagne flute she thought to herself, *Everyone at this table, I'm paying.*

All this time Catt couldn't bring herself to look in a mirror and it was shortly after this birthday when she met her killer.

If she'd been smart, she would have stopped trawling BDSM websites after the Toronto dog collar adventure. Besides, she'd already reported on these experiences in her last book of essays, juxtaposing the extreme, nuanced presence of BDSM games with the blankness of academic neo-conceptual art. These faux-naive arguments shocked most of the art world but received knowing laughs from her fans. The idea that *anything*—let alone the old thinking-cunt routine—could shock the viewers of sky Cable amazed her. As if Germaine Greer, PhD, Cambridge, had never posed for a beaver-shot in *Suck* magazine, using her body as proof that one could write feminist scholarship *and* want to fuck. "If there's a whore in the world, let them call me a whore," Greer had said blithely. Another one down the memory hole. It occurred to Catt that the epistemological groundwork for the war in Iraq had been laid by Paris Hilton's anal sex video. Like the great Easter egg hunt for WMDs, the question of whether the soft-porn not-quite-home video had been posted by a sleazy ex-boyfriend, as

Hilton claimed, or by one of her publicists, was irrelevant. The only point was, it was *there*. Once anything entered the mediascape, it was unstoppable.

Still, as a rhetorical strategy, Catt's miles were used up in this area. She knew she wouldn't be sharing the dog-collar adventure with the next generation of cutters … the whole thing had started to bore her. Logging in to CollarMe.com was a guilty recidivist pleasure she indulged, winding down from the tour. But one night she saw a post that made her think she'd found her soul mate.

DOMINANT REALM

I am a single but integrated and strict Dominant; although with a highly developed imagination, I am safe, sane, self-aware, and diverse in spirit and energy—fully in the headspace of Dom, not switch or conflicted. My life balance is achieved from a multitude of creative pursuits, verifiably accomplished, which originate in the same intuitive space where the BDSM identity resides. A background in neuromedical research is combined with creation of music and the visual arts are key aspects of my life.

My approach is based on an informed sense of timing and pace in progressing an active or latent submissive to higher states of experience and responsiveness from mild to advanced and demanding activities. I insist on discretion—and can encourage married, separated, divorced, sub-curious women 18–45 to respond as no risk or threat of disruption will result from any liaison which may occur. I do understand and am empathetic to the particular challenge of submissive women as well as submissive couples 'trapped' in their rational head about this recurring and enlarging need for surrender with facets of degradation, humiliation, and body training for usage by the Dom as he wishes. I also have considerable experience with the dynamics of outwardly assertive independent female personas—executives and other types—seeking a path of surrender and loss of control to achieve an essential balance which is central to real self-fulfillment. This also applies to women in relationships where their submissive nature and need to be fully controlled are alien concepts to their mate.

You should be refined, poised in demeanor, gracious and professionally formidable; as well as truly conscious in recognizing that any posturing and pretense will be a profound waste of time. You must be evolved enough to confront your recurring need for more than a 'play' dialogue. You must be truthful and not delusional—not overweight (this means not 'full figured', 'plump', 'ample' 'pudgy' or 'obese'). No druggies, or out of control drinkers. Not interested in any cyber-masturbatory pretenders, and will only respond to those willing to go offline mutually recognizing the possibilities of direct contact by phone to transcend email smokescreen and verify sincerity.

Prefer you are located in Los Angeles area.

Catt studied her killer's ad carefully. Back in LA, there was not much besides work to look forward to. Hank, the sixty-year-old maverick lawyer who'd been her partner in sexual friendship, had recently gotten together with Becca, a nice, divorced woman nearer to his own age. Given these facts, the Dominant Realm post struck Catt as extraordinary. Not only was its writer highly intelligent, he was intelligent *in the same way* as Hank and Michel and people of their generation she'd grown up admiring.

This is some heavy shit, Catt thought when she read it. Intense, but in a good way. The conjunction of powerful keywords (*intuitive space, alien concept, profound waste of time, transcend email smokescreen, verify, truthful and not delusional*) with the imperative voice established very high stakes. His use of the phrase "female personas" implied an awareness of the cyborgean nature of gender. Her face tingled with pleasure. And "informed sense of timing" … The micro-magnetics of timing; the art of speaking your lines just after the peak of an audience laugh was the only thing she'd really learned as an actress. Catt realized her killer was smarter than she. She was hooked, even before "poised in demeanor, gracious and professionally formidable" spoke to her vanity.

Later, after they'd met, once she surmised the black BMW was most likely her killer's primary residence, she longed to protect him. His situation was doomed, but she was moved by the way he occupied space. His autodidactic achievements in highly technical fields from electronics to neurobiology, his archaic use of the prepositional *who* instead of the dehumanized *that*, his accomplishment as a pianist and daily practice of yoga reminded her of the Asperger's boys who attended her readings. He was someone who could not quite live in the world. Mind stretched to a point that can't be conveyed without an effort involving physical pain … Sitting beside him, she watched his actions and speech unfold at a second remove, as if he'd been forced to watch himself in a mirror.

Well, this was the life of the mind in present America. Ninety-five percent of the students she met had no information or sense of any historic continuum. The rest were autistic.

After leaving the restaurant, Catt takes Stretch for a walk on the beach and then a long nap. She dreams she's in the car with her mother in upstate New York. Charged with first-degree murder for advocating abortion, she's about to turn herself in. They go into a church and browse through some books on sale in the nave—reading material for those about to be killed—but they only have cookbooks: *Plan Your Last Meal*. She thinks: *I don't want to die at the hands of these people.*

The sound of the generator kicking on wakes her at five p.m. She gets up and opens the curtains to a parking lot softened by pinkish-gold light. The sun's already dropped behind the rock hills.

"I've got good news and bad news," the Los Angeles broker tells Catt the next morning, when she finally reaches him on the Villa Vitta's front desk phone. The nerves around Catt's left eye respond with a frenetic dance. The twitch is like psychic incontinence, erupting every few minutes.

"Okay, I'm ready."

"So, the good news is, we're all set to close the eight-unit side on Friday. But the folks on the four-plex withdrew their offer—"

"Oh no."

"Don't worry, I've already written a backup."

Splitting the twelve-plex into two deals had been the broker's idea. The small complex was built on two legal lots and he'd judged, correctly, they could net more on two separate sales. The problem was, Catt's replacement deals on the thirty-six units spread all over Albuquerque were supposed to be closing on Monday.

"So I think what you need to do is talk to your people in Albuquerque and get an extension. If you want to accept the back-up I'll initial for you—"

"How much did we lose?"

"You're gonna love this. I upped the asking price $25K—"

"Blake, you're amazing." Her left eye twitches again.

"And the new buyers went for it."

Catt hangs up the phone, thanks Lourdes and hands her a crisp fifty dollars. She's just made $25,000, more than the price of her car, although by this point she no longer sees the numbers this way. Years ago in New York, she'd wavered for weeks about buying an eight-dollar lipstick, unable to get past the primitive math: one Chanel demi-crème equaled sixty minutes of temp office work, an eighth of her day. But now the numbers, unanchored to referents, exist by themselves. It occurs to Catt she won't be free of her killer until she gets rid of the twitch.

"It's like shooting fish in a barrel," she'd foolishly bragged. They were at her house in LA on the living room couch and she'd thought he, more than anyone else, would understand the game she was playing with paradox, a game that had come to define how she saw the world. Wanting to tell him something about her life, she had no idea then that the money she'd made could seem like a gallon of water to someone lost in a desert.

She considers the problem of timing: How can she stall closing the Albuquerque deals without paying penalties? Catt doesn't give a shit about the $25,000 but now, for the sake of the game, she doesn't want to lose any of it. The deals were like puzzles. The answer was always right there, you just had to move the pieces around until it emerged.

Lourdes thanks Catt for the windfall and tells her Raoul is gone for the day. Catt can't imagine where he has gone. She pictures the closest real town, a larger collection of dust roads and storefronts three hours away.

Back in room number 8, she decides to use funds from Friday's sale to close on the two cheaper buildings. She'll ask Edgar, the broker in Albuquerque, to get an extension on Mescalero, a derelict former Route-66-era motel, which shouldn't be hard. Mescalero had been empty for months. No bank would loan on the place. Set back on a now-sleepy road under some ancient cottonwood trees, three blocks away from the Santa Fe rail yards, the building had old casement windows set deep in its white plaster walls. Once the next-to-last major stop before California, Catt imagines Dustbowl migrants arriving in Albuquerque by jalopy and train.

Though she's indifferent to money, the buildings themselves exude romance, they offer a promise of history reclaimed. Looking for buildings that winter, catching Southwest Airlines's nonstop commuter plane every two weeks from LA, she could hardly contain her excitement. She loved Southwest's old one-class cabins with clusters of bench seats facing each other; they evoked card games and whiskey, the entrepreneurial spirit of the old west. Surveying her fellow commuters, she wondered how many of them were onto this thing? How many were looking for underpriced fixers after unloading their equity-laden stuff in LA at the peak?

It was such a sure bet, moving money from an inflated bubble to an under-priced, upcoming place. But when she tries to explain this to her Los Angeles friends, they look at her blankly. "Albuquerque?" her friend Luke Petit asked. "I've been there once. I found it incredibly sordid." For weeks Catt turned Luke's comment around in her mind but couldn't decode it. What was sordid? She saw only opportunity there. Luke had taken a tenure-track job a decade ago and slowly stopped writing.

His credentials were better than Catt's. Did that mean he'd won? His life seemed pretty boring.

Catt leaves the motel to call Edgar from a calling card phone outside the municipal building. He puts her on hold, makes a few calls. As she expects, all parties accept the delay. When she hangs up, the day feels suddenly flat. She thinks about leaving, but it still feels too soon to return to LA or even Campo La Jolla. Time, she decides, is the best defense against rage. Even if, worst case, her killer had tracked her internet search to the server in Punta Banda, if she waits another few days another pressing demand will arise. Knifing Catt will no longer seem worth the long drive.

She has a few hundred dollars cash in her room. She decides to use one of those bills the next morning to get a local fisherman to take her out to see dolphins and seals.

There is a recurring belief that to locate this, this margin of error, would be to trace a historiography of one's present amnesia—Catt wrote that night in her diary. *Can no longer remember the time before the person stopped being part of the process. Hallways leading to multiple doors. Behind them, a basketball court, loudspeakers, coaxial wires, folding tables and chairs. Conversion. Each door leads to a room. Set theories, in which the system eventually takes over.*

Later, rereading these words, Catt will wonder what she'd absorbed before reaching the Villa Vitta motel. The porousness of a delirious body. And later still, she'll realize the word in her killer's ad she should have paid more attention to was not "intuitive space" but "verifiable." He'd used this adjective in his post and repeated it several times on the phone. The first time they talked, Catt took pains to explain why she couldn't post photographs of herself on a BDSM dating site. She thought of her students. How disappointing would it be for them seeing her face while trawling BDSM porn? Her killer—still known at that point as "Dominant Realm"—didn't press her on this. He seemed more intent on her words and her voice. Their rapport was already sublime, he could take her appearance on faith. Besides, he couldn't post photographs of himself, or even—until their trust was secure—tell her his name. "There's a great deal written about me on the web," he explained. "An increasing amount. More and more every day. And all of it," his voice became grave, "verifiable." They hung up. A few minutes later he emailed his name. She jumped on the net, and everything that she read confirmed his prolific biography. Numerous websites described Nicholas Cohen's invention of the remote keyless device. His company website included a trailer for a forthcoming promotional Novanex DVD. Online trade journals praised the success of the miracle compound's clinical trials. Four pages deeper in Google, she found company filings for Umbrella LLC, the entity he'd told her he'd used for his cable media flips. She saw ads for his Halcyon Records triple album CD and a book on the nature of mind in the internet age, co-written with Daniella Koreli, who he'd described as his sometime-business partner and ex. He and Daniella had also compiled a print-on-demand business directory that could be purchased in English, Romanian, French and Japanese.

When i met You it was as if You could see straight through me, beyond things that happened, back to my childhood, Catt emailed him some time later.

In Your presence i could look through the past to a better more probable life. i saw what could have been.

She'd worked too hard building a life she didn't believe in. She wanted to be lost again.

You said: 'Answer me. Answer me truthfully.' But i couldn't do this. Pieces, excuses, falling away. You said: 'you see? The truth is so very simple. Why do you have to give false answers to get to the true?'

You told me to follow, and i wanted this very badly. To be blasted. You offered to teach me progressive devotion. You spoke to the evidence: the variable nature of my present truth. When You noted the fragility of my current life-form, i felt Your intelligence as something painful. To me and to You.

Catt was never afraid of the phrase "surrender control of your finances to me." It was part of the delirious game. The connection between them was palpable. They both knew the Master/slave roles were semantic and circular. Looking back, Catt was sure her mind changed over dinner weeks later at a restaurant in the Hollywood Hills. He gave her a copy of the new Novanex DVD and assured her, that by funding the next round of clinical trials she'd be "performing a service to all mankind" and joining an elite global network of prominent slaves. She paid the check quickly and left. She knew then he was psychotic and broke. Until then, the erotic haze surrounding their dealings had softened this knowledge, but his bold pitch brought it straight to the front.

Walking out of the restaurant, she was gripped by a fear that put her on notice. There was just one chance to do everything right. He knew where she lived, who she was. Her only chance to escape was to discover the truth.

Late that night, she went back on the computer and began digging deeper. As she cross-referenced the websites, the ads and reports, the word "verifiable" dissolved in her brain. Because what she found was a thick web of lies: Self-produced websites and vanity posts in online trade publications. Numerous patents filed more than two decades ago and still pending ... blog entries, anonymous infomercials, physician endorsements broadcast on space-rental webcast domains by doctors whose names couldn't be traced ... lies metastasized over the net, lies *verified* against other lies, a closed loop of baseless assertions. Oh, brave new genius of the twenty-first century ... Did her killer have a slave-pool of girls posting this shit on the net? Umbrella, his media LLC, produced North Hollywood porn and the scholarly articles on his CV were published in journals that didn't exist.

All the dreams Catt remembers since meeting her killer have been about death. On her third night at the Villa Vitta, she dreams she's outside a yurt in the Turkish highlands preparing a meal. Stepping inside, her not-quite-ex-husband Michel is there watching TV. He looks up and asks, with mild interest, *Have you come back here to watch me die?*

I was being poisoned then by the culture, but I didn't know it, she writes in her diary. And: *In order to arrive at the fundamental practice, one must shed certain elements: region, name, personal history, domesticity, gender. All personal histories amount to the same. Clues mixed in with the garbage. All clues lead back to the room ...*

On Thursday morning she gets up at six to meet Javier, an unemployed local who's agreed to take her out fishing. For a few blissful hours, Catt loses the twitch. Approaching an offshore island, a whole school of dolphins swims so close to the boat they can almost be touched. On the east side of the island, hundreds of seals sun themselves on the rocks, smiling little creatures flopping down into the water for fish, as playful as dogs. Catt misses Michel. During the dreamtime, they swam at a beach close to here with a seal. It was one of the few times the unhappiness lifted. Catt had a notebook and Michel drew cartoons of a long-whiskered seal smiling at them across the choppy waves. Catt's eyes tear up at the memory, crying is such a release. But then her eye starts to twitch.

Arriving back onshore around noon, Catt considers checking email at the town's one internet café but decides not to risk it. *Pushed to extremes, the machines become each other's prostheses,* as she later wrote.

Before leaving the restaurant that night in Hollywood Hills, Catt said No to her killer. She's very sure about this. Because sometime after, he called her and said it was very important that she return the Novanex DVD to his office right away. Even Catt knows that digital media is infinitely duplicatable. Why would he want the DVD back? The only possible reason was that *he already knew about her online research.* Had he bugged her hard drive? Hacked into the ISP server and somehow traced each keystroke back to her house?

Deciding to stop all contact with him, she'd tossed the unwatched DVD into a drawer, but as soon as her killer hung up, she put the thing on and took notes.

For the first half of the program, a succession of "clinical subjects" (grad students, housewives, software designers, TV-show hosts) describe the incredible changes Novanex made to their lives; changes, she remarked in her notes, deemed by our culture as protean: "Subjects report being more sexually active, alert, rested, focused, and happy and *able to work long hours at repetitive tasks on the computer.*" The last half of the show featured endorsements from renowned doctors. Catt wrote down their names: Dr. Jeffrey C. Barlough, Pharmacology Chair at USC Medical School; Dr. Karen Beale, Senior Medical Officer, United States Navy; Dr. Nathan S. Abramsom, Chief Research Neurologist, Albert Einstein Medical School, and a few more. Checking employee directories and the American Medical Association's physician registry list, Catt found that none of these people were doctors, nor—except for the coincidentally-named Nathan Abramsom of the Nassau County Blue Cross HMO—did they even exist.

Desperate to get the DVD out of her house, she drove to the Beverly Hills Wilshire Boulevard, office address, on her killer's site. There, she found a soon-to-be-razed, vacant cinderblock building with an unlocked front door. Upstairs, the number 210 door had a cheap Staples plaque for "Novanex Therapies." Except for "Dr. Nathan S. Abramson," in room 215, no other tenants remained.

Catt slipped the DVD under her killer's door and left that night for Campo La Jolla. Now she was obsessed. Instead of just hanging out she went to the internet café in town the next day, typing her killer's name over and over into Google, Intelius, High Beam. Eighteen pages deep, she found a collection of AOLStalker.com search engine logs stored on a *.ru* domain. Internet searches made on Nicholas Cohen by people all over the world recorded strange, deeply troubled associative streams:

Pussy smokes a cigarette, pussy blows smoke—penis exfoliation shaved pussy stories NICHOLAS COHEN *penis extraction* NICHOLAS COHEN *litigation mediacom pretty women with cocks worldcast net*

Albany sex protein diets property management NICHOLAS COHEN *lingerie sale …*

She found dozens of lists just like this and imagined people, no, they had to be women, typing these words not knowing their searches were being logged. And Catt's search right now—was it being recorded and traced?

That night, the Villa Vitta motel's restaurant is open for the first time since Catt arrived. She meets a party of schoolteachers who've just arrived here from Tijuana, a twelve-hour drive.

Strewn with Spanish Colonial tables and chairs, the restaurant is murkily lit with two chandeliers. Like every Mexican restaurant and store, the Conquistador keeps its doors literally open for business, which makes the room drafty and cold. Still, the evening is festive. Catt gave some of Javier's fish to Raoul, who's just back from Guerrero Negro, and he has the cook prepare them with peppers and onions. It's too much for one person to eat. Raoul asks if she'd like to share the fish with the other guests, and the teachers (all men) invite her to join them. Drinking shots of tequila, passing plates of stuffed lobsters, the teachers are having a fabulous time.

Fernando, the man at the head of the table, tells Catt they all teach at the same high school. Since the start of the school year, they've been saving up for this trip—a pilgrimage, really—to see the whales and their babies at Laguna Ojo de Liebre. They rented a big Econoline van and they're leaving at dawn for the lagoon, about three hours away.

"It's a once in a lifetime experience," a math teacher named Rafael tells her. "The whales swim two thousand miles from the

Canadian coast to give birth to their babies each winter. And there they remain, nursing and training their young for six or eight weeks, until they're ready to swim back to Canada."

"It is their homeland," Fernando explains. "Inside the lagoon, the whales are as trusting as dolphins."

"Nowhere else in the world can you come this close to seeing the whales," the geography teacher tells her. "They are aware of your presence—they swim right under the boats!"

Rogelio, the chemistry teacher, shows her the snapshot he took four years ago of an enormous gray whale three feet from a boat, the top half of its torso reaching out of calm lagoon waters into the sky. "The whale is a mystical creature." And then the conversation drifts into Spanish about impossible students and absent, ridiculous colleagues. Raoul brings out Javier's fish and they pass it around the long table. Wearing sports shirts and plastic pocket protectors, the men remind Catt of a long-ago time when teaching commanded respect as a profession. Living just twenty miles south of San Diego, they probably don't earn more than $500 a month but their camaraderie makes them part of an enviable foreign, parallel world. Rafael pours her another shot of tequila.

On the fifth day, her left eye still twitching, Catt's already thinking about how to fix up the new buildings. She figures it's safe to leave and she does.

Years later, after quitting analysis she'll come back to Laguna Ojo del Liebre to visit the whales but they won't impress her as much as the teachers.

2

PAUL: HIS FREEDOM

THERE ARE SOME PEOPLE who, seeing themselves as alien wherever they go, have never wanted to travel.

At seven thirty on a Thursday morning in March, Paul Garcia locks the front door of the blue house on Slate Street behind him. He presses the key tight in his palm before putting it back in his state-issued windbreaker pocket. His own door, his own key. How many times has he thought about this as he worked his way out of Level III Las Lunas State Prison, to Level II Santa Fe, and from there to the low-security Farm and parole?

Out less than two weeks, he's trying hard to establish routines. Routines are the key to sobriety, changing old habits to new. Paroled back to Farmington, he has to remember: the chaos that ended less than two years ago with his arrest is only *one drink away*. During the binge that lasted maybe six weeks, he'd spent nights and days stalking his ex-girlfriend Tanya and getting fucked up on crack. At the outset, his goal seemed really clear. He had to stop Tanya from killing their unborn child, and perhaps win her back. If he'd succeeded, he could've probably gone to a meeting and written the crack off as a slip. But once he took the first drink, he was into the zone. There was no going back. After that, he'd lost his job, and then gotten arrested for writing bad checks and credit card fraud. Legally speaking, the stalking and crack use hadn't come into the picture. And this was high on his Gratitude list, because if they had, he'd still be locked up in the Level III with the rapists and gangs.

Before this, he'd been sober a year and a half.

The March sky is Navajo blue. What a beautiful month! There's a thin coat of frost that will burn off before ten a.m. Paul closes the gate to the tiny front yard. Outside the bay window, a rose bush grows wild. It's like he's been airlifted here. He still can't get used to the place. His friend Jerry Koven dropped him off with the key the night he was let out of the Farm.

Jerry is one of Paul's oldest Farmington friends and also his biggest problem, he fears. He'd met Jerry in San Juan County Jail while doing forty-five days for his fourth DUI a few years before. Jerry was in for his second DUI and also possession of crack, charges that Jerry's attorney would eventually get dropped, but on the day he and Paul met, his wife Cris was playing a game, pretending she wouldn't post bail, because she was pissed. Now Jerry's his landlord, and also his boss. He and Cris own a furniture store called Casa Bonita. The blue house on Slate Street was new—something, apparently, he'd picked up on the side. Flanked by apartments, the old-fashioned blue bungalow was less preserved than ignored. Oil pumps, copper from decades of rust, run day and night in otherwise vacant yards.

When Paul leaves for work, most of his neighbor's blinds are still closed. These guys work nights in the fields, their big shiny trucks parked motel-style in front of their doors. Early on in the binge, Paul sold his Chevy S-10. For now, until he saves up for a car, he has to walk four miles and back to the store. He's glad none of these guys are up early enough to see. In Farmington, no one but the Natives, the winos and bums, ever walks. But at least he was *free*, and shouldn't he try to enjoy this? He'd been crossing off days ever since January 3, when the Parole Board granted him early release.

And now he was out. Sober since his arrest two years before in July, he had not lost one day of "good time" since arriving at the Level III. Determined to shave as much time as he could off the three years the judge had sentenced him to, he'd stayed out of trouble and done everything right. In addition to "good time," he'd earned extra release by going to Bible School, attending chapel two nights a week, and signing up for Therapeutic Community. In the end, he'd only wasted sixteen months of his life, plus the four months he'd been locked up in County Jail waiting for the case to be heard.

He'd nearly dropped dead when the judge gave him three to five years. It wasn't as if he'd *stolen* the fuel credit card, it was *his*. The card came with his oil field truck driving job. Sometime during the binge he'd stopped going to work. Only after he'd charged $937 in Circle K gas, smokes, and food had his bosses remembered to shut down the card. By the time Paul stood in front of the judge he'd been sober four months and the dickhead public defender had practically sworn that if he accepted the plea, he'd get off for time served. He wasn't a thief. Except for a few DUIs, his record was clean. Clearly, the whole thing was rigged. Halliburton, his former employer, owned most of this hideous dust and oil-field town.

Paul can't stand the desert. It's not like he'd *choose* to live here. Even though he'd grown up in Albuquerque, he said Oregon whenever anyone asked him where he was from.

In fact, his family fled the state shortly after his birth and he'd never been back, but the word summons pictures of towering evergreen trees, wild thickets of berries and grapes under cool misty skies and the life that might have been his if father hadn't lost his Jesuit college job after his mom became mentally ill. The last-born of six Catholic kids, Paul can hardly believe the loser flaked out on the couch who was his dad had ever been a Spanish professor ... or that his mom, an overweight screaming shrew, had trained as a classical pianist before meeting his dad. Paul's birth began the onset of her schizophrenia. His childhood was marked by maternal caresses inexplicably mixed with beatings and bricks thrown on his feet. "You little nigger," she'd hiss. His mother was Lebanese. She saw Paul as the spawn of his father, that "greasy spic bastard," that "son of a Mexican outhouse shitter." Disgraced when his mom called one of the nuns in the Spanish department a whore, they moved back to Albuquerque, where his Dad had grown up. For the rest of his life, he taught junior high and fell asleep every night on the couch.

Paul moved to Farmington with the cops after him six years before his last arrest, thinking his sister Rene might take him in. When she did not, he'd already run out of cash and could not think of where else to go, so he lived in his car for awhile and got a couple of jobs. In his heart, he despised the white trash that comprised Farmington, both high and low, but he learned to fit in and even picked up the drawl. He checks the box "Other" whenever he has to fill out a form that asks about race. In his thirty-eight years, he's only left the state twice.

"Seven days left!" Paul wrote on March 1 in the journal he'd kept since his first day in prison. "This is my last week ... I'll try and write in you every day." And then he'd gotten the flu.

Ten days out, even the flat stretches of Farmington streets are a jumble, almost too much for him. He still can't get past the unlimited feel of the dry, sun-warmed air on his skin. It's like being touched. (Paul doesn't like being touched.) The March breeze makes him dizzy. It's like being touched by a beneficent presence, or maybe by God.

Passing the high school on Slate Street and Locust, his stomach clenches into a knot. Swarms of kids everywhere, watching the weird old guy cut though their grounds. Short, prison-cut hair, new gray strands mixed in with the black, he feels like a slow-moving target, walking to work. With his broad chest and thick wire-rimmed glasses, it's like he's an alien freak dragging himself through a nuclear desert after the world has been bombed. Built like an athlete, he could pass for a regular Farmington guy despite his olive-toned skin, were it not for the dorky thick glasses he's worn since he was eight. He was always a nerd. His feet are too small. Each day his hairline creeps further back on his scalp. He looks like a satyr! He feels people's stares as they drive by in their cars, as if they could see the thick pelt of Lebanese hair on his back.

Oil field guys cruise past in their Yukons, F-250's and Rams while he trots on the side of the road like a dog. Can they tell that the clothes on his back are state-issued? His jeans aren't even a brand … they were hemmed by another inmate before he left prison.

First things first, he repeats to himself coming out of the schoolyard on Elm. *I've got to stop tripping.* Even though Jerry's only paying him $250 a week, that doesn't mean he can't hitch a ride to the mall for a nice pair of Levi's. It's still early days. *Get a grip, put a lid on those negative feelings.*

Still, it's a lot harder being sober outside than in prison. Cars whizzing past. *Just for today, I can choose to stay sober.* How many times has he repeated this sentence in meetings? But what do you do with your thoughts? In two weeks he'll be twenty months sober but he's been twenty months sober before and look at what happened to him. The old-timers who've been sober for decades and still come to meetings, there's something different about them. They're not just refraining from having a drink. They seem somehow free, as if they've reprogrammed their negative thoughts. Maybe that's what they mean by the spiritual awakening.

In prison Paul turned his will over to God but he's still the same person. Can you hate yourself and love God? Brother Charlie says no, because "God made the world and everything in it."

"You've got to watch out for disappointment," they say in meetings. "The past is the past, no point feeling guilty about it, because it's brought us to where we are now."

On his third night in prison Paul dreamt he saw a big orange van drive over a cliff and crash on the asphalt below. The van was loaded with uniforms, painted as bright as his ugly jumpsuit. He ran down the hill to investigate. Two young people sat on the ground, all shaken up and the truck was in pieces. He knew there was someone he knew in the wreckage, and he woke up in his cell to the sound of his own crying. He took this to mean he was, as they say in AA, "No longer driving the bus."

After that, he really did turn his life over to God. To avoid disappointment, he trained himself to eliminate hope. And this helped. The night before his release, his sister Pam changed her mind about picking him up, but he did not take a drink.

They'd only been planning this for six months! Clearly, Pam was still angry. On some level, Pam, the most functional of Paul's brothers and sisters, was, like their mother, mentally ill. Everyone thought the sun shone out of her asshole. She was Ms. Good to his Mr. Bad.

Forty-two, never married, Pam had put herself through medical school. She lived alone with her eight-year-old son in a gigantic new house that she adorned with framed family photos. Insisting their childhood was normal and happy, Pam was a zombie. Still, whenever he thinks about Pam, Paul gets a lump in his throat. He has to force himself to calm down. "The mind of an alcoholic is like a machine," his AA friend Curtis S. used to say, before he relapsed and drank himself to death in a trailer alone.

Instead of leaving the Farm with his sister Pam, a medical doctor, nicely dressed, Jerry sent Cris. *Uh-oh*, Paul thought, when she stepped out of the Navigator. Wearing tight jeans with rhinestones all over her ass and a pink Phat Farm hoodie, she looked like the wife of a gangster. Cris was Paul's age, ten years younger than Jerry, and the question running between them in Cris's mind since they first met was, *When are you going to fuck me?* This was Cris's brilliant idea for how to get back at Jerry.

Strapped into the gray leather seat, Paul stared at the broad expanses of space flipping past while Cris yammered on. Blunted daggers of light reached through the street-legal window tint. He knew then he was scared. As always, Cris was oblivious, bringing him up to date on all of Casa Bonita's exciting news: who was up for a bonus, who'd gotten engaged, how many living room sets they'd unloaded last week.

The light hurt his eyes. At least he didn't have to think about Pam any more. Somewhere in the move from Santa Fe Level II to the Farm they'd lost his prescription sunglasses, and now Cris was acting as if she'd just picked him up from the airport, not prison; as if he couldn't wait to get back to the furniture store after a long vacation. He'd worked for Jerry and Cris years before, and never imagined he'd find himself back at Casa Bonita. But in order to get parole, Paul needed a guaranteed job. Who would hire a felon except for a friend?

Fucked up as he was, Jerry Koven was one of the few people who answered Paul's letters from prison. He'd even written that he was thinking of opening a new store in Gallup. How would Paul like to move there and manage it? Paul had been stupid enough to let himself feel excited.

But now, Cris seemed to have other ideas. Some time during the drive, she told Paul his new job would involve turning the junk room in back of the warehouse into a scratch 'n dent outlet furniture store. "I *think*," she'd said, "Jerry's still clean. We can finally make some improvements now that he's not raiding the safe to buy crack."

Ugh, he'd thought. *But when am I leaving for Gallup?*

"And wait'll you see the house!" She meant the Alpine Drive palace she lived in with Jerry. "We've added a barbecue pit and a spa. Except—" (a deliberate flip of her hair) "—the asshole's still never around to enjoy it." (Long sigh.) "Who knows where he goes?" This was a reference to Jerry's habitual whoring. "I'm so glad you're back, Paul. I *need* you." The old Jerry and Cris routine. The only thing worse than Jerry's erratic behavior was Cris's enabling, which had always left Paul bouncing between them.

Outside the window, tall Byzantine shapes of red rock jutted out of the sand.

Before Paul moved to the Farm, he'd gone almost a year without seeing the sky. It was all very confusing. The world at medium-security Level III was so bleak: thirty minutes of yard once a day, unless the place was in lock-down, which was at least half the time. "Yard" was a cement slab at the bottom of forty-foot high cylindrical walls, topped off by electrified wire. The small patch of air above this was most often blue, although sometimes it was gray. For months, his only sense of the weather was in the distant gradations between blue and gray sky.

In the car Paul wished he could slow everything down and never go back to Farmington. Cris's hands flying off of the wheel and almost brushing onto his crotch, *I have to wait,* he kept thinking, *and see what God has in store for me.* But when they turned into the U-Store-It outside of town, for the first time all day he was happy. He had the key to Bin 138 in his windbreaker pocket. When he turned the key to the lock, he almost choked up at the sight of all his old things. *They've waited for me.* His rack of CDs, his boom box, his long-distance harrier trophy, his canvas collapsible hamper ... all were untouched, exactly as he'd arranged them all those months before. And then Cris took him to Farmington Heights to meet up with Jerry back at their Alpine Drive house.

Late afternoon found Jerry passed out in front of the new plasma TV. "Hah—at least the shithead's at home," Cris remarked. Still. Just because Jerry was comatose didn't necessarily mean he was high or hung over from crack. Jerry *was* actually brain-damaged, which, Paul assumed, was what led him here after a promising scientific career. "You better not wake him up yet," Cris advised and then disappeared. Upstairs the kids were banging around. Paul took a long uneasy bath. Finally, Jerry woke up and took him for steak at the Outback.

Born into a rich St. Louis family, Jerry Koven graduated magna cum laude from Wash U and went to the University of Chicago for graduate school. He'd been a geologist until his brain got tossed around in a near-fatal car crash. After that, when he could no longer keep his mind on the job, he moved here. His parents gave him a large lump of cash, which Jerry used to transform an old warehouse into Casa Bonita, *the home of affordable quality furnishing.*

About the only part of Jerry's brain that remained intact was the part that knew how to make money. He discovered a niche: extending credit to unemployed Natives who received monthly government checks. Brain dead or not, Jerry was smart, and that was the level at which he and Paul could connect. They kept each other amused with their bullshit. Paul wished he'd known Jerry before the crash but if Jerry hadn't scrambled his brains, he would have stayed in Chicago, and then they wouldn't have met.

"Haaah, Garcia, you hungry?" Jerry poked his fat finger at the laminate picture of a king-sized prime rib. "Gotta build you back up." He was already into his second Jim Beam. "We'll take two of those." The waitress was still standing there. "Pretty soon you'll be wanting some *real* pussy." Paul gripped his glass of ice tea until his palm froze. "Or is there some special boy?" He felt his face flush. Sex, like everything else, was controlled by the gangsters in prison. Only once had he seen two guys going at it. It was not something people did on their own just for fun. "Nah, Jerry, it wasn't like that." He could not begin to tell Jerry what it was like—boring and loud, with occasional flashes of violence—or how he'd sat on his bunk reading the Bible to keep out the noise.

"Paul, never mind, I'm just shittin' ya. But wait 'til we're out of here. I've got a surprise."

Paul chewed on his steak wondering what it might be. A platter of crack? He'd been out of prison less than twelve hours and things were already moving someplace he couldn't control. And this guy was his boss! So far Jerry hadn't said one word about Gallup. Instead, he was talking about setting him up at his getaway pad over on Slate. He'd let Paul use it for $400 a month. Does Cris even know about this? Until now Paul hasn't thought once about where he might live, but if Jerry charges him $400 a month for the rent, how's he going to save up for a car?

Each day here is filled with anxiety, Paul had written in his prison journal. Whenever things got really bad, he'd pictured himself living in Gallup. A new town, his chance to start over. When Jerry offered him full charge of the store and a share of the profits, he'd envisioned renting a mobile home outside of town and buying a horse. A pinto, maybe a dark brown Arabian. In Gallup, he'd ride his horse every day to the store. He'd build a lean-to for shade out in the back, and whenever business was slow, he'd hang out with his horse. He imagined the horse eating apples in two or three bites and licking the juice off his hand.

That night, Jerry parked in front of the blue house and tossed Paul the key as if he'd just won some kind of prize. "Go ahead, open it!" A fat Navajo woman sat on the couch, surrounded by dildos and condoms and KFC wrappers. "I'll leave you two to it," Jerry said as he walked out the door. This was the big surprise. The woman wasn't even really a prostitute, she was just another Farmington loser into Jerry for her last rock of crack or maybe a furniture payment. Typical Jerry. So cheap, he could not even spring for a nice, blonde Santa Fe whore.

After he forced himself to do what was expected, the woman curled up under the sheet as if she expected to stay there all night. By now it was four a.m. Desperate, Paul told his first lie since he'd turned his life over to God: "Listen, you've got to leave now. My mother's coming to visit from Albuquerque. She could show up any time." His mother was dead—he'd never once been to her grave since the funeral eight years ago—but that got the girl out. As soon as she left, he started to clean.

He cleaned for three nights. He found some old rags, some bottles of bleach and ammonia, and cleaned his way from the small covered back porch all the way out, until he reached the front door.

Halfway to Casa Bonita, Paul crosses a little green park. He feels safer here. Every minute he's walking the streets he risks running into old crack-smoking friends, or his dealer, or, worst of all, Tanya. He thought he'd put Tanya out of his mind, but lately his thoughts have been drifting. His sobriety felt *so strong* before he left prison, but now that he's out it's like reliving the first thirty days. He doesn't think he'd take a drink if he met Tanya, but he knows that he'd want to. What a drag, having to start fighting that off all over again. The only times he feels really safe are when he's at work or at the noon meetings. Dragging Jerry's old scratch 'n dent sofas around for minimum wage, he can forget his weird feelings. He has to stay positive. That's essential. But whenever he looks over his shoulder, *Hello sweetheart*, here come the old feelings of dread.

In the ten days he's been in Farmington, he hasn't once picked up his journal. And what would he write? In prison, he wrote in it every day. Not his feelings or memories, not about other inmates, that was too risky. Instead, he made lists. What he ordered from commissary (shaving cream, toothpaste, deodorant, the transistor radio he had for a week before the guards took it away). The books he picked off the cart (Dean Koontz, Stephen King, Larry McMurty, *Co-Dependent No More* and the Bible). The phone calls he made and received (Pam, Ravene, his cousin Mason, his sponsor Mike D.). Also, his letters, his Bible Study certificates, his workout routines and his moods: Anxious, Nervous, Trusting in God, but mostly Depressed. Paul has a record of every push-up he did while he was in prison but he cannot remember shit about what happened before his arrest. And really, what was the point of establishing facts? Thinking back might make him feel guilty ... and there was the chaos, waiting to suck him back in. In meetings everyone says *it's important to accept the past*, but accepting isn't remembering. He has to stay focused.

"Name one thing you're proud of," the counselor asked them in Therapeutic Community. Of course everyone mentioned their kids. And he'd been embarrassed, because the only good thing that sprang to his mind was working for Halliburton, driving a twenty-ton Class A oil field truck. Getting that job was something to be proud of. Seventeen bucks an hour, and he'd never attended truck-driving school. He just signed up for the test and then passed. At some point during the binge he must have stopped showing up because he cannot remember being fired from work. Was that before or after he took the first drink? He doesn't remember. The relapse started with crack. He hung on a long time before drinking, which was something else to be proud of, although he couldn't say that. Crack was never really a problem. His disease was addiction to alcohol. At some point during the binge he started using the card when his money ran out ... which must have been *after* he lost the job, but *before* he started dealing because after that, he would have had cash. Well not really dealing, he just sold a few vials on spec. At first he started using the card to put gas in his truck. Then a few groceries. Finally he was hanging out at the pumps, gassing up other cars for half price until the card got declined. Still, that wasn't how he got arrested. He'd already moved out of his place. The cops were not going to find him. No. He would never have gotten arrested if he hadn't had the first drink—

By then he was living out of his truck, but until the first drink, he had everything straight. He kept his clothes and his stuff in the toolbox, and bought a special wood box for hiding the crack. It could have continued like that forever if he hadn't run out the weekend his dealer went down to Albuquerque. No one had shit anywhere. Finally he drove over to Aztec to buy a few joints from an old stoner named Bill, but the town's weed supply was dry too. Bill asked him in and took out a couple of Budweisers. In the ten seconds it took Bill to walk from the fridge to the couch Paul debated the wisdom of drinking. Then he pulled off the tab.

Every problem Paul's had in his life can be traced back to drinking. *If I'd just stuck with crack, things would've been fine.* Leaving Bill's trailer he picked up a few quarts. The first one, he drank in the parking lot outside the store. After that, he started driving around, drinking more beer, feeling fantastic. He was in the back-country sailing over dirt roads, so he wasn't expecting a stop sign, much less a cop. When the pig turned on his lights Paul put his foot on the gas and hauled ass over a hill so fast he had time to hide in some bushes. Well that was alright! His little Chevy S-10 had just out-run the police. After waiting awhile, he figured he might as well make it a night, so he drove back to the store for a twelve-pack.

Driving around drinking the beers, he wasn't aware he was thirty miles over the forty-mile limit until he passed cop number two. Flat roads all around, there was no place to bail; he knew that he'd had it. By now there were empties all over the cab, plus the wood box with his pipe and a few empty vials. Slowing down, the red and blue flashing lights moving in closer ... no way would he pass a breath test, and this would be Felony DUI 5.

So when the cop shone a light in his face and told him to step outside of the vehicle, Paul decided he might as well finish his beer. He had nothing to lose. Enraged, the cop pulled him out of the cab, cuffed him and drove him to County without ever searching the vehicle. Crack is an evil addictive substance, but Paul's never had any *legal* problems with crack. Although in a way, it was drinking that *saved* him. After they booked him on DUI 5 they found an outstanding warrant for the fuel credit card. They were so happy about this, they never considered searching the truck. Thanks to his drunken behavior, he'd never been charged with possession or dealing.

This, Paul has come to believe, was all part of God's plan.

The park lets out in a new part of town built in the '80s with streets named for girls. Tiffany Court, Melissa Lane, Brittney Circle. It's strictly white Christian trash, kid's plastic swing sets and toys all over the yards, shiny new trucks outside the garages. If Tanya had not aborted his child, he would be the dad of a toddler. She already had two screaming brats from her last marriage, and her ex was a jerk. What was it about *his* sperm she found so repugnant? All of Paul's siblings had kids. Like Brother Charlie from God-Time, the group that led chapel in prison, had said, his rights as a father-to-be had been violated. The baby already had little toenails and eyes when she vacuumed it out. Life begins at the time of conception. They'd prayed about this in chapel.

If Tanya had done the right thing, he'd still be driving for Halliburton. They might have been living on Brittney Circle, surrounded by neighbors, with three screaming kids buried in car payments, house payments and credit card debt. Given a choice, he'd much rather live alone in a trailer outside of town with some dogs. At twenty-eight, Tanya was still in good shape, but not a whole lot else going on. Was the abortion part of God's plan? If she'd had the kid, he'd be stuck here the rest of his life. In two months, Paul will turn thirty-nine.

I've been thinking about paroling to Albuquerque, he'd written last year in his journal. *Instead of Farmington. Why shouldn't I go back to school? Study psychology?* In fact he'd misspelled the word and written "phycology," which was one more example of what spending eight years in this town does to your brain. His sister Pam was a medical doctor. If he'd finished community college, stayed sober and kept his old tech job at Intel he would not have forgotten that word.

I have all the time in the world, he wrote in the journal. *If I think positively I realize there are a lot of people my age who would kill to have a chance like I have. No parents, no wife, no kids, not even a dog! I have nothing holding me back. I might as well make getting my P.H.D. in phycology my long term goal. Why not have two doctors in the Garcia family? This is mainly what I've been thinking about.* He'd been fasting for God when he wrote this, a thing he did every Wednesday but told no one about. The previous night, a new guy with a reputation for narcing had been moved into their pod and everyone jumped him. Seven guys punching and kicking him into a corner until he lay half dead on the floor like a dog with blood running out of his mouth and there was nothing for Paul to do except sit there and watch.

Why would I want to go back and work for Jerry? he asked the journal. *The guy won't even write to me, plus he's doing drugs and drinking. Why would I want an environment like that? Plus I'm pretty sure as a Latino ex-con I'll be entitled to grants and other assistance.*

But so far that hasn't happened. What *has* happened is, he has had to leave work and show up at parole to pee into a jar three times a week. Who else but Jerry would let him do that? Even if Pam had let him stay at her house for a while, without a guaranteed job you can't get parole, and he didn't know anyone like Jerry Koven in Albuquerque.

An addict himself, Jerry knew all the angles. He'd pretty much saved Paul's life that time back at County. As soon as Cris bailed him out, Jerry had her petition the judge for Paul's work release. Instead of sitting in jail, the guards let him out five days a week so he could sit in the back room at Casa Bonita and bullshit with Jerry. When they got bored, Paul went out on the floor. He had a rapport with the Natives and made lots of sales. Paul was so good at the job that by the end of his forty-five days, Jerry hired him on as the manager. So this time, when parole needed proof of a job, Jerry hired him back.

Is this what I've waited almost two years for? The subdivision spills out four blocks from the store at the corner of East Broadway and Main. Paroling to Farmington was disappointing enough, but working for Jerry and Cris feels like losing five years and he doesn't see any way out. Shouldn't he be advancing? After giving Jerry $400 for rent he's making way less than minimum wage, $150 a week. Cars and trucks he'll never own whizzing past on East Broadway, the pawnshops and 99-cent stores right in his face. He's not even really making $150 a week because he has to pay for parole, twenty-five dollars a week. And then credit card restitution, fifty dollars a month ... Where was the future? While he was still at the Farm he'd imagined it like a movie. His life would be only one thing, curved into space like a screen, devoted to God and sobriety but now that he's out there are hundreds of other things going on, things that shoot through your nerves and have no place to go. Paul feels these complications erupting all over his body like scabies. Lately he's been having dreams about cliffs. He's in a car with a few other people driving up Blaylock Ridge to look at the sunset. As soon as the driver turns off the motor he knows something bad's gonna happen. The door opens. People push him out of the car, one of them grabs his arm and tosses him over the cliff, he's too weak to resist. After falling, he wakes up in a sweat.

Well. He hasn't been to the gym or picked up the Bible since leaving the Farm but at least he hasn't taken a drink.

First to arrive at the store, Paul turns on the lights and coolers. The store is a big metal building, eight thousand square feet arranged in dollhouse displays: Southwestern, Traditional, Spanish Colonial, Early American, King Master Suites, Girl's and Boy's Bedrooms. He puts on an Eagles CD and makes a fresh pot of coffee. This is the best part of the day, alone in the back without the employees. Jerry and Cris have it made. They hardly even come into the store and they took in $40,000 last month just selling furniture. And that's not even the main part of the business. The real money is interest on payments, and Cris deals with that from her home office.

Jerry had one good idea when he opened Casa Bonita. Before then, Farmington didn't even have a furniture store. People drove down to Albuquerque, or if they had money, over to Santa Fe. Most people who shop at Casa Bonita don't even have trucks. They live out of town on the Navajo reservation.

Both of Casa Bonita's revenue streams—selling the shit on EZ terms and then taking it back when buyers miss their first payment—are tied to the monthly emission of government checks. The showroom is busy the first week after checks. By the end of the month, Hector, the ex-biker Jerry hired to repo, will be making his calls and returning with truckloads of stuff.

Paul's first job today is to draw up a list of people for Hector to "visit." Hector is new. In the old days, Paul and Jerry did it themselves, pretending they were gangsters ... Jerry getting his rocks off on how far he'd come from his career in geophysical science. Even though Paul's past was not as illustrious, he was in on the joke. They were slumming together. Paul felt bad, of course, when the wife burst into tears, as if she had no idea her old man wasn't making the payments. He was always amazed at how meekly the deadbeats opened their doors and surrendered the shit. As if they'd known this day was coming, since the moment they bought the new dining room set. It was like: Free Will, or Fate? Secretly, Paul considers himself a determinist, which could be one reason it took him so long to turn his will over to God. If the script's already written, isn't the decision kind of redundant? But, as Brother Charlie explained, as God's soldier, Paul's job was to take care of the footwork.

Paul feels almost god-like making the list, imagining the looks on people's faces when Hector walks into their houses. He has to remind himself to be humble. He is merely the instrument of a greater fate … Like how, in the CNN special on lethal injections, they always had two med-techs on the IV, one to release the anesthetic, the other the poison. Since the bags were unlabeled, no one had to deal with the guilt because no one was really responsible.

Tripping like this, Paul can forget for a while that *this is not what he wants to do with his life*. But what is? In the last ten days, his personal goals have diminished from becoming a doctor to saving up for a car, if he's lucky. He looks at the creosote scrub outside the back office window. The salesmen come in, and the rest of the morning drains off into business.

Just before Paul leaves for the noon Brown Bagger's meeting, Jerry calls saying he might stop by later on before closing. *Uh-oh*. For the whole ten minutes it takes to walk to the meeting, Paul considers the reasons Jerry might want to see him. None seem very good. He's being fired? He hasn't been there for him as a friend? The trouble with Jerry and Cris is, there's never a reason behind their actions. It's like his childhood. One minute his mom would be playing Stravinsky, the next she'd be slapping his face. You Filthy Greaseball. He'd better watch out. At Las Lunas he'd seen the counselor Suzanne a few times, and she'd told him to summon his Nurturing Self to silence his Critical Self so his Inner Child could run free and recover. Well, at least she was pretty.

The walk takes him past Sheila Gold's Sun Country mall Drug and Alcohol Center. After each DUI, he'd sat through dozens of Sheila Gold's classes. Sheila definitely had more going on than Suzanne. She wasn't an addict herself, but she was a pretty good sport. She'd moved here from Boulder and gone into counseling after getting divorced. The point was, she cared … Maybe not about him *personally*, but about what she was doing. Sheila was smart.

Paul hasn't seen Sheila since he got back to town. He might as well stop in to say hi, but her storefront is locked. There's only one car outside her door. It's a black Nissan ZX, '81, with the t-tops, a total classic. Maybe she's gone out for lunch? Last he knew, she drove a Camry.

The black car has a sign: *For Sale By Owner, 82,000 highway miles, asking $1,200*. Could it be Sheila who's selling the car? It doesn't look like her kind of ride, but maybe she took it as payment from one of her clients. This car is the bomb. Black with gray pin-stripes, no major dents. Sheila Gold was a *friend*. She'd come to his sentencing date as a character witness, and been totally shocked when the old redneck judge would not let her speak. "I think the court has already heard enough about this defendant. We're running three months behind schedule." She'd even complained to the DA that a sentence of three-to-five years

for a petty, nonviolent crime was *inappropriate* and *dispropor-
tionate*. Clearly, this woman wasn't from Farmington. He'd
written to thank Sheila once he got to Las Lunas and she'd
written back.

Paul's heart beat faster. A whole new piece of God's plan
spread out before him. Maybe having this car would not be
impossible. If the Z was Sheila's, she'd probably let him make
payments. She wasn't someone who needed the $1200 bucks.
She'd trust him. He'd already decided he was finished with
trucks. And he would not let her down. Maybe twenty-five
dollars a week, he could swing that. God's will be done he could
be mobile again, and in an excellent ride.

The meeting takes place in a small Catholic church hall that's
seen better days. Twenty-odd people, most of them men, sit
around two folding tables. By the time Paul arrives they're
starting the shares. He finds a seat near the door and opens the
Big Book. The group is the same every day, mostly nice, a few
old retirees and people who work in downtown stores and
municipal buildings.

The only weird person is Alan, the attorney who'd tricked
him into accepting the plea. Only in Farmington can you go to
AA and see your old public defender. He'd seen Alan last Friday
and of course avoided him, but he's here again today. Alan
doesn't seem too pleased to see Paul either. He's younger, late
20s, and keeps his eyes glued to the book. What a pussy. Paul
would never have pegged him as a drunk, but Alan has got to
be pretty messed up to show his face at this meeting. How
many other ex-clients does he see in these rooms? Paul guesses,

plenty. He has a black leather jacket on the back of his chair. Either he rides a motorcycle or he thinks he's cool. In any case, he looks pathetic.

Today's theme is Resentment. *It is plain that a life which includes deep resentment leads only to futility and unhappiness. With the alcoholic, whose hope is the maintenance and growth of a spiritual experience, this business of resentment is fatal. When harboring resentment, we shut ourselves off from the sunlight of the Spirit. The insanity of alcohol returns and we drink again. And with us, to drink is to die.*

As always, the first share comes from an old-timer. Alice, a middle-aged lady, talks about the first days of sobriety. Three months sober, she could not understand why she didn't feel better. "I was so pissed off all the time … of course I thought my problems were everyone else's. I hadn't worked all the steps. Really until I got to Step 4, I was just a dry drunk. But I had a great sponsor. My whole life was falling apart. I just wanted to talk. I wanted to tell her all the bad stuff that my husband was doing, what went on in the house, but she did not want to hear it. She just said, Read the steps. Work the steps. And she was right. I'd been avoiding the Fourth Step …"

Paul feels depressed. He'd been so excited when he saw the Z. But even if Sheila lets him make payments, where will he find enough money to get it on the road? There's insurance, probably triple with his DUIs, and—new since his last DUI—ignition interlock. Jerry has one in his old Ford Explorer. You have to blow into the thing to start the engine and bring it in once a month to be monitored. How much does that cost? Plus, it's more time off of work. A freakin' drag. It's like there's two sets of rules. Money's no problem for Jerry, but he hates blowing into that thing, which is why he kept the Explorer. The only time Jerry drives it is for the inspection. The rest of the time, he's in his new Dodge Durango.

Alice continues, "I must have been technically sober a year before I got around to taking Step 4's moral inventory. When I got to the part about *resentment*s, believe me, that list was long! At first it felt really good, get it out! But when it was done, I didn't like how it looked. I drank to not care, and when I stopped, all the old resentments came flooding back. I had to ask myself: Can everyone be that wrong? Mostly, I was using resentment to keep hurting myself. And then something happened. I just let go ..."

Maybe, Paul thinks, it's his resentment towards Jerry and Cris that stands in his way. Instead of resenting Jerry's success, he could ask him for help. With a car, he could do a better job at the store. He could drive the receipts every night up to Cris—

Everyone stands and joins hands for the prayer. *Keep coming back*—Paul feels a resolve as his arms move up and down. When the circle breaks, Alan comes over and offers his hand, and *fuck this is weird*—

"I just want you to know, I felt bad about how things worked out."

Alan seems pretty sincere. But how bad could he feel, sitting in court every day while Paul was locked up? Then again, why should he waste his time hating this lawyer? He has to move on—

"Whatever, man. I know how shit happens."

He shook the guy's hand, and then nearly ran out of the room to find Sheila Gold.

Jerry likes the media room because it's the only dark room in the Alpine Drive house. He has a headache. Most days he has headaches. The wreck left him with no sense of balance—he wobbles around like he's smashed, even the times when he isn't—and no peripheral vision in his left eye. His mouth makes too much saliva and sometimes he drools. Because the accident left his lips numb, he does not always know when this is happening. Every day it's like his brain is spinning a roulette wheel. Where's the white ball going to land? Headache, chest pains, loss of motor control rotate around his body like a flock of lost birds. When he's drunk or fucked up, the whole crazy process slows down. The same things are wrong, but it's like he's in a beneficent haze. Today he's more or less straight, sipping a beer. Judge Judy's on TV. He doesn't remember making a plan to visit Paul at the store, or why he made it.

Door opens, it's Cris. "Oh, so you're in here." She's got her skinny arms crossed, cranking up for an afternoon bitch-fest.

Jerry regards the woman he married ten years ago. At ninety-eight lbs, she looks like a long-bladed knife, or maybe a sparrow on crank. They met twelve years ago at the Farmington bar that she tended, and it occurs to Jerry that the less Cris has to do, the more hyper she gets.

"So. Are you gonna pick Dustin up from practice, or would you rather just sit here in your own drool?"

"Lemme think about that." He lets out a belch.

"Geez you're a pig." Cris's size is definitely her strongest card, the only link between her and the women he used to date in Chicago. The meds have made him so *hefty*.

"Mmmmm." Apart from her size, she's an unbearably ignorant cunt. "Whaddaya want me to do?"

"Jerry, you're so unreliable. I've been working on repos all day while you watch TV, and you still don't have time for your own kids. You have no idea what's going on at the store. You don't even know what's going on in this house. Misty's upstairs crying her little eyes out over Brandon—"

"Over who?"

"Dumb-ass, her boyfriend. And I saw *cuts* on her arms, this is new, thin lines like she's been cutting herself with a razor. I don't want to leave her alone in the house."

Jerry does not know what to think about this. Dustin, Misty and Cris are part of a strange constellation set into motion a long time ago. "Maybe she needs some time alone with her Dad."

"Jerry," Cris snorts, "you're such a zero, you're around more for the kids when you're gone."

"Nice tits," Jerry says in a daze towards her tank top.

"What are you, brain-dead? Why couldn't we have met in Chicago, when you still had a life?"

"Bitch, you think I would have looked at you twice? I took you out of a trailer park and gave you ... all this!"

"The only thing you've given me," Cris snorts, "is the—" but before she can say clap Jerry's phone rings. It's Paul, asking if he still wants to hang out.

Jerry picks up his keys. Cris can stay here with Misty. "I'm going down to the store. I'll grab Dustin on the way back."

A safe in back of the Casa Bonita office holds this week's cash receipts. Cris gave the combination to Paul on his first day at the store with strict instructions to never give it to Jerry. But now, Paul shouts out the numbers while Jerry spins the dial fiendishly. When the door opens, he reaches into its depths for an assortment of sad fifties and hundreds: deposits and lay-away payments. "Heh-heh brother, we're safe crackers." Jerry finds this highly amusing, breaking into his own safe and a shudder of thought at the back of Paul's mind tells him *Something is wrong here* ... but the business is still legally Jerry's. "Twelve hundred? No problem. It's a signing-on bonus, you've earned it." The more Jerry gives Paul, the more he's sticking it to the sorry bitch that he married.

The evening ends in a bar. Paul orders a Coke, Jerry drinks two doubles, and this alone would be grounds for Paul to lose his parole. He's not supposed to be in a bar, but is it his fault his boss is a psychopath? Jerry is talking about friendship, how Paul's the first person who's understood him since he left St. Louis. After the accident, maybe he could have gotten a job in the field ... How depressing, driving around in a Jeep for $40 grand a year after being a project director. Instead, he opened the store. You could say the accident saved him. Besides, Jerry adds, I like pussy too much to camp out in the field. Paul fakes a laugh. The moment's already passed when he could ask for more money to get the car on the road, but—thank God— Jerry's good mood continues into the next day.

At ten, he sweeps into the store and takes Paul to buy the Z. They drive over to Frenchy's and wait while the blow car device is installed. Paul can hardly believe his good luck. Maybe it's not really luck. Has he finally overcome his low self-esteem? Instead of isolating, he reached out to his boss. From there, they head over to AAA. Jerry pulls more large bills from his wallet and they leave with insurance, car papers and Paul's new ignition-interlock restricted license.

It's mid-afternoon when Paul returns alone to the store and realizes he completely forgot the noon meeting. A slow wave of dread follows him into the showroom. For the last fourteen hours he's been swept into a dream that was really just the old Jerry in his high manic phase. Why did Jerry even buy him the car? There's only one reason: to get back at Cris. When she finds out Jerry's been in the safe, she'll have a fit. She'll blame it on Paul and enlist him in a new scheme, most likely sexual, to get back at Jerry. Or else she'll blame it on Jerry, she'll blackmail him in some way, and what will Jerry expect in exchange?

Free for less than two weeks, he's trapped in their game.

But then it's not like that at all. Days pass without a peep from Jerry or Cris. The time changes, the days become longer. Driving around after work, Paul sees the good side of Farmington. Girls notice him in the car. He bags the Brown Baggers and drives out to Aztec to attend his old eight o'clock meetings with Mike D., his best friend and sponsor. With life reaching close to his hopes, he forgets about Albuquerque. If things stay on track, he might get a dog, ask for a raise, even rent his own place.

That spring, he does new things in Farmington: things he'd never thought about doing before he got sober. Before the relapse, he'd smoked pot occasionally. Amazing how much stronger, more in touch with himself he feels by abstaining. One Sunday he drives to Shiprock, an enormous cathedral of stone reaching up from the desert floor of the Navajo reservation. How many times has he driven past here and never seen it? The big rock has wings; it looks like a dinosaur bird. He gets out of the car. Seventeen hundred feet high, the rock is a labyrinth of caverns and pinnacles. Fast moving clouds break the sun into shadows of mutating color. The rock is protected by a Navajo curse. No one has ever succeeded in reaching the summit.

Driving home, he remembers Ravene. They'd met in Sheila Gold's Drug and Alcohol class. She was there for DUI 2 while he was waiting in County. With his sentencing date coming up, he didn't dare ask her out. Besides, he was still only several weeks sober. Still, they'd exchanged letters a few times when he got to Las Lunas. He'd sent her a Valentine's card and she did not send it back—she even thanked him. Then again, by the time he got to the Farm, she'd stopped writing. For a long time he'd felt anguished. Rejected, he figured that God was just doing some housecleaning. Maybe Ravene just found the whole prison thing too depressing. He thinks about calling. He rehearses the outcomes. What if she turns him down? What if she has a boyfriend? On Wednesday he decides he has nothing to lose. He calls from the store and she agrees to go out with him Saturday.

Suddenly, this seems worse than if she'd refused him. He hadn't planned for a yes. Except for Jerry's surprise, he hasn't been with a woman since Tanya. Is he supposed to sleep with Ravene? Does he even want to? Yes and no. Ravene doesn't really know anything about him. What will she think when she sees the hair on his back? The horrible scar that runs straight down his torso? He can always turn off the lights. If she wants to stay the whole night, what will he do in the morning? Isn't this just his Inner Critic talking? Anyway, who the fuck is Ravene? His hairy back is part of what makes him himself and if it's too gross, she can get lost. Yes, if he keeps thinking like this, maybe he can stay sober.

When he picks Ravene up on Saturday night, she stumbles out of her trailer like she's just done a line, all giddy and manic. Red flag. All those months at Las Lunas, Paul imagined Ravene as someone cool and desirable, but now she seems kind of scary with metal all over her face, a short skirt and a tube top. Over dinner he acts really polite. Even though he's rehearsed the whole sex thing about five hundred times, he takes her home early.

After the Ravene disaster Paul starts thinking again about leaving Farmington. If he stays in this town, he'll never meet anyone. The only foreseeable exit is getting Jerry and Cris to send him to Gallup. Towards that end, he throws himself into work at the store, finishing the outlet, setting up competitions between salesmen, helping out on the floor to sell stuff. The take shoots up by thirty percent and it seems like everyone's happy. But then, before Paul even raises the question, things fall apart in one day.

When Hector stops coming to work, Jerry decides he and Paul should do the end-of-the-month repos together. Paul isn't crazy about this. Busting into people's places and scaring old Navajo ladies is not what he signed on for. The more Paul resists, the more Jerry presses the issue. "Garcia, it'll be dope! Real wild-west shit, like we used to." When Jerry tells him to pull all the files and meet him in the parking lot Saturday morning at 8, Paul has no choice but to be there.

I don't want to be doing this, Paul thinks to himself, but the only way to stay sober is to do everything right. He gets to the store at seven thirty and makes coffee for himself and Jerry. He pulls all the files and sorts them in geographical order. This time, reading the names on the contracts, he imagines the looks on people's faces when he and Jerry start hauling their stuff out the door, how embarrassed they'll be in front of their kids and neighbors. He feels really bad about this, but it's his chance to pay Jerry back without doing something illegal. *Everything happens for a reason*, Paul repeats to himself, sipping his coffee and waiting outside the store for Jerry.

He waits half an hour. Finally, Jerry's Durango skids over the parking lot curb and nearly bucks to a stop as he slams on the brakes. *Oh fuck. It's eight thirty a.m. and Jerry's still high.*

His boss lurches out of the truck. Wearing the sweatshirt he slept in, Jerry considers the smug asshole employee standing outside *his* store in a sports shirt and neatly pressed chinos. Jerry's vision is blurred, but not so much that he can't see his old buddy Paul has turned into a jerk-off. The clipboard ... the mug straight from Starbucks. Paul is making it very clear he's above what goes on at Casa Bonita, but who does this shit think he is, with his AA meetings and faggot talk about God? Paul looks like a Youth for Christ leader, he won't even use the words *Jesus Christ* any more as a curse—but who does he think's paying his bills?

"So dickhead, whassup? You ready to roll?"

"Excuse me?"

"Ex-*cuse* me?" Jerry mimics. Where'd Paul come up with that? He sounds just like Misty, or one of the other bimbos-in-training at the Farmington Young Cunts Academy. "Hawww. No excuse for a sorry cocksucker like you."

Paul feels adrenalin pump into his fingers. "Jerry, what the fuck?" But he can't do this, he needs to calm down. "Listen man, let's just back off for a minute. You had a bad night. Just let me know—are you high?"

"Last I heard, asshole, you were working for me. Which makes what I do or don't do, none of your business. Your business is to take care of my business and from what I can tell, you're not doing much of a job."

"What are you talking about, Jerry?"

"Didn't I tell you to pull the files? Can't you even do that? Where the fuck are my files?"

"Jerry," Paul says, waving the clipboard, "what do you mean? The files are right here." He's starting to shake but he remembers Rule number five of the AA Dos and Don'ts. It says, *Don't be a doormat.* Or was that a floor mat? He's been thinking about buying new floor mats for the Z. "Jerry, I think you better be careful about how you're talking to me." God-damn—shit, now he's taking the Lord's name in vain—why is this happening? It's like something started to roll down a hill and now he can't get it back. But if he lets Jerry push him around, it will only get worse. "Jerry, I think you should take back what you just said."

Jerry can hardly see straight, the hard morning light sinking into his brain like an alien probe. He lets out a belch. "Ohhh, I see. Right. Now we're taking shit back? Well how 'bout I take back the car?"

"Jerry, you gave it to me!"

"Yeah see about gave. The car belongs to *my* business. If I hadn't bought it you'd still be walking all over town. Maybe then you wouldn't think you're so great. You'd still be locked up with your sand nigger friends if Cris hadn't signed for parole. And you think you're better than me? Shit. I built this business from nothing. You're forty years old. You can't even wipe your own ass."

The racial shit flies over Paul's head but it's four weeks until his thirty-ninth birthday and except for the Nissan ZX he does not own one thing to his name. And now with the felonies, except for Jerry, who will even give him a job? The whole thing makes him want to collapse. Standing here being screamed at by a raging crack-head makes him feel like he's six years old, and he just wants to cry. Instead he throws the clipboard onto the ground. "I'm out of here, motherfucker."

"You think you can leave? You can't leave!"

But Paul's already started his car. While Jerry stands in the parking lot trying to figure out what just happened, Paul heads out to Aztec to talk to his sponsor.

Paul, they decide, is in danger. He needs to get out of town. Mike D. helps him call Pam, who tells him he's welcome in Albuquerque. First thing Monday morning, Mike will find Sheila Gold and together, they'll talk to parole. Surely Paul's parole officer will agree that Paul can't stay on the job if his employer is using.

From Aztec, Paul drives back to the blue house on Slate Street and piles all his stuff into a couple of trash bags. He does this very quickly. Then he takes off the t-tops and starts driving to Albuquerque.

3

TRANSIT

ON THE LAST THURSDAY in April, Catt is driving to Albuquerque with Stretch and she cannot shake the cold she's had for more than a month since they slunk home from Baja. "The cold is the cure," she'd assured her diary after being sick for ten days but this is ridiculous. The cold moved from her throat to her nose and settled down in her lungs, its permanent residence. The doctor has warned her of walking pneumonia but she has to be there, her deals are all closing tomorrow. After the closing, she'll own thirty-three units—thirty-six, counting the condos—free and clear, with about $200,000 tax-sheltered dollars left over, providing the money is spent on improvements.

Wheezing along the I-40, Catt considers how broadly this word might be defined. Vehicles, travel, research, design … "Whatever you do, there's only a ten-percent chance you'll be caught," her ex-boyfriend Hank had advised her. "That's the statistical chance of an audit!" A jubilant cynic, Hank had done mega real estate deals for developers until an accident left him in traction. After that, he'd switched sides and devoted himself to good causes. Coaching her every step of the way, Hank found Catt's projects amusing. In the midst of all this, Tisa, one of

Catt's former mentees, a very political girl from Australia, had emailed to ask her how she planned to respond to George W. Bush's reelection.

"I'm gonna keep my head down!" was Catt's reply to this ludicrous question. It was painfully clear that staging a Noah's Ark of repression was part of the Bush regime's domestic policy pageant. Like everyone else, Catt had observed one or a few of each species—an Oregon lawyer, a Texas philanthropist, a musician, a handful of blue-collar workers—plucked from the social landscape and charged under the Patriot Act as state enemies. The prominence of these victims and the frequency of the arrests varied, but it was just enough to keep the whole population on the same terror alert posted at airports and harbors. *We can fuck you up good*, was the message. As everyone knew, the days of the public political trial were a distant historical memory—you could be sentenced to twenty years in federal prison and no one would blink, so why be a martyr?

In Catt's world, the artist Steve Kurtz had been the lucky martyr. Typing her credit card numbers into his online defense appeals, Catt was surprised by how much of a nonevent Kurtz's arrest had been in the art world. A fifty-eight-year-old SUNY Buffalo college professor, Kurtz's work had never been A-list or blue chip: it was didactic and topical. The guy was a crusty old hippie; he did not even have a good gallery. The art magazines—even the ones who'd refocused their brands as "political"—maintained radio silence. Because Kurtz's art work had nothing to do with *the politics of representation*, his story was left to Fox News, AP, and Reuters. His friends and supporters—the ones who'd received grand jury subpoenas—were strictly C-listers, with their tenure-track jobs in SoCal's least cool MFA programs.

Catt wondered if Homeland Security retained an art world consultant. Curatorially, their selection of Kurtz was impeccable. He had enough of a name to send a powerful warning, but he wasn't important enough for anyone to gain points by defending him.

In April 2005, four months into Bush's return to office, Michael Jackson stood trial in Santa Barbara for child sex and *Saw 2* had just hit the multiplexes. Film critics who once wrote for reputable magazines blogged to a handful of readers about the "new sadism." Last year's Abu Ghraib scandal had already been recycled as porn; *Abu Gag!* (The Best Throat Fucking Ever Lensed) was up for AdultCon's Grand Jury Award. While Homeland Security made preemptive arrests, any attempt at addressing the present, right down to this statement itself, now felt sadly preemptive.

Driving to Albuquerque, Catt is aware of two things:

She had to get rid of the cold and, if she is lucky, the twitch;

Her life might be better if she spent less time on the computer and more in "real" life.

To help with the latter, she'd decided to go out to Albuquerque and run the construction herself. Giving her money to a large, stupid ATV-riding white general contractor who hired illegals at minimum wage to do the real work offended Catt's sense of aesthetics. Instead, she'd built her small empire working with Titus, an Irish Sioux Indian she'd met at a lumberyard during her first year in LA. She'd just bought her first falling-down house and was determined to replace the asbestos siding with nice cedar shingles, but none of the white guys would touch it because asbestos was cancerous, so she'd decided to do it herself. *I mean, it's ridiculous*, she'd confided to Titus, leaning over the counter. *A few flecks of asbestos mixed in with tar just sitting there on the house since the Second World War? There's more cancerous stuff in the Los Angeles smog.* Titus held similarly libertarian views. In his forties like Catt, he exuded a wise aura of patience and calm. He and his wife Sharon had recently moved from Sonoma looking for work. The lumberyard paid him twelve dollars an hour. Catt offered him fifteen, and together they removed the asbestos and fixed up the house. When they'd finished, Catt took out a loan and bought another few fixers to keep Titus in work. Each time she flipped one, she gave him a bonus. Watching him ponder a mechanical problem was a beautiful thing. Like her, he thought for himself, and had not finished high school.

By the time the twelve-plex in Victorville sold, Titus was doing high-end renovations for architects, artists, and curators all over LA but—ever loyal to Catt—he'd offered to take time off from his business and come to Albuquerque to fix the new buildings up. Unlike Tommy, he'd never accompanied Catt on her short scouting trips in the winter, but she knew he could fix anything. Titus would bring out a small Victorville crew, including his grown-up son Brett who'd had some trouble up north and Sharon would come along for the ride. That made four, maybe five, and Tommy and Reynaldo, the Victorville maintenance guy, were coming out too, in the red truck she'd bought for Reynaldo to use on the job. Catt figured she'd just give Reynaldo the truck when they were through since his maintenance job would be over.

For the next five or six weeks, Catt and the crew would live in the three empty condos she'd bought. It would be like camp. No emails, no phone calls, no setting up meetings with friends ten days in advance. Her Outback is crammed with airbeds, foam mats, thrift-store dishes and pots. There's barely room for the dog. Hanging out with the crew would not completely replace the aboriginal life she once knew in London and downtown New York but it was a reprieve from her lonely life in LA. At least she wouldn't be surfing the web seeking out other killers.

Running the job on-site meant she could keep control of the books and eventually figure out what to do about Tommy. The guy was either inept or an out-and-out thief. At any rate, Tommy knows all too well what kind of money is floating around. He'd already hit her up for a "loan" of $10,000 before the closings ... a request Catt couldn't decline because Tommy had all her receipts and tax records for 2004 and 2005. And as they both knew, but never discussed, the returns Tommy filed on her behalf were, if not cooked, at least somewhat ... unsubstantiated? Hell, even keeping her head down she could end up in prison for fraud and there'd be no organic tomatoes or humanely raised chickens. The threat Tommy poses, if she let herself follow that thread, leads to the same place she'd been with her killer. To lower your guard, to surrender, to allow yourself to be conned ... she knew in the end both men could win because they wanted to win more badly than she did.

But then again, maybe not. If all goes according to plan, they'd finish the job by the first week of June. She has no other plans for the summer except to take some time off and travel. South India, maybe Nepal?

But nine hours into the drive on I-40 East this triumph is too far away to even enter her mind. The cold will not quit. Coughing so hard she can't catch her breath, she feels small and exhausted.

Who, she thinks, can I talk to? In Arizona, near Kingman, she digs in her bag for her phone and punches Hank's number.

Upon his sixtieth birthday (which coincided with the reelection of George W. Bush) Hank shut down his public policy lobbying firm and announced he'd entered the mentoring phase of his life. Which was a joke. Hank had always felt most alive when giving advice. A short, squat man with classically handsome American features sharpened by age, Hank called himself *consiglione*. Reaching him at the end of another bad day, he is only too pleased to be the *Consiglione* of his ex-lover's cold. "Catt," he drawls, "what I want you to do is pull your little car off the I-40 and stop at a Walgreen's. There's one just east of Kingman." Hank had once run successful campaigns for some of America's first progressive black politicians. His advice is highly specific and programmatic. "You got that? Now, you're going to need to spend thirty dollahs"—(Hank's money-voice reverts to his Southern origins) "—that's right, don't be so cheap, on an assortment of over-the-counter flu and cold remedies. Nyquil, Tylenol 3, you know the kind. They come in nice, bright shiny boxes—"

Catt was dazed. More than advice, she wants his sympathy. "But Hank, you know I don't believe in those things," she sighs dreamily. In his day Hank had believed there was no problem he couldn't solve, and it saddens Catt to see his brilliance reduced to curing a cold. "You know?" Slipping back into her old mistress role, she thought she could turn the faucet back on to his blind adoration. "They're full of corn starch and dyes, they're all the same shit garishly packaged in about two dozen brands—"

"Ahhh, you're such a snob."

At the height of his infatuation with Catt, Hank had seen this as a positive thing. She was his Pamela Harriman, which, Catt had thought was quite a stretch … although in Hank's downtown LA political world, her bourgeois-bohemian life did seem faintly glamorous. To Catt, Hank's world seemed wildly exotic. In New York she only knew artists. If she hadn't moved to LA, she would never have met someone like Hank. She knew he was still angry with her for vacating the mistress slot in his life, and for what? To meet killers?

"Yeah," she complied. "Hank, I know—half of America doses themselves on this shit because they can't afford to stay at home sick." Hank's mom had been a small-town legal secretary. Catt's was a bookkeeper. Both she and Hank were the children of sober, intelligent parents, the cream of the working class, who had only two kids, took summer vacations and went to the theater.

"I'm still madly in love with you." Hank's voice was a distant squawk on the phone … his sign-off line in their thousands of phone calls. Catt felt a bottomless loss. Where would she go? Between Kingman and Flagstaff there was only Williams …

"Hank, I'm really—sick." But Hank had a call coming through and her cell phone cut out.

Fifteen minutes later, Catt pulled into a mall. Hank was right, there was a Walgreen's. A few exits past Kingman, the landscape had drastically changed. Tall evergreen trees lined the road and outside, the gray dusk was blustery cold.

Catt dug a cardigan out of her bag and entered the over-lit store, filling a basket with pills, syrups and gels. The register flashed $32.12. Hank had forgotten the tax. She let Stretch out to pee and poured some of the cherry goop into the screw-top measuring cup. Why ask for advice if you're not going to take it?

She held her nose, swallowed. Before Hank shut down his firm, his billable rate was $600 an hour. For years in LA they'd kept each other amused, shocking his friends. "This is Catt Dunlop," he'd introduced her once to the mayor. "We trade sex for legal services." She'd always be loyal to Hank. He taught her everything.

By now it was practically dark. Sweating and coughing, she called Stretch back into the car. The medicine hadn't done shit. The wind howled and big clumps of wet snow swirled in the arcs of the parking lot lights. Could she drive through this? For how long? Stretch was all wet. She could not find a towel. The adrenalin pushing her forward was gone. She was losing her will. She started to sob in front of Walgreen's.

She reached for her cell and punched one of the few numbers she knew by heart: the last sympathy stop, her elderly parents. Married for decades, they'd merged into one voice. On the third ring, they picked up the phones they kept side by side. Before admitting defeat, Catt tried to convey the extent of her efforts. Her deals were ready to close. When they did, there'd be almost $200,000 left that she could access whenever she liked. It was a 1031 construction exchange, one of Hank's tax angles.

"Oh," they replied.

Why weren't her parents impressed or even excited? They'd been poor most of their lives, and now she'd finally made some real money. She remembered how crushed her friend Giovanni had been when, after achieving a stunning success in the art world, he returned to New Zealand and his old friends had nothing to say to him. Hadn't he done it for them? Making every right friend in cities all over the world, there had not been a day when he hadn't remembered the grandiose plans they'd made in their teens. And he'd been faithful to that. He'd achieved them. But they couldn't imagine the five thousand small steps it took to reach his success. All they could see was, he was no longer like them.

"But I'm still sick," Catt continued. "I can't shake this cough. And it's snowing. Maybe I'll stop for the night soon, maybe in Flagstaff. Instead of driving straight through like I'd planned."

"That sounds sensible dear," her mother said.

"The beginning of wisdom," added her dad.

Snapping the phone closed, Catt drives back onto the freeway, coughing and blinded by snow. Forty-five minutes later she exits in Flagstaff and finds a sleepy rundown motel for thirty dollars.

Sometime during the sixteen months he was in prison, Paul's sister Pam moved from her nice Southwest adobe luxury tract-home in northwest Albuquerque to a larger and nicer one two or three subdivisions away. Paul's been here five days. He can't get his bearings. Running from Jerry felt almost the same as running away from the law. Scared but excited, the danger lifts him up out of dread and pulls him forward to the unknown. Except for the great room, Pam's new house in Las Lomitas Heights seems exactly the same as her old one. Outside, the same freshly-poured black asphalt streets, the same long cement driveways, the same three-car garages set about thirty feet back from the road.

At quarter to nine it looks like a nuclear bomb has been dropped on the subdivision: kids at school, parents at work. Paul sits at the breakfast bar between the kitchen and great room drinking coffee and reading the paper. A comfortable scene, but he woke up this morning with the old feeling of dread. Pam's been incredibly nice about letting him stay here, almost *too* nice. Last night she took him to 24 Hour Fitness. She even bought him a card and said "Stay as long as you like," but what does that mean? A week, maybe two?

She has a new boyfriend, which makes Paul at least not totally useless. On Sunday she asked him to watch her son Raymond, which should have been cool except Paul knows that Raymond dislikes him. Each time Pam visited Paul at Las Lunas, she brought Raymond along, which on the surface seemed *nice* until, Pam being Pam, she made some remark about "scaring him straight." At eleven, Raymond still has a room full of little kid's toys. Things with Pam can change overnight, and then where will he go?

So far parole's been pretty cool. They had no issues with him leaving Farmington after he said he was staying in Las Lomitas Heights with Dr. Pam Garcia, his sister, a medical doctor. But the work situation is bleak. The job board at parole had only one posting, twenty hours a week at minimum wage. He's applied to Target and Wal-Mart and about ten other places but each time the interviewer sees the tick on the *Yes* box below *Have You Ever Been Convicted of A Felony?* the person's face changes and he knows it's all over. Thank You Mr. Garcia We'll Call If We Have Anything.

Paul never had trouble finding a job all the years he was drinking. If he was in Farmington his sponsor Mike could probably still hook him up with a job in the fields. But most of the jobs here are corporate, like Intel and Sprint, or chain businesses. He needs to start looking in places where the felony thing won't be an issue. Most restaurants are out, because parole won't let him work anywhere liquor is served. A little mom 'n pop place, some hole in the wall—a garage, maybe a junkyard? But he's got to be careful. If they find out he's working for someone with a criminal background, they'll revoke his parole.

Snow fell in giant white clusters overnight while Catt slept.

She wakes up to bright morning sun seeping through thin faded curtains. Outside, warm amber light turns the parking lot snow into slush. She sees a hippie café across Route 66, vacates the room, throws Stretch in the car and goes in for a coffee and muffin. Flipping her phone open she sees the mailbox is already full. It's only nine thirty—who could be trying this hard to reach her? Not Hank, not Michel. Her throat tightens. Then she remembers. She'd taken out a newspaper ad to start running this morning in Albuquerque, where she should already be. She'd written it almost as carefully as the first email she sent to her killer.

Property Manager Wanted: Alert, creative person or couple needed to manage 36 units. Duties include leasing, light maintenance, bookkeeping. Must have handyman skills. Excellent compensation includes free apartment, salary and possible profit share.

God, she'd been so sick she forgot it was Friday and the whole thing is starting today. The café is cheerful. She drags a spiral pad out of her bag and hits *1* for voicemail, unleashing a roll call of the unemployable. Old men, young men, men of indeterminate age with accents so thick she can barely make out what they're trying to say. Since she'd forgotten the ad she'd never changed the outgoing message—*This is Catt. Talk!*—and most of the callers seem angry and startled. *"Ma'am? Hello Ma'am? I'm callin' after the Manager job—have I got the right number?"* *"I've only got a few minutes left on my phone so you can't call me back, I'll try this again tonight from my aunt's."* A lone female voice says, *"I got fired from my last job and I'm havin' problems with childcare. I don't really have any experience property managing but maybe you'll give me a chance?"* Of the seventeen rambling messages, two are at least in the ballpark; men with experience, tools and reachable phones who hope Catt will "pass on their information to the person in charge."

Draining her coffee, Catt writes down their numbers. Maybe this won't be so easy. Once she's settled in Albuquerque, she'll rethink the problem. Try Craigslist or flyers around the university. In a city where so many people work for minimum wage how could she *not* find a quality person with these generous terms? There's no point in rehabbing the buildings only to leave them with a property management company who'll cheat her and overcharge for repairs while letting the apartments run into the ground. She needs someone like Titus who *cares*, who, like them, wants to do some small good in the world, rehabbing apartments in low-income neighborhoods to make them as nice as they can possibly be. Someone she can trust to collect and hold the cash rents, so she can set things in motion and leave.

Fully alert, she heads back onto I-40 East. On the highway, the snow still hasn't melted. Stands of snow-laden Norwegian pines line the road. Tall yellow stalks of Scottish Broom on the median poke through banks of plowed snow. Driving into the light, sun glints on the iced evergreen needles, the sky is deep turquoise blue. At eight-thousand feet, it's like watching two seasons collide. For the first time since leaving LA, Catt feels like she's on a real road trip. When the phone rings, she's recalling the Mishima novel she read in her teens, *Spring Snow*, the strange dialectic between nature and human emotion, so perfect it's hard to believe that a person wrote it. She feels far away from her life when she flips open her cell, *Yes, hello?*

"Hello ma'am. You placed an ad in the paper this morning?" The caller's deep, grounded voice brings her back—

"Mmm, yeah. That's right—"

"—for a property manager."

"Uhhh, yeah. I'm—we're—looking for someone to manage thirty-six units."

Paul glances down at the circled ad—"alert, creative"—what kind of job asks for that? "Well, the position sounds very intriguing." His use of the word pressing a switch in Catt's brain. Now she's totally there. Was his opening "Ma'am" maybe ironic? "I've recently moved back to town and I'd like to apply." "Oh? Where are you moving back from?" (Combing her mind for impressions to share when he says San Francisco, New York, or LA—) "Farmington."

"Uh?"

"Yeah. I guess you're not from the state. It's a little oil and gas town, up by Four Corners."

She thinks of the movie *Five Easy Pieces*. This is a total surprise. "No ... I'm from LA."

"Right, the 213 on your phone—" And now she's intrigued. The guy's really quick, but there's a directness and presence behind his voice, as if he's talking to her, specifically. Actor-ish, almost, but in a good way. Warm but not fake. She thinks of Ron Vawter, Jim Fletcher—great New York actors she's known who grew up in remote rural places and never lost that identity despite their careers. "Actually I'm not from LA, I grew up in New Zealand … and then I lived in some other places … But I've been in LA for ten years."

Just then a call comes blipping through. She still hasn't mastered call waiting. "Listen, uh, what's your name?"

"Paul Garcia—"

"I'll call you right back."

Catt slows down and parks next to an off-ramp to take the next call. The caller, a man in his forties, has just lost his on-site management job because the owners are selling. Eighty-four units, he's had the job for eight years. He has excellent references. Leasing, repairs, contracting bids, profit and loss, he's done them all. Mechanically, Catt takes down his number and says she'll call him back later. Then she hits redial for Paul.

Still in Pam's kitchen, he watches the phone and picks it up two seconds past the third ring.

"Hello Ma'am?"

"It's Catt. So where were we?"

"LA?" She laughs. "Actually I'm just outside of Flagstaff." Why is she telling him this? It seems important to stay on the phone long enough to figure out who this person might be. "I'm driving out from LA to close on three buildings."

This doesn't sound right. She imagines the picture unfolding in the applicant's mind—tough Orange County late-forties blonde in a new Mercedes. "Actually I'm not a full-time investor. I mean, it's not what I *do*. I teach history and cultural studies. I write about art, I do other things. This is more like a hobby."

Paul's never heard of cultural studies. He doesn't know what to say about that. She imagines him taking it in.

"The buildings I'm buying are pretty distressed, so we're planning on rehabbing them right away. Tommy, my business manager, will be out tomorrow. We've got a crew coming out from LA. Our plan is to restore the apartments—they may be run down but they have some fantastic architectural detail—and get them ready to rent. So the manager we hire ideally might be involved. Have you done any construction or maintenance work?"

"Yes ma'am. I've got my own transportation and tools. In fact, one of my jobs back in Farmington was to restore mobile homes."

Catt hears restore. She doesn't hear trailers.

"And you'd be willing to live at one of the properties?"

This could be a way out of Pam's house. It sounds almost too good to be true. "Yes, absolutely. I've just moved to town. I'm at my sister's house. I haven't really got settled anywhere yet. Actually, to tell you the truth, I left Farmington in a rush. There were some problems at my last job, so I'd rather not give that as a reference. But I've got plenty more. I am pursuing a life of rigorous honesty now. As soon as I find a job, I'm hoping to go back to school, maybe part-time."

There, Catt thinks. *A life of rigorous honesty*. He's a recovering alcoholic and most likely newly sober. That's what she heard in his voice, the rawness and urgency a person feels when they're trying to start a new life. Paul's voice brings her back to herself ten years prior when she moved to LA to start her own life. "When do you think you could start?" She tells Paul she'll call him back in a few hours, flips the phone closed and is confused to notice she's no longer on I-40. It's like she can't get out of Flagstaff. Did she drive off the ramp before calling Paul? Circling back, she calls Tommy, who has some kind of municipal job that leaves him plenty of time to take care of Catt and his other clients on the government's nickel. "Tommy? Listen, you won't believe this but I think I've just found the right guy—"

"Oh yeah? Do *tell*—"

"—for the management job."

"Did we close?"

"No I'm still in Flagstaff. I had to stop for the night. You remember the ad? Well about twenty-five hicks called up for the job, it was like being back in East Fletcher, I almost gave up— but then this other guy called. He seems just right. He seems like someone we can deal with."

"Girlfriend *slow down!* You know the manager job is a major staffing decision. He'll be reporting directly to me—"

"Yeah but what we did not factor in about the apartment is, the only people who aren't set up in a place there are the homeless. Uh, I guess it's not like New York or LA. This guy Paul Garcia has just moved back to town. For him, living at one of the buildings would be a positive."

"Okay Catt I hear yah. You just better not make any big moves before I get to town."

She tosses the phone into the glove box. Outside the highway descends thousands of feet. Her heart leaps ahead of her mind, as if she's opened a door to the future. The light is still dim. What she sees are just shapes. There's an energy moving inside her, the same way she felt when she started writing, as if she'd been kidnapped by an idea. If Paul takes the job, the whole scheme might fall into place. The idea of people working together, whether on a film set or construction job site, was in some way utopian. She thinks of the pictures of villagers tilling

March fields in the Middle Ages: a small cosmos, everything held in its place. For six weeks instead of sitting in front of a screen, she'd have something to do, with other people. Not forever, of course. Eventually, she'd fly back to Albuquerque every two months to pick up the rents, which Paul would collect, and she'd use to invest in some other project. Approaching the Petrified Forest National Park, she takes out the phone. Waiting for Paul to pick up, it's as if their positions have changed. Even though he's the one who needs a job, she really wants him to take it.

Paul is still assessing his change of luck when the phone rings again. Catt asks him to meet her and Tommy at one of the buildings on Sunday morning for a first interview. He writes down the address. Estancia Drive, number 256. He doesn't know where it is, but he'll find it.

As soon as she gets off the phone he feels dizzy and lost. Five days ago he was in Aztec, ready to crash on his sponsor Mike's couch with Mike's two screaming ADD kids ... and then here at Pam's. He does not know where he is. Who is this woman Catt, and the guy she talks about, Tommy, is he her husband, her boss? He'd never once thought about working in real estate. What first comes to mind are Farmington white-bread Republicans.

But Catt and this Tommy seem more like entrepreneurs ... And maybe they're offering him a chance to get in on the ground floor. *This* was a change. At parole yesterday he'd had to wait almost an hour, until the only male officer could come into the bathroom with Paul and watch him pee into a jar. Most of the parole officers were women, but two-thirds of the clients were men. Anyway, the guy, Officer Hanson, who was of course white, stood watching him at the open stall while Paul unzipped his pants for him. He was wearing his job interview clothes. At that moment, parole felt even worse than being in prison. No orange jumpsuits, no cuffs, but the attitude was, *we hate you now and forever*. When he'd tried to explain this to Pam, she said, "Everyone gets what they deserve."

Shit, even though Pam's a doctor, she's hardly been out of town. Paul imagines himself with a briefcase, flying out to LA to meet with his bosses on a business trip. Catt and this Tommy were probably stupid enough in their own way—her delight in the "fan*tas*tic architectural detail" in some, most likely, crack den deep in the war zone—but at least it was a breath of fresh air. He wouldn't mind getting rich if it's part of God's plan.

Crossing the New Mexico line, Catt realizes she's no longer coughing. She's awake, her head's clear, I-40 cutting a straight line across the mesa. Just east of Gallup, white horses graze among red lava rocks. The temperature outside is seventy-two degrees. She can't remember the cold leaving her body. Weird. Somewhere back on the road between the flurry of calls, the Scottish Broom stalks and the snow, it just disappeared.

4

DOG-EARED DREAMS

LUNCH, DRINKS, MAYBE BOTH? Edgar Moreno asks Catt when she finally arrives to sign deeds. Walking into the dim late-Friday hush of Satellite Investments her heart was still racing. Following Edgar past empty work-stations she told herself, *I've arrived, I'm no longer moving.* The twitch near her left eye thrashed around while she was reviewing the papers, but this, she assured herself, could not be a warning, simply a consequence of slowing down. Because all the omens so far today have been favorable.

It's a gorgeous spring day in Albuquerque, cool breezes masking the heat of the blinding sun on the mesa. En route to the Satellite office in Old Town, she saw lilacs in bloom, tulips and daffodils lining the walkways to well-preserved turn-of-the-century houses.

When Catt signs her name on the last dotted line, Edgar hands her the key rings. It's still not official—she has to sign papers with the 1031 guy this evening—but close enough. They decide to go out for omelets and margaritas at Camacho's. They take Edgar's truck—an old unrestored Silverado, the perfect accessory to his beige Armani suit—to the old-school Mexican luncheonette that had been one of their meet-points last winter.

Now that she's no longer driving, Catt feels like she's stepped into another dimension. She can barely keep up with Edgar's account of why they're not in his (silver, broker-esque) Lexus ... his car was in the shop being detailed because of the lingering smell left by an old high-school buddy he'd picked up hitch-hiking. *Man, I think the guy was living under a bridge.*

This was congruent with Catt's highly favorable impression of Edgar. Driving around town in the Lexus during her winter trips, he'd told her about his South Valley childhood, his high-school athletic career that led to an NYU football scholarship. Wisely, he'd majored in business, and then moved back to start Satellite when he realized an NFL draft wasn't imminent. They'd both been in New York in the mid-'80s and gone to some of the same bars and clubs. At thirty-four, he's a decade younger than Catt but he's supporting an ex-wife, two little girls, and his elderly mother.

Still, the West-Central strip between Camacho's and Satellite looks different to Catt than the last time she'd been here, in March. During those feverish buying trips, Edgar had put her up at the Azure ... an Old Town boutique hotel that limply modeled itself on The Standard. Even then, it hadn't completely escaped Catt that she was one of the hotel's very few out-of-town business clients. Several floors of the hotel were reserved for "permanent guests": people living in over-priced rooms paid for by Social Welfare. At the time, this hadn't bothered her but now passing the Azure in daylight, she sees that it reeks of poverty: the corroded aluminum frames of its modernist windows annealed by spring light.

Last winter, simply putting a coat on and looking up at the thousands of stars in the sky outside the airport had made her excited and happy. But now she sees other details she'd missed: there are no *youths* in sight outside the American Youth Hostel across the street from the park, which she'd found so provincial and charming, a hippie throwback. Half of its derelict residents are selling drugs in the park. The rest are passed out on benches. And the vintage Route 66 hotels with impeccable names—the El Sol, the Aztec, the Stardust— are actually flophouses.

Still, even today, when the keys in her bag make her no longer just a voyeur, the town's dereliction stirs Catt towards a mysterious beauty. Less than a half-mile away, old adobe farmhouses sit in big overgrown yards with chickens and outbuildings. It's as if *no one wants it* ... pieces of time that have been left to slumber away un- ravaged by, as Michel would put it, the violence of capital. Catt feels an almost sexual thrill in these places. They are fully alive, holding onto their secrets ... the *inconnu*, the undiscovered. She wants to swallow it whole, as if the past can be penetrated simply by walking through it.

Michel had flown out to join Catt on that last March trip to Albuquerque. He understood his estranged wife's magical thinking. Over the years, he'd expanded his baseline of normal. But this delusional flight to a Mexican town from a man she insisted on calling her killer? This alarmed him. "I need to pull out of this, find something to live for again," she'd sobbed to him for weeks that winter, over the phone. "I have to get out of this sink-hole of sadness." Clearly whatever life she'd made for herself in LA was driving her crazy. He was relieved when she threw herself into this real estate venture, and thought he should support it.

But how could Michel, an indisputably recognized intellec- tual commentator, understand her dilemma? After coming back from the tour, she'd played a cameo role in a friend's video art piece: a Druid priestess fellating a tree, in a blonde wig and long purple dress cut down past her tits. Wasn't she getting a bit old for this? A reviewer of her last book accused her of giving him "blue balls." If only she'd attended an Ivy League school, her work might have been read as *serious* cultural criticism, not the punch line of the last dirty joke in the world. But what was dirty? It was like the cutters and suicide girls who signed up for her classes ... their slutty outfits and exposed navel rings were not especially *sexual*. Girls their age were *supposed* to look slutty, and the g-strings and tube tops they bought at the mall weren't a proof of their narcissism, but a means of staying under the wire! It was like, when her friend Giovanni died of a heroin overdose, the art world fell over itself to depict his death as the tragic bad luck of a casual user. G. adored smack. It was the *yin* to the *yang* of his ambition. But to admit that he was both a prodigious success *and* an addict would force them to look at the psychic cost of traveling from a small town New Zealand Juvenile Hall to international art world fame in less than two decades. For two years, he couldn't afford a car in LA. Even though he spent hours each day commuting to his elite MFA art school on public transit, he forced himself not to resent his trust-funded classmates. "There are more than enough rich and talented people to fill all the slots in the art world," he said wryly. Catt enjoyed watching her students because they had to live in the world, and she was curious how they would do it.

By the time Catt met her killer, some of her dreams had come true and some had been abandoned. "I need new dreams!" she'd wailed to Michel. And, having missed her 45th birthday, he'd brought a beautiful cake with him from New York with an original poem written in icing: *Dog-eared dreams / Fire inside.* But even then, at the Azure, she'd wondered if new dreams were even possible?

Over drinks at Camacho's, Edgar tells Catt that her friend Tommy's friend Jill has called his office six times trying to shake him down for fifteen percent of his commission. "Jill says, since she's a broker and she gave Tommy my number to pass on to you, she's owed a referral. I mean, can you believe it? I've never talked to her in my life, my information's online, anybody can see it." Voicing surprise and outrage, Catt considers the threads of this latest scam. She's never met Jill, but Tommy's mentioned her as the lesbian partner of his co-worker, Camilla. She imagines Tommy preparing the script for Camilla to pass onto Jill, extorting money they'd split, what, 50/50? And then Tommy would wring his hands, whining about being placed in the middle. "She even threatened to have me investigated. Well, pigs will fly before that fat flaming fuck—" (They grin. Joining Catt on one of her trips, Tommy had put one hundred dollars of sushi on Edgar's check at a restaurant)—"gets a dime of my money."

Albuquerque's Old Town has been on the verge of renewal since Edgar Moreno picked up a football. If he hadn't attended NYU, he would have remained pessimistic about the district's potential, which, he sees now, would have been the more realistic assessment. His client Catt Dunlop insists the SoCal real estate boom is an illusion, about to fall apart any day now. But what does she know? Still, he's hoping she's the first wave. Her flips accounted for half of Satellite's business this quarter.

He doesn't want to be in the house when Pam and Raymond get home, so Paul decides to check out the five o'clock meeting on

San Mateo and Central. Pam didn't have room in her three-car garage for his Nissan ZX, so he has to blow-start the thing in front of the neighbors. Luckily there's still no one around. The black car looks different outside Pam's house from what it looked like at Casa Bonita. It looks like a heap. Here, the gardeners drive shiny Dodge Rams and the cleaners have Accents and Sentras. Paul wonders what the neighbors are thinking. Except for the gardeners and cleaners, he hasn't seen any other Hispanics. Have they figured it out? That he's the ex-con, black sheep relation of the good Dr. Pam?

A warm feeling of hatred surrounds his body, his face flushes. The old Paul Garcia would have just had a drink. Weird how he hasn't been to a meeting since he got to town. He'll have to use different pens to sign the five empty slots on his AA meeting card before going back to parole.

He puffs up his cheeks, blows and hums into the blowcar device's plastic mouthpiece. First try, the thing blinks green for a pass, and he starts feeling better once he gets out of Las Lomitas Heights. Roadwork on Coors—the drive's gonna take forty minutes. But at least he has somewhere to go, and the meetings make him feel cleaner.

On the southeast corner of San Mateo, St. Bridget's church straddles the edge of the UNM campus and the start of the war zone that's spread like a red tide from the old County Fairground. During the Route 66 era, the motels and bungalow courts around the Fairground were lived in by seasonal drifters who worked the game-booths and rides. Now they're terrariums for gang members tied to Juarez, illegal immigrants and welfare recipients from Arizona and Texas who've moved here for larger New Mexico checks.

It's 5:15 when Paul arrives at St. Bridget's and he nearly bags the whole thing—he hates being late, hates anything that makes him conspicuous—but he sneaks into a seat at the back of the Community Room. About thirty-five people, the place smells of Lysol and floor wax. Someone hands him a Xerox of the twelve steps, and he's almost relaxed when a guy in the front catches his eye and half-waves. Fuck. It's Frank Harwood.

The last time Paul saw Frank Harwood was at Santa Fe Level III, where Frank was nearing the end of a nine-year Manslaughter Sentence. Even at Santa Fe, Frank had creeped Paul out particularly, which was saying a lot because there was no end of skanky shit there. And it wasn't as if Frank had done anything heinous. He'd crashed into a tree! Of course he was drunk and the passenger died, which was bad, but he hadn't *tried* to kill anyone. The problem with Frank was, he was pathetic. From the first day, Frank hovered around like they were supposed to be *friends*, as if Paul could give him protection. The guy had been there eight years and he still hadn't figured it out. The Negroes, the Natives, the Latinos, the Aryan Brotherhood, the Others ... Frank hated them all, and they hated him back. Before the car-wreck, he'd been in insurance. Paul knew the last thing he needed was a buddy like Frank. But avoiding Frank made Paul feel terrible. He knew *exactly* what Frank Harwood was feeling: before he'd stopped attending, he'd been one of the class geeks at his school.

Seeing him now brings the whole sordid thing back. When will this shit be *over*? He can hardly stand to remember the twelve months he waited at Santa Fe for the check charge to be calendared: the closed-circuit cameras, the floodlights, the twenty-foot walls, the fear that stayed in your blood like a drip feed. So much for fresh starts. This is supposed to be Alcoholics *Anonymous*.

If it weren't for Pam, Paul would have gone straight to the Farm, where he belonged, with the white-collar guys and the potheads. He had no priors, he'd been charged with a nonviolent crime. If Pam hadn't promised to pay off the checks, and then changed her mind—

—But once she did, they had to keep him at Level III while the new charges were pending. *Of course* the first thing he did when he ran out of money was write a bunch of bad checks, it seemed safer. He only started using the card when merchants stopped taking the checks. Still, the DA didn't catch up with the checks (a misdemeanor) until he was already in San Juan County Jail awaiting trial for the credit card fraud (which was a felony). He was already sober eight weeks and the DA had been really nice, actually sympathetic. She'd offered to drop the whole thing if he could come up with restitution.

Of course he didn't have it—with the interest and penalties, it was almost $3,000—but he knew Pam did. And he felt really *bad* calling collect from the jail to ask for a loan. But she'd said *Yes*, and that night he felt amazing ... as if God was letting him know his new life wouldn't be bad now that he had his sobriety.

He didn't call Pam again, and she didn't visit. He kept on believing she would take care of it ... until his court date, when the nice DA stood up to tell him and the judge she *still had not received payment*. Now she'd *have* to write up the charge for the checks. Later, Paul found out Pam had taken Raymond on some stupid Disneyland trip. And when it came time to be sentenced, the judge read out some regulation, *Any prisoner with pending charges will automatically be classified to at least Level III* ... if Pam had just said *No*, like she meant, the whole thing would have been settled.

At the front of the room, the leader is reading about the 9th step, "making amends," from the Big Book.

Paul thinks: I have to try and stop feeling so bad about Pam. And then they open the meeting to shares.

Of the twelve Steps, Step 9 is the only one that leaves room for interpretation. Following on from Step 8 ("Made a list of all persons we had harmed, and became willing to make amends to them all,") it says:

Made direct amends to such people wherever possible, except when to do so would injure them or others.

Of course there's no crosstalk allowed, but people are struggling within their shares to reach some consensus about what "except" really means. As an example, The Big Book cites an extra-marital affair: better, they say, to just quietly *end* than make a *public* amend and risk the end of your marriage and hers—but, as one nicely-dressed lady observes, old Bill was a notorious womanizer and maybe *this* part of the book is less than one hundred percent canonical? Canonical is a word Paul cannot remember anyone using in Farmington. He'll look it up later.

But, he thinks, it's not just the word "except" that's confusing. What about "other"? Didn't the alcoholic himself count as an "other"? This is the word he focused on most when he was working the step with Mike D. back in Farmington. Because if the alcoholic wasn't careful about not making amends that would injure *himself*, didn't he risk slipping back into the old negative thoughts and self-loathing? And Mike had agreed.

Paul is still thinking about this when they stand to recite the Serenity Prayer at the end of the meeting. Before he can find his way out the door, Frank Harwood is there, shaking his hand warmly—*Garcia! I never thought I'd see you again.*

Frank Harwood looks bad. In prison, he always looked scared, but now he looks defeated. He's wearing a navy-blue blazer, ten years out of style, double vents, a jacket he probably had before he went in. *Heh—here we are, on the outs.* "On the outs"? Please. What is he watching, some after-school special? *So, how's freedom treating you?*

Suddenly Paul wants to stick it to Frank, for no reason he can explain, much less justify. He takes a deep breath and he smirks. "Oh, I'm in discussions with some out-of-state entre-preneurs. They're based in LA, and they want me to manage their real estate assets here in Albuquerque." Where the fuck did Paul come up with that? He sounds like the pre-prison Frank Harwood. And Frank smiles a bit, he's still too dim to completely decide whether Paul's bullshitting. "Well, that's great, man. Maybe we'll meet up for lunch, when I'm more settled." And then he goes into the whole sad diatribe: lost his house in the divorce, barred from selling insurance because of the felony, clerking somewhere for minimum wage ... "Well—" Frank pulls himself up, "—at least I have my sobriety."

Blowing into the mouthpiece, Paul feels ashamed. Not only did he make this guy feel bad, he just told a *lie*!—Well, maybe a half-truth. But there's no such thing as a half-truth if he wants to stay sober, and now he'll no longer have God on his side. Fuck, how did Frank make him do it?

Half-buzzed after leaving Camacho's, Catt struggles to keep her eyes on the road while following Mapquest. Stu, the 1031 guy, has promised to wait in his North Valley office 'til six. The light over the still-snowy tops of the Sandia mountains is pink.

Leaving the freeway, she circles the same four blocks twice trying to find it. Can this be it? A tiny cinderblock building behind a vegetable wholesaler? She's talked to Stu dozens of times, but she never pictured the wizened old guy in a white nylon shirt who opens the door.

Stu (recommended by Edgar) does nothing but move money around, though from the look of his office you'd never know it: cheap veneer paneling, two old metal desks, papers all over the place and ancient columns of file cabinets. Stu reminds her of a Times Square burlesque booker she used to work for, or maybe her uncle Seymour.

"Have any trouble finding it?"

She says no, and they step into the dimly-lit room to sign papers.

Another thick pile of binders and papers she doesn't bother to read—Hank's already reviewed them—so while signing, she starts chatting with Stu.

"Thanks for backing me up on that thing with Caruso."

"Caruso's a jerk."

"He was threatening penalties, $300 a day, when the first seller walked on the four-plex."

"Pure bluff. That guy is leveraged up to his eyes and that place on Tulane? No bank would lend on it."

It occurs to Catt that all the real estate guys here know each other's business. "Really? Why?"

"First thing he's upside down on the place, then he got busy elsewhere and stopped filling the vacancies."

"Well I think the building's fantastic."

"Yeah, Hal Price? It's the one that looks like a gigantic space-ship? He built that when he was just starting out in the '70s.

Sold it to his secretary. You should see the place he built later on for himself in Nob Hill—it's even crazier."

Catt looks up from the binders. "You're from New York?"

"Brooklyn. Moved out here with my wife for health reasons in '82. I was supposed to semi-retire. Then I got into this. I ended up buying some units, too."

"Really? How many?"

"Last count, just short of 300."

Catt can hardly believe she's in this seedy office, sheltering hundreds of thousands from capital gains tax, and the whole thing is *perfectly legal*. She feels a warm rush of gratitude towards Edgar and Stu. Thanks to them, instead of funding the war in Iraq, she can give bonuses to the whole crew and donate to Amnesty. A long-ago boyfriend once warned her: *the bill will come due*. Did he mean her whole life, or just her ambiguous marital status? But she isn't in debt to anyone. In a few minutes, she'll walk out owning thirty-six debt-free units and another $200K to use for improvements. Stu's in a back room raking it in, while middle America drives to a nice business park and signs its life over to Countrywide Mortgage.

Stu's approach makes her feel like she's just joined a cool, old-school club: the anti-Starbucks. People who've made money, but grown up without it. People with millions of dollars in liquid and real estate assets who still comparison-shop for a hairdryer and bring their own lunches to work.

She purses the side of her mouth so Stu won't notice the twitch.

Now he's feeling all anxious again about his sobriety, about the past, about work. Too anxious to go back to Pam's, Paul decides to do a drive-by past 256 Estancia. The pre-interview drive-by is a critical part of the job-getting strategy, and it works. Before prison, Paul never had trouble getting a job, no matter how wasted he might have been, no matter how broke.

Once, back in Albuquerque, coming off of a crack binge, he woke up in a boarded-up building deep in the war zone and decided to clean up his act. He borrowed a friend's wedding suit and answered an ad for a micro-contamination specialist. They were looking for someone with an engineering degree. And even though he'd never finished community college, even though he'd been *fired* from Intel for showing up drunk to his assembly-room job, they ended up hiring him. And for a while, it went really well. The bosses were two guys his age. Within a couple of months, he learned everything there was to know about clean room fabrication. They even promoted him to take charge of a new plant in Phoenix.

The trick was to bond with the people in charge. Show up on time, be alert and act like you've already been offered the job. Don't want it too much. Wait, listen, observe all their little habits and gestures. Humans—the most grotesque animal species—emit unbearable levels of psychic noise. Easy enough to figure out what they expect, and then just feed it back.

Paul was twenty-nine when he stopped working for Klean-Tech. He wonders if he'll ever regain the confidence he felt during those years. But now he's sober, and maybe his problem is, he's just been setting his sights way too low because of bad self-esteem. In prison, the therapist told him his co-dependency issues all stemmed from poor self-esteem. *I want you to look in the mirror and say* I Love You *out loud* ... Which was a joke, the mirrors were made of aluminum, you couldn't see anything clearly but maybe she wasn't as dumb as he thought. Because if Paul thinks hard, he can picture himself in the future: Ralph Lauren sports coat, nice pair of slacks, getting out of a roomy-but-sporty sedan. He's a college professor! Maybe even a dean, or else a forensic psychiatrist. The police enlisting his expertise with the criminal mind to track down the serial killer, predict his next move ...

Estancia Drive is located in an old part of Albuquerque: east of Coors Boulevard, a few miles south of Las Lomitas Heights. The lots on both sides of Coors are under construction with new subdivisions: nice, but not as fancy as Pam's. Places for people who work in the huge business parks further north, Intel and Sprint. The new malls are finished. People can start buying stuff at Home Depot and Target before they move in. Paul's never hung out in this part of Albuquerque, but as soon as he turns right off of Coors, it all looks deeply familiar: old duplexes and four-plexes, small stucco homes with dirt yards ... like the place he grew up, on the northeast side of town.

The building at 256 Estancia Drive is a skinny low stucco rectangle with five doors and five rusted swamp coolers up on the roof. The back yard—a wide swathe of gravel and dust—must be the parking lot, but there are no cars. Either the building is vacant, or nobody's home. Or else they're too poor to have cars.

Paul stops and gets out of the Z. The front yard is gravel with one enormous overgrown tree with roots sticking out of the ground. Across the street, there's a mom 'n pop store with a hand-lettered sign: Appliance Repair. Beside it, an old guy sits out on a lawn chair drinking a sixteen-ounce beer.

Now he's confused. The drive-by is not giving him any useful information. Why would anyone come out from LA to own a building like this?

Catt remembers last winter: After leaving the Villa Vitta motel, she'd hung out for a couple of weeks at her getaway place in Campo La Jolla before going home to LA. By this time she was no longer fleeing her killer: more like, her *life*. Hank's thing with Becca was almost official, but he still had the key to her place. He could show up any time, and an intense conversation that began in the kitchen could end up in bed. Since they'd never weighted the sex thing with meaning beyond the rest of their friendship, it was hard to turn off. But didn't the fact that she'd nearly got herself killed amount to some kind of wake-up call? They'd become so dependent upon each other—and even if sex was not on the list, there were still all the *calls*.

Since the first GWB election, Hank had watched his access to power gradually wane. Finally, last year—in '04—he'd shut down the firm. He was semi-retired, with too much time on his hands. Even at the height of his powers he'd phoned Catt two, sometimes three times a day to debrief on this-or-that intrigue or deal. And she'd found it fascinating. Working sixteen hours a day, he was never too tired to deconstruct power in its most absurd and intricate detail. Hank was one of the most brilliant people she'd met, and by far the most driven, with an inexhaustible need to be understood. Less busy then with a career of her own, she'd been his Boswell.

Hank was less busy now, but he'd gotten used to their calls. He likes to read whole *LA Times* stories out loud—not the political news, where he and his friends were once featured—but more local things, California Lifestyle. How did it get to this point? He and Catt no longer bother discussing the real news, which is increasingly buried in short columns at the back of the paper that nobody reads: *CIA Send Terror Suspects Abroad For Interrogation … White House Says US Does Not Export Torture.* Pointless to ruin the day. Anyone with the most casual interest in these events has already gleaned the most horrific details online, months before the official report of the 'facts.'

But still: Catt was too young to give up, and she couldn't spend forty-five minutes a day talking about self-help and water-less plants. Hank had spent the best part of his life designing programs to house the homeless, promote civil rights and affir-mative action, and now he feigned a passionate interest in Zen. It was all much too sad. That winter the word "rendition" had just begun to be used, but they rarely talked about this. *This ren-dition program is fully authorized, so the CIA is not doing anything illegal that has not been authorized by the president,* announced CNN. Were she and Hank the last people around who knew what "tautology" meant? And if so, who did that help? If Catt disappeared long enough maybe Hank would spend more time with Becca, or find another writer to call.

Back at Campo La Jolla, after deciding not to abandon herself to her killer, Catt remembered she had another cata-logue essay due in this week. This one is for a Swedish museum—a country she's never been to, an artist she's never met. The curator, whose English isn't too good, wants her to write something discursive about The Female Brain, a subject she's never considered before. Was the brain gendered? She had no clue. Still, she knew the drill: write a few pages about the artist's work; compare him with some more-famous contemporaries; then, throw in some quotes from a couple of cultural theorists—their names mostly started with "B"—the trick was to pick the right ones. Benjamin, Baudrillard, Bourriaud were too dated. Better to go with Badiou.

Outside it rained. Catt found that *her* female brain kept circling back to her killer. Once he asked her to drop the DVD at his shell-office, he must have known she had his number. But then where had he gone? Would he be waiting outside her house in LA?

After three or four days of these thoughts, she called Michel.

She hadn't seen him for two or three months. He'd just gotten back to New York from a conference in Belgium. The last time they'd talked, she was busy researching her killer. He hadn't followed her flight to the Villa Vitta motel.

She wonders how all this could have happened, without telling Michel. For the first time since she'd moved to LA, they wouldn't be spending the summer together at their place in East Fletcher, Vermont. In fact, they were talking about selling the place. Was he seeing someone? In the past, that wouldn't have mattered. Just last winter, they'd met in Quebec at Christmas to cross-country ski and taken turns placing calls to their respective lovers from the phone downstairs at the lodge.

Despite this new estrangement, in the beginning she'd kept him apprised of her romance with death.

To Michel, Catt's rant about sexual slavery, Romanian websites and computer surveillance coming from three time zones away had been deeply disturbing. Over the years, he'd come to favor the long view of mental illness—to see it as a form of heightened awareness, a collision of incongruous signs—but rarely encroaching upon his actual life. But now his not-quite-ex-wife sounded, in fact, certifiable, wanting to *surrender control of her assets*, which (not to make too fine a point), after all, were half his.

The more Catt considered her seduction and flight from her killer, the more she thought it had something to do with her unbreakable bond with Michel. At bottom, Michel understood everything. Surely he's thought about this?

Outside the window, she watched small rocks in yellowish rivers of rain wash down the dirt road. She picked up the phone.

To the extent Michel's thought about this dilemma at all, he's assumed it was over. *But*, Catt insists, *how can it be over? Haven't you thought—? Why would I be willing to take these incredible risks with a stranger?—and I wanted to give him the money, I mean, I must have wanted to die—*

—Why do you act so crazy for something, *chaton?*

—*Because I'm so disappointed and sad!* (pause) *I mean, in the beginning, what roped me in was I really believed we had this incredible psychic connection, like, like—*

—Well psycho sounds much more like it. This guy is a sleaze, a sleaze with incredible psychotic powers. The schizophrenic is a dangerous ghost. So it's interesting to meet this kind of guy, but dangerous to get too attached—

—*Michel have you considered my death wish might be a somatization of the death of an understanding, between you and me?*

The phone disconnects. Catt sobs. She still sees herself and Michel as an oddly distinguished old couple. They redial.

—*Chaton*, I'm thinking of you. Why do you always have to go for these things?

—*Michel why do you always have to deflect?*

—Tell me more.

—*I'm tired of being alone*—

—I gave you what I could. Maybe the reason you were attracted to me is the same reason you go for these freaks.

—*It's a bad trade!*

—But the difference between us is, he's not going to be there for you. And I will.

They talk for another half-hour. But when they hang up, she can't shake the feeling of defeat and dread.

On her first night in Albuquerque, Catt sits up late at night on an air mattress on the floor of the cheap one-bedroom condo she now legally owns. Six hundred square feet, two rooms with gray wall-to-wall carpet, and white mini-blinds overlooking a xeriscaped courtyard. A Ponderosa pine tree outside the bedroom's lone window. The apartment seems like the place you'd buy for yourself if you were a secretary heading into your first Saturn Return with no prospects of marriage. Weightless but present, cocooned by the strangeness of this, she's a long way from New York or LA or anything she can explain to her friends. "It begins here," she writes in her diary.

Light outside the window wakes her up around six. The day starts in a purposeful rush of lists and strong coffee. Her plan is to turn one of the vacants at 256 Estancia into an office. They'd start work at Estancia, and then move over to Tulane and Mescalero: landscaping and paving the yards, patching walls, replacing the urine-stained carpets with saltillo tiles, repairing the heating and cooling, replacing the roofs. To her, it's a *plus* that the buildings are vacant: no bank would loan on unoccupied properties, which is what makes them so cheap, and they're ready for upgrading. She has no taste for evicting the poor to make way for more stable tenants who'll pay higher rents.

She'll stay alone here in apt. 216. She'll put Titus and Sharon and Brett in the condo downstairs. The rest of the crew can stay with Reynaldo in the two-bedroom across from the pool, the one she'd bought for just $22K and promised to sign over to Tommy at the end of the job as a bonus. Tommy was cool about the crew using it, and she booked him a nearby motel room. Having Tommy off-site is actually better. Titus thinks Tommy's a thief, whereas Tommy believes that Titus is ignorant, and also homophobic.

At ten, Catt takes Stretch for a walk to the park. Another perfect spring day. Less than a mile south of the UNM campus, the houses en route have anti-Bush signs in their drought-landscaped yards and Tibetan prayer-flags strung between columns of their adobe porches. There's a Prius in every third driveway. Why were the condos so cheap? Nob Hill South is a classically affluent neighborhood, the unattained dream of her parents—a place of pound-rescued dogs, whose residents favor large yards over garish additions to their well-restored modest homes. *I could easily live here*, Catt thinks. She imagines herself handing out Halloween candy from one of these doors and joining the local chapter of Amnesty. And the park ... five or six blocks of shaggy deep lawn and stately old pepper and cottonwood trees mixed in with Japanese maple and deciduous larch. She takes Stretch off his leash and sits under the broad trunk of an oak.

How long has it been since she's talked to a tree? In her youth, certain encounters with trees opened doors to emotion—could even set off crying jags lasting one or two weeks. She and the tree facing each other, perfectly balanced … the whole of its history entering her through her eyes … but the balance is terribly fragile and this makes her weep. How long can anyone open their heart to a tree? It's as if she's been offered a glimpse of something too huge, the empty space of a poem that she'll never write.

Sated and happy, she walks back to the complex where Tommy, Reynaldo and an elderly Mexican man are waiting for her, blasting the a/c in the red truck and passing a gallon of water. They've been driving all night.

Catt waves. The men get out of the truck. Always the dresser, Tommy's gone over the top with the southwestern motif. He wears a Tombstone string-tie with his Gap button-down shirt, held in place by a gigantic cluster of turquoise and silver. Every inch of his plump, forty-two-year-old fingers and wrists are covered with Navajo jewelry. The belt on his Dockers is studded with abalone shells and mother of pearl. His companions wear t-shirts and jeans.

Tommy gives her a hug—"We thought you forgot us! Thank *God* you're back!"—and walks her a few steps away, not quite out of the other men's earshot.

"Girlfriend, listen to me: we've already got a situation. You see that old man? That's Reynaldo's uncle. Reynaldo told me about him this week, he says he's a roofer. So—it's not like we were planning on bringing a roofer, but I say okay, alright, we'll pay him a hundred dollars a day—that's me looking out for you—and if he's no good Reynaldo can deal with it, it'll be on his back. But when they show up to leave, I see the guy's like, sixty years old, he cannot speak one word of English, and I say *sorry*, Reynaldo, you better tell this uncle of yours he is *not* coming with us. Then Reynaldo threatens to walk, which leaves us one person short, so I give in. I say, alright."

Catt glances back at the truck. Reynaldo's uncle looks like one of the Oaxacan migrants who work in fields around Campo La Jolla. He could be seventy. Then again, he could be forty. "Yeah, Tommy. No problem."

"Well that's what I'd say! You'd think after that Reynaldo would be one happy camper. But he hasn't said *two words* to me since we left San Bernadino. He's been sulking all night. Instead, he and the uncle have been gabbing away nonstop in Spanish all night—I tell you, my head!—and when we reach the Arizona state line, the uncle starts grabbing my arm, apparently, Reynaldo tells me, he's afraid of the Border Patrol and wants to go back! Reynaldo asks me if I can't make some kind of detour—*right*, through Colorado? How could anyone born here not know the most basic geography?"

Catt thinks: Tommy looks like a latter-day Liberace.

"So the uncle spent most of the night hiding under a blanket and Reynaldo just sulked. And I told him, Reynaldo, if you keep this up, you will *not* be leaving here with this truck!"

Ah, so that's the point of the story. Still, Catt finds it hard to believe Tommy wants the red truck for himself. It's almost seven years old. Catt bought the red Dodge Dakota with Reynaldo in mind when they hired him: what would a nineteen-year old Chicano from Victorville most like to drive? It looks like a penis on wheels. Reynaldo's kept it well lubed and buffed.

Catt's eye twitches violently. She's already forgotten the park. They go out for breakfast. Tommy shows her the impressive array of ledgers and markers he's bought to keep track of her money. Then, the men sleep and she hits the thrift stores.

That night Catt dreams about June Goodman, a writer she'd known in New York. In the dream, June was still in her early twenties and teaching an algebra class. The students applauded. June was shockingly beautiful. Standing at the back of the room, Catt was kidnapped by two shadowy men. She wakes up and sees an arm reaching towards her through the window— but it's just the branch of the pine.

The next morning, she and Tommy meet Paul and even though Tommy protests, she offers him the job.

"I was feeling pretty hopeless and down when I moved back to Albuquerque," Paul will remember much later. "I was, you know, a thirty-nine-year-old person moving in with my sister. I'd just gotten out of prison and I was on parole, and I didn't think I could get a job. I was—well, I was very self-conscious? Down on myself. I mean, I knew I had my sobriety, and in the background that's always a good foundation, that's always a good thing to hold onto and continue to have hope with, but— that's underneath. On the top was, just me feeling worthless, moving in at thirty-nine with my sister and knowing she didn't want me to stay there for long. And nervous about how I would move out, because all I could think was, Gee, in order to move out I'm gonna have to somehow come up with first month's rent, security deposit, all that stuff, be able to turn on the utilities? It just wasn't going to happen!

"I didn't know what I was going to do. Anyhow, my first thought was, I've gotta look for an apartment complex or some-thing that needs a maintenance man where they would give me an apartment as part of the job. Or—I just need to get *any* job.

"When I saw the ad in the paper I'd already gone around and applied for jobs at places like Wal-Mart, some gas stations, a couple of restaurants, even a couple of fast food restaurants and always in the back of my mind was: what am I going to do when they ask, Have you ever been convicted of a felony?

"When I saw Catt's ad in the newspaper, it said everything there I was looking for, apartment included—I thought wow, this is too good to be true. I thought there had to be a catch, like it wasn't real—I'd do a lot of work and there wouldn't be an apartment after all. That's what I thought was happening. It would turn out to be some kind of scam. But I thought I'd check it out anyway, so I did, I called. So, Catt answered the phone and she sounded different than what I was used to, maybe a little like—lighter? Full of energy, and hope and good-will, and I thought wow, what's going on here? Is this really real? Is this something happening?

"And of course I wanted to make a good impression. The day I went for the interview, I remember I cleaned up my car really nice, got it as shiny as it could possibly get because I wanted to make a good impression. I pulled up at 256 Estancia, and Catt and Tommy were there. I think I talked to them for a while, and then they asked me to leave and come back in an hour. What was I going to do for an hour? I just drove around. And then I came back, and they said: 'You're our new manager.' And I said, 'Right on!' I mean shit, they didn't even ask me about felonies. And the next day I started the job."

5

LAND OF ENCHANTMENT

TOMMY KNOWS HE'S IN TROUBLE when he's left holding the cart while Paul and Catt speed shop at Wal-Mart for janitorial products. They run through the aisles grabbing buckets and brooms like teammates on a stupid game show. Whenever he opens his mouth they trade secret looks, as if he was their junior high school principal.

Catt can't believe how much fun she is having. How long has it been since she made a new friend? On the outside, Paul seems really solid and stable, but he likes to talk about some of the weird arcane stuff she's more or less made a career of. During his first week on the job they exchange views on UFOs and extraterrestrials, the migration of souls into animals, and high art—which, they agree, is distinguished from kitsch by one's acceptance of unknown outcomes. Tommy lurks in the background and glowers.

Meanwhile, work proceeds. Titus and his family arrive along with his helpers, Jason and Matt. By the end of the second day, the base office is finished. Trucks arrive with supplies, and Titus's crew moves on to the rest of the building.

Staying alert, Paul struggles to pick up the cues. They're paying him $600 a week, but he still doesn't know what his job is. They don't want him doing construction. Titus already has that well covered. It's more like, he's an assistant to Catt? Or else he's being trained to take over from Tommy, become the new manager?

During his second week on the job, they send him to pick up samples of landscaping gravel at a nearby quarry. The young lady's face behind the counter looks familiar, but he's been gone for eight years. Why would he know her? Then he remembers. She came to the Farm on alternate Sundays to visit Malone, her husband or boyfriend. Malone's wife doesn't recognize him. Or maybe she's just being cool. At any rate, he's relieved to get back to the job. None of these out-of-state people know anything about him.

When he returns with Dixie cups full of gravel, Catt waves to him from inside one of the units. Dressed in old jeans and a bandanna, she's painting white window trim. Since the first day on the job, Catt's had the unshakeable feeling that she and Paul are playing a series of games, maybe scenes from old movies. Like the neighborhood boys she recruited for games as a child, he's super-attentive, as if he's mind-read whatever script she thinks they're playing. He walks up to the window to give her the rocks; she takes them, and suddenly they're in a country & western biopic. *Sweet Dreams? Coal Miner's Daughter?* She's the young pregnant wife; they're fixing up their first home together. Talking about gravel, practically blushing, she gestures him in. And then the film changes. Arranging cups full of samples, they're in the Evidence Room. He's the young cop to her plucky district attorney.

These fabulations help Catt throw herself into the job with the same abandon she gave to her killer. Working sixteen hours a day, she sets up accounts, hires subcontractors, makes hundreds of tiny decisions about colors and floor tiles and windows. With Paul on the scene, Tommy has taken a break from his supervisory duties and instead made himself useful, disappearing for most of the day to look for dented fridges and stoves, salvaged building materials.

Every night after work, Paul goes back to Pam's and Catt has dinner with Titus and Sharon. They talk about Brett. At twenty-two, his future is gravely uncertain. There's an outstanding warrant for his arrest back in Sonoma. Drunk, high, or upset, he drove into a neighbor's fence. Titus hopes he'll use the money he makes on the job to turn himself in, post bail and pay restitution. Sharon (who isn't Brett's mother) thinks it's time for Brett to step up to the plate and face his responsibilities. Brett has a four-year old. His ex-girlfriend's mom, who took custody of the child when her daughter was arrested for meth possession, has been threatening legal action for unpaid child support. Titus wants to teach Brett a trade. Until now, the only job Brett has held, when he's worked at all, was as a waiter … and what kind of job is that for a man?

Brett is clearly ill-suited to working construction. He disappears every night. And no one knows where. Unlike his dad, he's classically handsome, verbally quick and tormented.

Cautiously, Catt suggests other scenarios: perhaps Brett could do graphic design, maybe culinary school? Every day on the job, she and Brett talk about noise bands, graphic novels, and comics. If he'd grown up in Marin instead of a trailer park outside Santa Rosa, he might have been one of her art students.

When Tommy catches Reynaldo and his uncle drinking in one of the condos while everyone else is at work, he puts them on a bus back to San Bernardino. Now they have one extra vehicle. Over lunch, Catt and Tommy decide that the best thing to do with the red truck is to give it to Paul to use as a maintenance vehicle.

Paul can't believe his good luck. Even though he's busy all day, he still doesn't really know what the job is. But he has a company car! No one seems to care if he drives it at night back to Pam's house. He doesn't have to embarrass himself anymore blowing into the LifeSafer. He decides to work even harder. Still, he wishes they'd hurry and finish Estancia soon and start work on Tulane. This is where Tommy and Catt want him to live, because—hard to believe—it's in an even worse neighborhood.

When the landscaper's bid for Estancia comes in at $35K, Catt and Tommy ask him to hire some local workers and do the job on his own. Finally, Paul has a chance to prove himself. He puts an ad in the paper. Knowing the locals don't all have cell phones, he gives the address and a time, ten a.m. to report for interviews. Two guys—a nineteen-year-old white kid, and a middle-aged Native—show up early. Since it doesn't take much except physical strength and work ethic to wield a shovel, and these guys must want the job more than the others, he hires them. And they do a good job, everyone's happy.

Later, Paul learns that the older guy, Joe Stillwater, has just gotten out of Las Cruces Level IV State Prison. Evan, the white kid, did jail time in Texas. His first managerial task on the job and he's just hired two ex-cons? He's worried what Catt and Tommy will think, but by the time they find out, Tommy is gone and Catt doesn't mind. In fact, she approves of it.

Spring ends abruptly that year, just as it has every year Paul can remember in Albuquerque. The cool wind disappears overnight, leaving the city to bake in its natural state: a sweltering desert with dry air so hot you can barely move through it. Between now and mid-August, the only relief will be the monsoons. Every two weeks, the monsoons arrive out of nowhere. The sky changes from blue to tornado gray, and wind rushes down from the mountains. Weeds and debris scatter the highway. Rain pounds the cars like ten thousand nail guns and for a while you can breathe. But then, the sky clears as abruptly as the monsoon arrived, and it's back to the furnace.

On one of these hot summer days, Paul and Catt drive the red truck to the Best Buy at North Valley Plaza. Catt has no reason to be there. She could have continued her work, given Paul petty cash and told him to pick up a digital camera. Instead, she sneaks out of the office behind Tommy's back. "But Catt—do you think we can get away with this?" Paul asks as he backs the Dodge out of the yard, and they laugh. By now there's no doubt in his mind that Catt's the real boss. It's hard to believe: this woman owns all these apartments, and she acts like they're ditching school together.

Five days ago, Catt found a dusty silk rose on her laptop. The stuffed, red fabric heart on its green plastic stem was embroidered with three words: *I Love You*. Titus was in the office when she discovered this Valentine's Day Wal-Mart relic. She blushed, but then quickly recovered and put the rose in the glass where she kept her markers. Since the Day of the Rose, whatever charged *thing* that's been going on between her and Paul has escalated. Did the rose come from him? Catt likes Paul, she respects him. By now she has gathered how badly he needs the job, so it's hard to imagine him taking the risk of such an open flirtation. Did Brett put the rose on her desk? Brett knows she's been taking his side against Titus and Sharon. But Brett's way too cool to treat Catt like some favorite elementary school teacher.

It occurs to Catt that she's never been given a rose by someone she hasn't already slept with. *So it must be Paul* ... but he's already told her he's in AA, and she's seen the LifeSafer thing in his car, which means he's had at least one DUI. So maybe it isn't. Why would someone trying this hard to rebuild his life risk an affair with his boss? He already knows that she lives in LA and isn't divorced. Plus, she's several years older than he is.

"You better drive fast," she deadpanned. "I mean, floor it! Tommy saw me walk out of the office."

"Yeah, well. He better not try giving you shit."

"Too right. You know what Brett told me? Tommy asked him out for coffee last night. He told Brett he had some ideas about his future. Brett thought they were going to Starbucks, but instead they end up at a gay bar on Central. Which is, you know, no big deal. But then Tommy came on to him."

"Tommy's a freak."

"What Paul, are you homophobic?"

"No he's a *freak*—not 'cause he's gay, although I've never seen a gay person acting like that. It's like he's rubbing your face in it. Have you ever wondered if he's really gay? There's something dishonest about him. How did you get involved? He acts like, maybe you owe him something?"

"No .... I don't know. I've known Tommy a long time, since I started doing this. I met him in Crestline, at the place where Michel and I did our taxes. And then Tommy quit and offered to be our personal business manager." Catt leans closer. "By then

Michel was back in New York and I was taking care of our finances, but he was never in one place for long. Bills kept getting lost." Paul's hand brushes her thigh when he shifts down to fourth. "It was confusing ... It seemed easier then to just let Tommy take care of things."

By the time Paul and Catt arrive at the mall, the rose is no longer a mystery. But there's no way Paul can make the next move. She decides to risk it. Before he can get out of the truck, she puts her leg up on the dash and looks him in the eye. "Paul, what I need to know, I mean, seriously—is this going to interfere with our work?"

Oh shit. Now he's being busted for sexual harassment. Her platform sandals are dangling over the wheel, rather provocatively.

"Because if it is—"

He'd better stay calm. "Of course not! What do you mean?"

"This flirtation between us." He squints at her through his thick, state-issued glasses. "I mean maybe I'm wrong—"

"No, no you're not." Shit, this is excruciating. "But okay. What, what were you saying?"

"Look, I know on one level I'm your employer, and that's real, that won't go away. But we don't really know each other ... So, I just wanted to say, I'm someone who has no problem compartmentalizing. You know? Keep a strict church/state separation. I mean, what I'm trying to say is, whatever happens between us, I would always keep those things separate."

"Well then. I think I should ask you out on a date."

"Okay ..."

"Then how about Friday?"

Did this just happen? Neither of them can quite believe it.

They're in the mall parking lot, still at work. This is getting way too intense.

"Great. Now let's go buy a camera."

Browsing the aisles, Paul tries to summon an interest in lenses and digital memory. As if proving a point, Catt takes her time, looking around for the best deal. Shit, if he had her platinum card, he'd just pick the best one in the store and be done with it.

But where is he? It's like he's fallen into a warp. Paul's never owned a credit card in his life, but suddenly he's feeling sorry for the pimply young white Best Buy associate, working forty hours a week for minimum wage—a job Paul couldn't get because of the felony. But now he's the—companion?—of a wealthy Los Angeles woman. No, that isn't right, Catt is cool. She might even need his protection. He just needs this day to be over so he can call Sponsor Mike.

By the time they exit the store, the deal's sealed.

Later on, Paul and Catt will discover they had the same epiphany in their late thirties, waking up to an awareness that the present is totally open, there isn't a script, everyone's just making things up as they happen. Paul was in a group holding cell at San Juan County Jail when this happened. Catt figured it out at an upstate New York writer's colony.

"The important thing is, don't tell Tommy."

"No," Paul repeats, "Don't tell Tommy." It's uncanny the way that Paul seems to mirror her words and her gestures, even her intonations. It's like being fed back to yourself by an alien. He's already described himself to Catt as a perpetual Other. But it's not Paul's ethnicity that makes Catt feel like the professor from heaven or hell. It's the fact that he's never been out of New Mexico!

"What's it like to be you?" Paul will ask. "What's it like in New York? Where is Belgium?"

But happily, Paul mirrors her goofiness too. He looks at her solemnly. "But Catt, what will we do about Titus?"

"Ahhh, I think he already knows. Titus is like an old sea bass. He's been swimming around on the ocean floor for decades."

Paul hasn't been on a date since that night with Ravene. He wishes time would fast-forward and that he and Catt were already together, just kicking back, and he did not have to do this.

"You better watch yourself, brother. Fucking the boss is the best way to get fired," Mike had commented. And then he'd stupidly talked it over with Pam, who asked, "How *old* did you say this woman was? And she's *married*?"

Still, Friday night after work, Paul goes home, dresses up, takes the tops off the Z, and picks Catt up at the condo. He's already planned to take her for dinner at his favorite restaurant, then maybe a drive to the top of the Sandias. And hopefully that will be that, he'll be home by ten thirty.

At Las Cartegnas, a Mexican family place where you can't get a drink, Catt struggles to eat refried beans and chile rellenos. This is a far cry from her life in LA. The restaurant is full of overweight, badly dressed people eating huge plates of food in unflattering lighting.

"Remember Brigitte," Michel warned when she called to report on her Friday night date plans. Brigitte's life was a cautionary tale, almost a code word between them. At thirty-eight, she'd left her two-decades-older philosopher husband for a truck driver she met while he was a Distinguished Visiting Professor at Berkeley. Three years later, she woke up in Fresno knowing she'd made a mistake. She had no one to talk to. By then her ex-husband had married an even younger American writer and they became academe's new power couple. Meanwhile, Brigitte—who'd taught at the Sorbonne and enjoyed access to all of Europe's intellectual life while she was married—struggled to pick up a few community college classes. "Prole life," Michel chuckled, "can be pretty boring."

Paul smells musky-sweet, drenched in something she guesses is Old Spice cologne. Nice, she thinks, that he made an effort. He picks up the check, overtips. So far, the evening has gone just as Paul planned it, but he's dreading the moment when they get into the Z and Catt has to watch him blow into the mouthpiece. No surprise, she's never been in a blow car but at least she turns it into a joke—"here, let me try it." She fumbles around, and fails so many times the car almost shuts down.

Driving up to the crest of the Sandias, the temperature drops as they gain elevation. Up here, the night is chilly and pleasant. Distant lights from the city cut through the darkness. They kiss, fumble a bit, and then Paul drops her off at the condo.

The next night they get a motel room. And this is great, but he gets dressed in the bathroom, relieved that she doesn't expect them to spend the whole night together.

On Sunday she wants to make dinner for him at the condo. This is better than sex. How long has it been since a woman made him dinner? Also, it's less problematic. Afterwards they keep the lights off, so she still hasn't seen the horrible scar, but in the morning there's no way to avoid it. Catt already knows he's in AA, so he decides to confront the problem and tell her about the accident that happened when he was wasted one night (he doesn't mention the crack) and she acts *surprised*, pretending that if he hadn't pointed it out, she wouldn't have noticed. How had he forgotten this most basic aspect of female behavior?

All in all the courtship lasts three days. After that, they're together.

The whole crew is relieved when Tommy flies back to San Bernadino. Now they can relax. For the two weeks (it feels like two months) since the job started, they've been living under the weight of his strangeness.

On Friday, the day Stu cuts the checks, Tommy calls Catt from his office, very distressed. He can't really talk—no, he has to tell someone ... When he got home Wednesday night, his partner Ron dumped him.

"Ron says he can't put up with me always leaving this way, he says I'm not available ..." Catt's shocked. "Tommy, that's unbelievable!" From what Tommy's said in the past, he and Ron have been together eight years. How could this short time away derail their relationship? "Oh Catt, it's okay, I've seen it coming ... But the point is, he wants to wrap things up right away and his name's on the house! He threatened to take me to court if I don't cash him out—the only good news is, he'll settle for $22K, which is a *lot* less than half of the equity. Until you gave me that condo, the house was the only thing that I owned. And I was planning on doing it up! Southwest contemporary, make it really adorable—"

Catt says nothing.

"But the only solution I see now is, I can get Ron off my back if you cash me out of the condo."

Catt wonders if Ron even exists. She's never met him. Her throat clenches so tight she can hardly breathe, just as it did when she was fleeing her killer. Tommy is shaking her down, it's so insultingly blatant. But then she forces herself to turn the problem around, examine it from another perspective. No doubt this is extortion. But didn't the problem reside in her offer to give him the condo? *That's* when she gave away $22,000.

If she keeps the condo herself, rather than give it to him, doesn't it come out the same? In fact, maybe better. She can rehab the place, rent it for six hundred a month. The numbers are good, more than a twenty percent cash-on-cash gross rent multiplier.

That evening she asks Stu to write Tommy the check. She doesn't tell anyone. But who would she tell? Her life in LA is already a memory.

Except for Hank—whose calls she dodges—none of Catt's friends, ex-students, or interns bother to call her in Albuquerque. And if they did, what would she tell them? Each long day is completely absorbing. Throwing herself into finite and solvable problems (trash pick-up, squatters, utility meters), her vision constricts to the few miles between buildings. She's seized by a sense of the possible. In Albuquerque, jurisdiction over each of these problems can be traced to an actual person.

At Tulane, she installs a wrought-iron gate around the trash dumpster to stop the rest of the neighborhood from dumping their garbage. When the garbage truck driver refuses to open the gate, she writes to the sanitation commissioner—*please support our attempts to improve the quality of life for our tenants in this troubled neighborhood*—and cc's the mayor. Within days, the driver apologizes.

When Titus discovers a handful of drunks squatting in the vacant Mescalero apartments, he wants to call the police or an eviction attorney. Catt sees another solution. She sends Paul to the building to offer each squatter $1,000 cash if he'll leave by the end of the week. Titus is furious. He's working twelve-hour days in the heat for less money. Why is she rewarding the dead-beats? They should be punished. But she's already looked at the numbers: evictions cost $750 and at least two months lost rent while they grind through the courts. Cheaper to buy the drunks off, and also nicer. The squatters accept, and construction begins. The plan is to transform the old flophouse into a haven for musicians, artists, and writers.

Finally Tulane is ready and Paul moves into a two-bedroom apartment. Catt helps him unload his belongings: a clothes hamper, a few pair of jeans, his GED, a middle-school athletic trophy, and a box full of photos.

On their first night in the apartment they look at the photos. Paul has a few snapshots from both of his marriages, but most of the photos are of his dogs. They sit on the futon, and Catt looks at dozens of pictures of Janey, a German Shepherd (poisoned by Paul's ex-wife's former boyfriend), and Ruggo, a liver-spotted Dalmation (hit by a car and found dead by the side of the road two days later). None of Paul's dogs ever died of old age. The deaths of his dogs, like his cars—wrecked, repossessed, and impounded—are deaths of chaos and poverty. Looking at the photos, he comes close to crying. He hasn't taken them out since before he went to prison. He'd made up a scat song for Janey. Ruggo was Paul's lucky dog, he was almost a brother.

Looking at the photos, Catt sees two large dogs on a dusty patch outside a small trailer. "It was the happiest time of my life," Paul remembers. "The time between DUIs four and five. I was living alone with the dogs outside of town in that little single-wide trailer. I was only drinking at night, I still had the truck-driving job. I was paying my bills. Every week I bought one or two new CDs, I still had enough money left over when I cashed my paycheck."

Catt can't imagine this as an idyll of happiness. Each new scene Paul reveals from his past is littered with devastation. His parents are dead. Cars, repossessed. His former best friend got one of his sisters pregnant when she was fifteen and then vanished. And yet he seems perfectly cheerful. Like her dog Stretch (rescued from certain death at the city pound), he's adapted.

Never once does Catt consider this new romance rash or impetuous. It was all very fluid. She remembers how devastated her colleague Danielle had been at the end of a three-month relationship that mostly consisted of talks about *where it was going*. Throughout the three months, Danielle had spent hours decoding the meaning of a weekend away with her boyfriend. Was it a sign he was *ready to take things to the next level?* Unlike the collar she'd worn on the book tour, to Catt this was *truly* degrading. Since the first day in the red truck, she and Paul have not spoken once about their relationship. Like the job, it's just there. It's something they're doing.

They paint the apartment deep blue and green, and scour Craigslist for furniture. Of course Paul hasn't earned enough yet to pay for this stuff, but he's already rented the rehabbed Estancia apartments. He collects the cash rents, and they drive around spending it. She's aware that their financial relations are fraught, perhaps even vulgar, but sees no alternative. She has it, he doesn't. Neither of them care very much about money. Instead, they crack jokes. What will become of this stuff if they break up? If Catt comes home one night and finds Paul with a new girlfriend, will she scream, *Bitch, get out! That's my couch you're sitting on?* Will she sob to Danielle, *and that's* my *TV they were watching?*

"Ahhh," Paul will comment, "the poor *precariat*"—he's heard Catt use that word—"they're up to their ears in credit card debt, the only thing they possess is each other." She finds this brilliant.

Who is this woman? Paul wondered. Tommy refers to Michel as a "European intellectual." Maybe she is one too, though he's never met any. Once while they were fooling around, talking shit, she looked him in the eye and said, "You think you're smarter than other people." Uh-oh, he thought, here it comes. But then she continued, "And you're probably right. But what can it be like to be that intelligent and have *no information?*" One of those questions you're not expected to answer. Less than two months after arriving in Albuquerque, he has a good job, a free apartment, a company cell phone. All this is obviously part of God's plan, a reward for being sober.

"What is it like to be you?" Paul asks sincerely. He's never traveled, he's never known any "intellectuals." Since Paul doesn't share any of Catt's cultural references, their conversations are always direct. But he is so *present* ...

"Why did you come here?" Paul asks her one night in a restaurant. He's worried she's getting bored. "Albuquerque isn't your place. I mean, you're a cultural critic. There's all this stuff about you on the computer. Why didn't you go to New York, or one of those other places?"

"In LA, I met someone who wanted to kill me."

That's too dramatic. She takes a big gulp of her drink.

"I mean, maybe not literally. But I had a death-wish."

She tells him the story of Dominant Realm, her flight to the Villa Vitta.

"He wanted me to become his slave, surrender control of my finances, but then I couldn't—"

And how is he taking this? Except for Hank, Michel, and her close friend Bettina, she hasn't told anyone about these events, because there's no way to talk about them, she hasn't yet arranged them into a narrative.

"I think maybe what stopped me was friendship. I mean, if you're a slave you can't be anyone's friend because how can anyone trust you if you're not responsible for your actions? And then it's false—if you're an adult you can't pretend you're a baby. The whole thing started out as a game, meeting people online, the power exchange. I was alone and bored in LA. It wasn't a death-wish, more like the opposite."

By now she's quite drunk. "People think the BDSM is so heavy but most of the people who do it are totally sweet. From the outside, running away to the Villa Vitta was totally crazy, but there was a logic. I mean, don't you think that craziness always happens within a logic? There are all these systems out there, each of them has its own rationality."

"Oh, Catt. I don't think you're crazy. You were just being silly."

Stumbling out to the car, Catt touches the left side of her face. Nothing. How long has it been since the last twitch? A week, maybe longer?

Paul thinks maybe this is the moment to talk about prison. But no, she's too drunk. He'd just have to do it again. When you're drunk you forget things.

Two days later, walking Stretch to the park, Paul finds an opening. Catt's chattering on about dishes, Fiestaware, which color to buy—turquoise or orange?

"*Not* orange."

"Why?"

"I don't like that color."

"Why not?"

"I've got some pretty bad memories of that particular color."

And then he tells her everything—the drunken binge, the fuel credit card, the public defender, prison—or almost. He can't tell her *everything*. Bad enough he's a convicted felon.

Catt steps into a cloud of compassion. So this is what she heard in his voice, that first time they talked on the phone when she was in Flagstaff. She cannot imagine spending even one day in prison. She's never done anything she couldn't talk her way out of. Paul spent sixteen months in state prison for defrauding *Halliburton*? Of less than one thousand dollars?

Meanwhile she's amassed tens of thousands by working within the tax code's gray zones. Unaware of his former employer's massive war crimes, Paul seems ashamed of stealing less than an art gallery spends on an after-party.

Shortly after Catt met Michel, she'd been stopped in New

Jersey for driving an unregistered car with an expired license. Instead of locking her up, the police chief brought her coffee and magazines, and let her sit in his office. Michel paid her bail and the judge let her off with a warning. In the same court, the same judge sentenced a woman to twenty-nine days in jail when she could not pay the fine for bouncing a check to a supermarket, which she wouldn't have bounced if she had any money.

The fragility Catt sensed around Paul wasn't just the result of his shyness, or recent sobriety. It was something more serious. If the world tells you you're garbage, you are. And how do you even begin to recover?

When Tommy fired Reynaldo, Catt didn't know what to do with the red Dodge Dakota. That night, she looked for the title and signed it over to Paul. She wasn't using it anyway.

6

BEGGAR'S BANQUET

DURING MEMORIAL DAY WEEKEND, Catt buys a twenty-five dollar bike at a yard sale.

Drowsy with heat, the deep quiet streets of Nob Hill remind her of childhood summer vacations. Instead of driving to the gym twice a week in LA, she bikes around town running errands. From the bank to the food co-op to the used bookstores on Central … She's forgotten Nepal. Instead of the Himalayas, she looks up at the Sandia mountains.

Since sending the check, Catt's heard nothing from Tommy. With Tommy out of the way, she enjoys the illusion of limitless time. Each day unfolds unobstructed. Nights, she plays house with Paul at Tulane. Each morning she visits the job or goes over the leders with Sharon. She eats lunch with the crew. Then she turns off her phone and retreats to her one-bedroom condo.

During these long afternoons, she remembers the aimless intensity she felt in New York in her early twenties. Newly arrived from New Zealand, she worked at temp office jobs and attended a few acting classes. Life was eventless but full. She had no ambition beyond supporting herself in New York and she'd achieved it.

At one of these temp office jobs, she met Seth Morgan, a poet. She'd known poets before in New Zealand, but none of them were as brazen as Seth in declaring Poetry as their vocation. "Poetry," said Seth, quoting Ted Berrigan, "is a full-time job. Poets don't take vacations." Like her, Seth lived in the East Village. When the job ended, he invited her to stop over. He lived with his wife and two little kids just a few doors away. After college, they'd moved here from West Virginia so Seth could be around other poets. And he'd met dozens of them: people like Seth, in their twenties, who worked as infrequently as possible and mostly hung out in his apartment. Seth often stayed home with his kids (his nonpoet wife had a job) and there was usually food in the fridge. Their apartment was HQ for the St. Mark's Younger Poets. The Older St. Mark's Poets stayed home a lot too. Often, the Younger Poets paid ceremonial visits to their apartments, but these visits weren't reciprocated.

Not a poet herself, Catt rarely went along on these visits, but she found the scene at Seth's house very comforting. The poets neither had nor spent money. Books were stolen or shared, drugs were bartered. Unlike the girls in her acting classes, who were approaching adulthood in frightening ways (brunches; dinners at expensive restaurants; credit cards, cocktails, and dating) the poets moved as a tribe between several apartments. People gathered at Seth's every day to drink beer and smoke pot and talk about poetry. Conversations gave way to collaborative poetry writing, and the poets all worked on each other's magazines.

No one except the poets read these magazines, but the selection was highly competitive. The editorial branding of each stapled 'zine was life-defining. Even though Jarrett and Damien practically lived on Seth Morgan's sofa, their magazine, *Avenue*, rejected his poems continually. *Avenue* was founded to advance Jarrett's brilliant—and to Catt, incomprehensible—formalist aesthetic. She found Seth's poems equally incomprehensible, but his work apparently was incomprehensible in the wrong way. Shut out of *Avenue*, several girls and the lone gay boy in the group started *Phlegm*. With its punk rock aesthetic, *Phlegm* was occasionally read by nonpoets. Its editors soon started bands to escape the poetry ghetto.

The poets took many drugs, but sexual mores were highly conservative. Couples had kids. Straight single boys lived alone in the "boy's dorm," an unheated E. 12th Street tenement, and the straight single girls shared two or three bigger and nicer apartments.

Of the unattached women, only Terry Stiles lived alone. Her poems were in everyone's magazines, but she'd already set her sights higher. She could stay up all night with Jarrett translating poems from the Greek with a shoplifted dictionary, but unlike the boys, she wasn't content to work in a book store for minimum wage. Though she was friends with the *Phlegm* crowd, she had no interest in playing in bands. She was a poet, and needed all of her time to become one. Arriving from Boston, Terry had come out as a lesbian. She dressed like a boy. She supported herself selling speed, which she got from a Forest Hills dieting doctor.

Terry was brilliant. Like the nerdiest poet boy, she could parse influence from imitation over centuries—from Catullus through Herrick and Pope; to Mallarmé and Kurt Schwitters through her older contemporaries. Her poems were open and pliant, but they were also aware of themselves as physical objects. Sitting on Seth's couch in her actress-y clothes, Catt felt vaguely embarrassed beside Terry. Terry was always and only herself. Mostly, Catt studied how to become other people.

More than two decades later, where were the poets? Some were no longer alive. The more ambitious Young Poet boys had gone back to school and become editors, academics and diplomats. Drifting into their thirties, the girls had become proofreaders, nurses, and paralegals. The poets who'd become most successful were those who'd made clean breaks with their youths. Except for Terry. Twenty years sober, she was still Terry Stiles, a respected poet. She'd broken up with numerous allies and girlfriends, but never herself. The last time Catt saw Terry, she was directing a writing program in San Diego.

Drifting once more in Albuquerque, Catt considers Terry's decisiveness. Why hasn't she told Hank about Paul? Terry was never afraid to end things with her lovers. Catt was unable to break up with anything.

Throughout these long afternoons, Catt reads and naps shamelessly. Sometimes she walks a few blocks to swim laps in a city pool. Her primary goal is to stay out of the car and move around sparingly. The longer she stays in one place, the closer she feels to stepping inside a parallel timescape … something more viscous, internal.

Often, she feels like she's in *Meshes of the Afternoon*, a black and white experimental film she used to show to her art students. A dreamy but pointed magnificence … Maya Deren, the filmmaker, inventing surrealism by trailing around a florid and transient Hollywood neighborhood with her hand-held Bolex, sometime in the 1940s. When Deren steps into a dark Spanish-style room, the camera stops down abruptly and the frame seems to contract, the reverse of a dilating pupil.

The movie was timeless, and yet irreducibly locked in its time, cocooned from the Second World War in a Freudian bubble of locks and skelton keys, signs and symbols ...

"Deren uses specific cinematic devices to convey deeper meaning," Catt read in a used book she picked up on Central. Which was so stupid—as if "meaning" was ever a thing. Deren didn't *use* anything. Rather, she willed herself into a parallel time whose contours can only be seen by its inhabitants.

Within this bubble, Catt reads the old notebooks she'd brought with her to Albuquerque ... notes about nineteenth-century London she'd made before she'd abandoned her thesis. Havelock Ellis, Margaret Sanger, Eleanor Aveling Marx ... the Bloomsbury social reformers who'd led unthinkably adventurous lives as scholars and activists. Eleanor Marx, the only one of Karl Marx's five children to assume the mantle of intellectual activism, speaking herself hoarse at trade union halls but translating Flaubert on the side because she longed for beauty ... Margaret Sanger leaving a husband and three little children for exile in London when she's indicted for mail fraud after publishing birth control pamphlets. Maybe, Catt thinks, she could do something else with these lives, this information. Something maybe not quite academic, but less empty to her than art writing. Perhaps, instead of her own, she could use these other lives to tell a story?

While Catt dreams, Paul drives between buildings, showing and renting apartments. As the summer progresses, he feels increasingly pressed to fill all the apartments. Catt's paying him $600 a week until the construction is finished, but when she's gone, he'll be paid ten percent of the gross rental income. This seemed like a good deal when they hired him, but even with the units full his income will shrink to, maybe, $1,400 a month ... barely enough to live on. He's already decided to go back to school full-time in September. Catt's cool with that, they've decided to pay someone else to do maintenance. All he has to do is pick up the rents and fill vacancies, which shouldn't take more than 10 or 12 hours a week. Plus, he has the red truck, and the free phone, and the free apartment.

But, as he's finding out, even $600 a week isn't really enough to pay his expenses. Parole is thirty-five dollars a week, and there's another $120 each month when he takes the LifeSafer in to be monitored. He'll have to pay car insurance (expensive, with his DUIs and Ignition Interlock license), and also the bounced check restitution. If he doesn't keep paying them off— a hundred dollars a month—they'll revoke his parole. Too depressing to even think what he owes: with interest and court fees and fines, he'll be paying restitution forever. After all these expenses, he'll have about $800 a month to live on. Without Catt in town, he'll have to buy his own food, pay for all his books, gas, clothes, and utilities.

Paul has no idea how he paid for these things before coming to Albuquerque. Maybe Jerry took care of it? Farmington's already a blur, he cannot remember. But his dependence on Jerry is over. And Catt won't be here. She'll move back to LA, and then to Chicago to teach Cultural Studies in the second semester.

Once everyone knew that he was with Catt, Tommy had sat down with Paul to talk about bookkeeping. "I'm warning you, brother," he'd smirked. "You'd better not get too attached. For as long as I've known them, Catt and Michel have had an *open relationship*. And you know what that means. She'll be on to the next guy once the summer is over."

Why was Tommy saying these things?

"Just remember, you're fuck buddies, and then you won't get hurt. But between you and me, that girl has a *very healthy libido*. Not that I blame her. She and Michel, well—they just come from a different culture. You know … *European*. In fact, it's likely Michel's taste runs to boys. That would explain all his travel."

Even though Paul had just started the job, he knew this was crazy. Michel had stopped over in Albuquerque on his way to New York. He'd taken Paul out to dinner, and Michel was an excellent guy. A world famous philosopher, but not stuck up at all. Tommy was trying to scare him. Maybe he was afraid that with Paul on the scene, Catt and Michel would replace him?

Still, even forgetting whatever game Tommy was playing, Paul can't stop wondering what will happen to him when Catt leaves at the end of the summer. If he can't even get by on $600 a week, what will he do when it's less? How will he pay for books and tuition?

It never crosses Paul's mind that he could sell the Z, or find a roommate, or get a part-time job waiting tables. He and Catt have purchased an exquisite black leather couch off of Craigslist. Italian, designed by an artist … The couple who sold them the couch had just moved down from Santa Fe. He was a psychiatrist, she ran an art gallery and they lived in a huge architect house at the foot of the Sandias. *These* are the kind of people he's moving with … Catt and Michel aren't just rich, they're pretty famous—he's typed their names into Google. If Paul wants things to continue, he has to blend in to this atmosphere. Finish up his BA, maybe travel and then go to grad school. This will take years. Until then, he has to observe and do what's expected … not be scrounging around in his old ways for extra money.

Five weeks into the job, Catt invites the whole crew to Florino's, an upscale North Valley restaurant, on Saturday night to celebrate. It's still early June, and the work is more than half-finished. Evan and Joe, the two local guys, are surprised by this invitation, but they show up in dress shirts. Tommy arrives on the Southwest nonstop that afternoon unexpected, dressed in full Wild West regalia to "be part of this thing" and "check over the leases."

Sitting at the long table with Paul, Titus, Sharon, Brett, Jason and Matt, Joe and Evan, and even Tommy, Catt floats on a small cloud of happiness. The job has created this group, however provisional.

Over drinks, they go round the table, each person saying which of the buildings he or she would most want to live in. Catt picks Mescalero for its old plaster walls and the pepper trees outside its louvered windows. "Oh, you just want to get high," Tommy laughs. "Picking the street that's named after mescaline—" But Joe Stillwater tells them Mescalero isn't a drug, it's the name of the last band of Apaches who held out against the Navajo. "How do you *know* this?" Catt trills. "I'm Mescalero." The whole table looks at him; his powerful arms covered in black ink tattoos. "Well, anyway, half. My dad's side of the family." Then he pulls a folded up paper out of his pocket: a drawing of black thunderbolt lines. "This is our chevron. After Titus got me helping him over at Mescalero, I started thinking about that part of the family. My Dad is deceased, so I talked to my uncle. My uncle knows all about it, because he's spent time on the rez. There's only one Mescalero rez left—about two thousand people, down by Tularosa. So I asked him, and he made me this drawing."

Catt's heart is close to bursting. Four weeks ago, Joe Stillwater was an unemployed unskilled worker. Now he's part of the group. He's not just showing up every day at the job, but actually caring about it. And isn't this proof of her hypothesis? Titus, who is a quarter Sioux Indian on his mom's side of the family, is intrigued by the actual drawing. They've been building adobe walls at Mescalero … If it's okay with Joe, maybe they could stencil the chevron on the front wall, make it kind of an emblem? Joe nods, and tells Titus he'll cut one and bring it on Monday.

Paul and Catt exchange glances. They'd been talking about hiring Joe as the maintenance man, and this clinches it. He's already told her Joe Stillwater's story.

At the end of Joe's first week on the job, thinking he'd keep him on the crew, Paul asked Joe if he had any references. And Joe said no. Then he confessed that he'd just gotten out of prison. Unfazed, Paul replied, "Oh. Which one?" and Joe said, "Las Cruces." Paul didn't ask what the charge was. Instead, he told Joe that he'd spent time himself in Las Lunas. Joe knew right away that Las Lunas was Level III, and he knew then that Paul knew Las Cruces was Level V, maximum security. So he told Paul:

"After getting divorced, I was sharing a place here in town with my mom and my sister. One night, my sister's ex-boyfriend showed up there drunk, wanting to talk to her. He had a gun he was waving around. My sister and mom were both there in the room, and I didn't think twice. I had a knife and I went for it. I did fourteen years. The public defender pled it to Manslaughter."

Looking over the table, Catt realizes that everyone here except for herself and Tommy has been incarcerated, homeless or both. When Titus and Sharon moved down from Sonoma, they lived in their van for two months, both working full-time until they could save up enough for an apartment. Cops in his small Texas town showed up at Evan's mom's house on his eighteenth birthday to arrest him for assault. At sixteen, he'd gotten into a fight with a classmate, but they'd deferred the charges two years so he'd go to jail, instead of receiving probation as a juvenile. "Yeah man ... happy *birthday*! I'd just finished high school, and the guys they locked me up with were really scary." Evan, his mom, and his three-year-old son moved to Albuquerque just to get out of Texas. His son's mom stayed behind. She was, like Brett's ex, a meth addict. Brett—who still hasn't decided whether to turn himself in on the warrant—lived alone on the beach in his van when he was sixteen, with an eight-month-old infant. The Victorville painter Jason's son Matt spent part of his teens in San Bernadino County Juvenile Hall for spray-painting graffiti. Even the vendors she's hired have records! Zack, the artisan-hippie who built a straw bale wall for them at Tulane, remembered Paul from the Farm. Zack had served eighteen months for Possession With Intent To Sell—a few marijuana plants in his back yard. Was this Prison America?

Catt never set out to do social work, but apparently everyone outside the art world has either lived in a van or been incarcerated. None of these people see any connection between their sad, shitty stories. Instead, they're ashamed. Except for Paul, who blames The Disease Known as Alcoholism, they put it down to back luck and misfortune.

By the end of the evening, Tommy is sloppily drunk: making loud toasts, knocking over glasses with his turquoise bracelets. This is strange ... Catt's never once seen Tommy drunk. The games Tommy's running demand his full concentration. Why did he come back to Albuquerque?

The next morning he phones Catt from his hotel room: *I need you. You've got to come over right now. I can't talk on the phone. I'm too upset. There's been an accident.*

Uh-oh. Bracing herself for more trouble, Catt jumps in the car. She arrives to find Tommy slumped on the edge of his bed, chain-smoking. The door to his room is wide open. A portrait of anguish, sweat on his forehead. *Thank God you're here Catt. I've been robbed. They took all my jewelry! The cops have just left.*

Stepping into his theater, making all the appropriate noises—*at least you weren't hurt*—Catt's mind races forward as she recites her script. *Tommy try and calm down, tell me what happened.*

His eyes move between Catt and the floor. *I woke up early this morning and went out to do my laundry. You know?* She nods. *There's a little laundrette a few blocks down on East Central. Well, I walked into the place. It was empty. Even then I got a bad feeling, I should have just left, but I think, no big deal, it's Sunday morning. So I put my clothes in the washer. Sit down to wait. And then two men, they were Latinos, walk into the place empty-handed. I look up. They come closer. Then one of them takes out a gun, a little silvery thing, and he tells me: Look down. Now give me your wallet. I do that, what else can I do? And then the other one says, Now give me your jewelry. And then they left. Catt, they took everything! The jewelry was a present from Ron. Some of the pieces were vintage, I mean, it's worth thousands. But that isn't even the point, it's the sentiment—*

The best lies begin with a fragment of truth. Catt struggles to find it. Tommy is only here for two days, so there's no truth in the laundromat part. Maybe he went to a bar after the restaurant? Picked someone up who took off with his stuff?

—And now I don't even know how I'll get home! If I'm not in the office first thing Monday morning, I'll lose my job, I already

took too many days off last month to come out here. Of course the first thing I did was to cancel my credit cards. I flew out on a voucher, I was gonna purchase the return at the airport—

Resisting the obvious, Catt wonders why Tommy doesn't call Ron. Couldn't Ron buy him a ticket?

Oh Catt I can't tell Ron about any of this! It would just make everything worse. The jewelry wasn't insured! The cops don't see any hope of recovering it. You should have seen them: a couple of rednecks, they couldn't care less. They don't even think it's a Hate Crime. And then there's the money. I had $500 cash in my wallet and you've been so amazing, so generous—

Five hundred cash: the daily ATM limit. *Tommy, I know you must be devastated about losing the jewelry. But at least cash is just cash. Why don't you let me replace it?*

Compared to the scale of the drama, the adrenalin pumped through her body, Catt feels she's gotten off cheaply. They drive to an ATM. She gives Tommy the cash and drops him at the airport. She doesn't offer to buy him a ticket. Perhaps they both won? He got her for $500 but this time, she set limits. But then again ... she doesn't feel safe. Tommy is out of control. What will he think of next?

Alone all afternoon at the condo, she can't read, she can't think. Paul is out showing apartments. She wishes she could step back into her old life as an art critic. For the first time since arriving in Albuquerque, she calls her home phone in LA to pick up voicemail. But none of her old friends have left messages. Just a few robot-calls. And then a male voice—

This is a confidential message for Ms. Catt Dunlop from Countrywide Financial Services. We'd like to tell you about some exciting new loan products available to homeowners just like yourself that can be easily accessed, even if you're facing foreclosure—

She snaps the phone shut and calls the 800 number. *Hello, Beneficial Finance*—isn't Beneficial a sub-prime lender?—*Yes, that's right.* There must be some mistake. She has a loan on her house in LA but it's current—*You'll need to discuss that with servicing—*

A half-hour later a recorded voice tells her—*Your loan is ninety-six days delinquent and has been placed in pre-foreclosure—* But Tommy was paying the mortgage. Her next call is to Tommy—*The number you've reached is no longer in service.* Catt still hasn't filed last year's taxes and her spreadsheets, her leases, her bank statements, receipts, and credit card papers are all with Tommy. She'd considered the extent of the risk before authorizing him as a signer on her business checking: worst case, he could get away with about $10,000 before she figured it out. Compared to the benefit—*she would not have to think about money*—the risk seemed sustainable. Even if Tommy disappeared with her papers, they were replaceable.

In the coming months, Catt will discover unpaid credit card bills and dozens of payments from her business account to eBay and QVC shopping. Confronted, Tommy will threaten to report her for tax fraud. She'll propose a deal: if he returns her papers, she won't go after him for embezzlement. She'll hear stories from his former Crestline employer about property deeds signed over to him from an elderly, now-deceased former client. Shady, but not prosecutable. One afternoon she'll receive a call from a blocked number, and it will be Tommy, no longer charming, speaking to her in a voice so deep it's almost unrecognizable: *Bitch, I'm in Indio. If you want your shit back, it's here. I'll be at the Chevron. I'll wait for two hours.* For the first time, she'll be frightened. Her father will offer to drive out from his home in Palm Springs to retrieve the papers. He'll find Tommy waiting. Not saying a word, Tommy will toss two cartons of unsorted papers into the trunk of his Hyundai. By then it will be dark, and her father will drive forty miles back to Palm Springs, barely seeing the road because of his cataracts.

Everything, Hank told her once, *is replaceable.* But at what psychic cost?

The next weekend, Catt has to fly back to LA for what she describes to Paul as a "speaking engagement." She's been asked to appear as a guest on Cross Currents, an ironically old-school talk show held at a gallery. The host, an old anarchist, has rebranded himself as a "media ecologist."

Twenty-two people sit in the dim auditorium on a perfect June Saturday. Most are MFA students. The others are vagrants.

Tobias, the host, has been doing the show on and off for two decades. Conceived as a "community event" at the local bookstore, when the store went out of business the show moved to a gallery. Short and wiry, with shaggy gray hair, Tobias looks like an elf. He's also encyclopedically brilliant. Years ago, Tobias hosted Cross Currents events with some of Catt's early heroes: Frank Zappa, Carla Bley, Captain Beefheart. In those days, his show must have drawn a big crowd: young couples with kids, people with regular jobs, as well as the usual artists and writers. A General Audience that *rejected the blandishments of a reality defined by TV,* as the program notes put it, or who just wanted to get out of the house on a Saturday.

No community, no event, Catt thinks, adjusting her mike. In 2005 people have long stopped attending these things, but she feels bad for Tobias, still putting his heart into it. As Paul often put it: *The definition of insanity is doing the same thing over and over while expecting different results.* Catt can vaguely remember a time when Tobias might have conversed on network TV with Dick Cavett ... But now his language, the definition itself of "media ecology," sounds almost autistic. The more marginal an ideology, the more fervently held the belief.

The premise of an "alternative media" is, let's face it, a joke. For the past several years, while she built her career, Catt sensed that all cultural dialogue was really a cipher ... for something else ... a means of obscuring the thick toxic cloud under which we were all living. Everyone acting, for professional reasons, as if these things matter. But even now, two and a half years since the Iraq invasion, you can't raise your eyes without seeing American flags and lapel pins, even in cities. The endless debate about "prisoner abuse" (only the hard-core leftist blogs called it torture) halted, to everyone's great relief, by the Abu Ghraib show trials. This is what Catt wants to talk about with Tobias. Pregnant with Charles Graner's baby, Lynndie England lost her plea bargain when she naively remarked that she *didn't know her actions were wrong.* She'd gotten off-script.

In order to reconcile these abhorrent photos, the American people needed a *monster* to blame, not a stunned zombie.

Tobias wants Catt to talk about sex. Was she *really* as abject as she appeared in her writings? Wondering if she'll have to summon French theory for the rest of her life to explain her brief, girlish adventures, she performs as expected and deflects the question.

At the end of the afternoon, an MFA student introduces himself and asks Catt to write a catalogue essay. He's enthusiastic about her performance a few minutes ago with Tobias. Catt cannot fathom why. She's already blocked it from memory. The MFA student's show is at a conservative mid-market gallery. Unlike most of her supporters, the artist appears affluent, gym-toned, and completely untroubled. She wonders if this is a portent.

On Monday morning, she stops at the bank to freeze her accounts before returning to Albuquerque. The teller is horrified by Tommy's activities, and asks if she plans to press charges. *I can't imagine*, the woman offers, *how it must feel to be betrayed by a former employee.* Well, thinks Catt, worse things have happened. That morning she'd read an *LA Times* story about the preemptive arrest of a Muslim doctor, who'd "planned to treat wounded terrorists." Even here, deep in downtown Los Angeles, she can see four American flags through the bank window and two in the lobby.

With a few hours to kill before catching the plane, she stops to buy Paul a present. Browsing the racks of a Los Feliz boutique, she feels old and poor. Finally she finds the right shirt: a vintage silk print with pictures of horses. And it's the right size! All in all, this is the high point of the trip.

Ever since Catt left for LA, Paul has worried that the trip home will make her come to her senses. Maybe she'll break up with him over the phone? Or will she wait, and do it in person in

Albuquerque? Still, his face lights up when he sees her emerging from the airport's secured area. And she's waving! Catt's eyes mist up when she sees Paul standing there, with the uniformed chauffeurs and extended poor families. Except for her parents, no one has ever met her in the lobby when they picked her up at an airport. A big hug: "You came back!" "Paul—you really know how to meet a plane!"

This makes him feel good. In fact, Paul's never met a plane in his life. All morning he debated whether to bring the small gifts that he'd bought to the airport—a tiny stuffed bear, a dozen red roses. Finally he'd decided against it: too cheesy, probably something Catt and her friends wouldn't do. And he was right.

The unspoken question floating between them for weeks disappears even before they get into the red Dodge Dakota.

7

SOCIO-GRAPHICS

PAUL MOVES INTO THE CONDO with Catt when a disgruntled tenant breaks into the Tulane apartment and slashes his tires. Just being there now makes him anxious. The guy was a crackhead, no way of knowing when he'll be back. He leaves early each morning for work, leaving Catt free to read, nap, and write in her notebooks. Evenings, they work on her taxes.

Catt starts telling her friends what she's really doing in Albuquerque. They can tell by her voice that she's happy, but it doesn't seem right. Shouldn't she take things more slowly? Some of her colleagues are dating people they've met on match-making sites. Determined not to repeat the mistakes of their youths, they're reading books about courtship and marriage. Their words wash over her.

On one of their walks to the park, she tells Paul about the connection she's had to trees since she was a teenager. The way certain trees speak, almost pour themselves into her. Emotion floods in and she's no longer anyone. Sometimes she weeps, but it's not a bad sadness. To Paul, this sounds mentally ill, but he doesn't dismiss it. Instead he sits next to her under her favorite oak, and then he feels it too—the tree is no longer outside, it starts to enter him. *Oh Paul,* she says softly. The whole thing is amusing, but at the same time, serious. He imagines the whole cosmos contracting, shrinking down to *one single thing*—just as he'd imagined it would be if he saw an alien. For sure, Catt's way into trees, but what gets to him more is the image of them sitting there with the dog, just one speck in the universe. It's a really intimate moment, even closer than sex. He can't think what to say back, so he just says *Oh Catt*—and then they start laughing.

Most Sundays they drive out of town to explore New Mexico. They visit forlorn tourist parks from the 1960s. They drive through the Navajo rez, climb mountains, and walk through the lava fields taking pictures of rocks, forgotten towns, and each other. These trips, Catt thinks, are *dérives.* In its new engagement with "the political," the art world has rediscovered mid-century French Situationism, reprising the language of Debord and his friends minus the pleasure. Hundreds of artists, their *practices grounded in socio-graphics,* displaying photos of buildings, dioramas, and flow charts, like old-fashioned grade school geography projects. She thinks of André Breton describing the day he met Nadja, "On one of those afternoons we knew so well how to waste …" Does her familiarity with other centuries make these drives more enjoyable? Possibly. Catt can't imagine a present that isn't associative. She feels *supported* by history, almost literally. For Paul, content is all on the surface. Nothing relates to anything beyond itself. Without culture, the subject is isolate … Can there even be conscience without interiority? Lynndie England: *I didn't know my actions were wrong.* The Big Book and the Twelve Steps of AA offer behavioral models, not ethics. And this makes Catt fearful.

The only time Paul really feels free is when he's driving. Losing himself while moving forward, so long as he's on the move, there's no more dread, no more panic.

During these Sunday trips, Paul and Catt invent car games and make up new verses to old cowboy ballads. They decide to be "permanent boyfriend and girlfriend." To Catt, this sounds so dumb it's perfect. Therefore, she believes it. They make plans for the future. In September, Paul will go back to school. He'll get a BA in psychology. They'll visit every third or fourth weekend, flying to each other's cities. As soon as he finishes—two or three years, with the credits he earned at community college—he'll move to LA and go to grad school. Maybe USC, maybe UCLA. After that, they'll turn Catt's LA compound into an alternative psychiatric facility.

Talking about these future plans makes them miss each other *already*. Secretly they're both relieved. Who could continue at this intensity?

Titus and crew finish the job at the end of July and go home to Victorville. With Paul's first semester on the horizon, Catt gives him a chunk of the August rents to buy clothes, an office PC, and a laptop. She expects him to be delighted and grateful. Instead, he asks for another $800 to put a toolbox on the Dakota. When she refuses, he's furious. He never *asked* Catt for a laptop. What he wants is the toolbox: Dodge regulation, not salvage, not aftermarket. *It's for the business!* She's shocked. Until now, Paul has mirrored her language, her gestures, and worldview so perfectly, how could he possibly want this stupid consumer accessory? The longer they argue about the Dodge toolbox, the more Paul regresses: "Mason, my cousin, has a sharp new aluminum toolbox on the back of his Silverado. Mike D. has one too! You don't understand. These guys really *know how to take care of their tools*. It's a sign of being professional."

"Paul, that's absurd." She's already met Mason, a thirty-nine-year-old, shifty-eyed hick with five kids and a yard full of gas-guzzling vehicles. "Besides, that's not your profession. You're the manager! We hired Joe Stillwater to do maintenance."

"Why are you being so mean? I'm trying to take care of things here, I'm running your business. I've already got a new Skilsaw and drill kit. Now I want the toolbox!"

She shrugs and gives a small laugh. "Out of the question."

This is a side of Catt he's never seen. "Motherfuck! I can't believe you are even saying this. I'm busting my ass every day to take care of your shit and the crackheads that live in your buildings, while you freakin' live in a dream world. Get real, we're in *Albuquerque*. This is not some organic farm. If I leave my tools in the bed they'll be gone in two seconds—"

"Then lock them up in the cab."

"Yeah, *right* ... You want me to stand there like an asshole, unloading every time I get out of the vehicle?"

Given Paul's past, this doesn't seem like an unbearable hardship. Trying once more, she reasons, "Paul, it doesn't make sense. You're not even supposed to be doing maintenance. You're going to school. We're paying Joe $1,400 a month—"

Suddenly he wants to hit her. She's so smooth and glassy. Paul knows he'd better get out before something worse happens. He storms out, slams the door, and just drives—twenty, thirty miles over the limit—until he ends up at a meeting.

As alcoholics, we can't expect our problems to go away just because we've stopped drinking, someone reads from the book. *Drinking is just a way to put our problems on hold …*

Four hours later he returns to the condo with flowers. They don't mention the toolbox again. *So what if he's immature,* Catt rationalizes. If he were mature we'd be negotiating each phase of this quote "Relationship."

On their third-to-last weekend, they drive up to Farmington to visit the grave of Paul's dog and all his other old places.

Ruggo, the lucky Dalmatian, was buried on a dirt hill a few yards from the highway. It's too scrubby and hot to sit on the ground. Rusted hydraulic gas pumps line the horizon. *I'd kill myself if I had to live here,* Catt thinks at the gravesite. Each place they've seen—from Jerry and Cris's Alpine Drive palace, to the county jail, mobile-home park, and Casa Bonita—is equally dismal. *There is nothing in this town to want.* Which must be poverty at its most elemental. She adds a few rocks to the gravesite.

Paul takes an iced tea out of the cooler and sits on the tailgate. Weird. He'd been closer to Ruggo than to anyone in the world. They shared a deep understanding. All these years, he's never been back. And now he doesn't feel anything. They look up towards the grave. Maybe bringing Catt here wasn't the greatest idea.

"At first I didn't believe he was dead," he tells her. "He'd been gone for eight days, but there were times when he'd gone off before. I put flyers with his picture up all over the place, so when this lady called and said she thought she'd seen him by the side of the highway, I got really happy. I figured he'd been hit by a car. I mean, why would she bother to call if he wasn't still living? Maybe she hit him. So I thanked her and went out to get him. Why was I always expecting the worst? Maybe good things can happen.

"When I got near the place, I saw the back of his body hunched up. It was right where she said, just off the pavement. His head was tucked into his chest—the brown spots on his neck looked like the number seven, which I always thought signified luck. But when I got out of my truck I had a really bad feeling. Because he didn't look up, he wasn't moving. I swore, no matter how bad he'd been hurt I'd take care of it, even if it meant selling the truck. Cars were driving by fast. I felt sick. I did not want to look. But there he was. He'd probably been dead just a few hours.

"His body was already stiff, but I still picked him up. When the blood started coming out of his mouth, I just started bawling. The road was so close to where I was living, why didn't I find him? I'd never let myself cry like that before. Then I buried him here, where we used to go walking."

"I'd cry if we broke up," Paul says on the long mellow drive back to Albuquerque. Each day brings them closer to Catt's departure. But he can't keep this sweet, sad feeling for long. He's too anxious about the hundred bad things just waiting to happen.

"I keep feeling like the other shoe's ready to drop," he says when they're close to the city. But she's oblivious. "I just keep worrying how I'm going to make it. I mean, I know I get to keep ten percent of the rents and that's really generous, I mean really, beyond my wildest dreams, and I'm incredibly grateful. But what's going to happen when you go back to LA? Is eight or nine hundred a month enough to go back to school on?"

All summer they've been together, never thinking about money, buying whatever they needed. Until now, Catt's never once thought about Paul or his finances as a separate entity. And she's shocked—not by his question, but by the idea of anyone living on $900 a month. She knows she couldn't do it.

Now that Tommy's out of the picture, Paul has just taken care of most of the things he used to do—balancing checkbooks, paying the mortgage and bills. In a sense he's already taken over from Tommy. If Catt and Paul hadn't met, she'd be in Nepal and Tommy would still be stealing.

"Maybe you could do Tommy's job, too."

"Really? That would help out a lot, make things easier."

"Yeah. I mean, you're already doing stuff that he used to do." But then she doesn't know what to say next. It seems confusing to talk about salary. What was the number? The $800 month Tommy got paid, or what he took on the side? After Tommy paid the big bills, Catt spent maybe $1,500 a month? That was about what it cost not to have to think about money. Why shouldn't Paul have that freedom too? "So maybe instead of keeping ten percent of the rents, you could just take what you need. For your expenses." Her mind was racing ahead to the worst case scenario ... like Tommy, he could probably embezzle a month's worth of rents before she found out. But Paul's on parole, he'd never risk it. "I mean, within reason," she adds. He wouldn't have access to her savings accounts or property titles. "Of course I'll have to talk to Michel, see if he's cool with it."

"Wow, Catt. This is … *amazing.*" He's just been adopted by two wealthy college professors.

"I mean, we'll be totally trusting you." But the three buildings in Albuquerque are already making a profit, more than she needs. She has no interest in shopping. She and Michel are indifferent to luxury but, as children of working-class families, they're aware of the cost of the freedom to *think.* Why shouldn't they share it?

The first step to implementing this plan is to add Paul's name on her business checking account as a signer. But at the bank the next morning, the teller refuses. *Chex-Systems won't accept Mr. Garcia's name.* Catt is outraged. Paul feels nauseous. *He has twenty-six unpaid checks dating back to '03 … The only way you can add this individual's name is by waiting six months after he makes full restitution.*

"Why didn't you tell me about this?" Catt asks through her teeth as they exit the lobby.

"I had no idea! How would I know they'd ban me?"

"I mean about writing the checks in the first place! How can someone write *one bad check after another?* I mean, after the first, you must have known they would bounce—"

"Catt, I was fucked up! I didn't have any money. You think I'd do it sober? I've been paying those checks off every month since before I went to prison. I'm still paying them off. I just didn't tell you."

"No—"

"I mean, it's bad enough I was in prison, I just thought you didn't need to hear it. Besides, it's too depressing. I'll be paying those checks off forever."

"How much do you owe?"

Everything's swirling. He needs to calm down, take this slowly. "I really don't know. Catt, it's not like I lied—"

"How *could you?*"

Oh fuck, here it comes. "How could you owe money to the point that it screws up your life, and *not know* what you owe?"

"I could find out at parole."

For a moment she softens. Then her rage finds a new outlet: if Paul is paying the debt like he said, why wouldn't the bank let her add him as a signer? It was *her* risk. How can anyone hope to start a more normal life if they can't even bank? Is he supposed to keep his money under a mattress?

Later, when Paul phones parole, he learns that he owes $3,962.67. He reports this figure numbly. "Is that what you wrote?" Paul doesn't know. Catt makes him call back for a breakdown. The checks totaled $1,857. The rest of the money was interest, court fees, and penalties.

This, Catt thinks, is injustice. *If you punish the poor by making them poorer the cycle is endless.* That Friday she brings some construction receipts over to Stu and returns with a cashier's check for $3,962.67.

No one at parole asks where Paul got the money to pay off this debt. Instead, they reduce his parole status to Minimum. Now he no longer has to come in once a week. Once every three months, he'll report on the phone. Besides wiping the debt, the money has saved him $2,400 a year on parole fees and urine analysis.

With the checks paid, Paul has disappeared under the wire. He still needs permission to leave the county, but doesn't *county* sound almost like *country*? So when Catt has to fly back to LA for a few days, he doesn't think twice about joining her.

And LA's a dream. A late summer Monday, all the people his age are at work, and Paul's driving up PCH in a rented convertible! It's a perfect eighty degrees, sun spilling across the incredible deep blue of the ocean. Everything is clean: white seagulls, white stucco houses flanked by flowering bushes Catt says are called bougainvillea.

In every respect, LA is the reverse of New Mexico. It's all so much lighter. The tall buildings, the beautiful curves of the freeway. It's like stepping into a movie ... *Mulholland Drive*, *Reservoir Dogs*, *Pulp Fiction*. He imagines himself living here as a UCLA graduate student, encountering Gwen Stefani or Uma Thurman at Whole Foods or the farmer's market.

Even meeting Catt's friends is less scary than he expected. Of course the first thing they all ask is, *what do you do?* At first Catt leaps in with, "he's an animal therapist," and then he starts saying it too. Everyone plays right along. No one cares, anyway. Already, he's had "sessions" with the dysfunctional pets of the two troubled girls Catt describes as her interns. All you have to do is describe the girl's problems while you look at her pet. Despite their MFAs and rich parents, they're totally insecure. Shit, perhaps he could do this.

At Topanga State Beach, he takes out a roll of bills to pay the ten-dollar parking fee. Money means nothing. The sand on the beach is so white, it's like he's stepped into Baywatch. He can hardly believe at this same time last year he was living behind concrete walls and electrified wire. He takes off his shirt and walks into the waves, baptizing his new self in the icy Pacific.

Albuquerque comes crashing back when they return. Someone broke in to Paul's old Tulane apartment and left the door open. This time the desktop computer and TV are gone, and the word *Asshole* is sprayed on the black leather sofa. Was it the same crackhead who popped the lock last time? Another? Or someone else from Paul's past? The message is so specific. Could it be Tommy? A warning? This time, even Catt's frightened. She remembers her killer.

Paul needs to get out of Tulane. Catt's leaving soon. He can live at the condo.

But then again ... on their many walks to the park, Catt has seen a For Rent sign on a perfect old house, a three-bedroom bungalow on Dartmouth built in the 1930s. Even before Tulane got scary, she'd imagined them reading in front of the fireplace. Her LA compound isn't really a home. Camping out in the guest house, she rents the main house to a pair of celebrity stylists who've ripped out her hibiscus and daisies and planted Himalayan bamboo. The front yard is littered with Buddhas. She and Michel have just accepted an offer on their old house in East Fletcher. Soon, they'll no longer own it. How long has it been since she's lived anywhere? The rent on Dartmouth is just $850 a month. They could easily rent the condo for six. For just $250 more she'll have a real home again.

Catt leases the house. She wants to be happy. They move in just in time for Paul to prepare for his first semester. He picks up the student handbook and reads out the names of the classes: Psych 101, Brain and Behavior. *I'm a student*, Paul tells himself over and over. With credits for the community college classes he attended two decades ago in a crack haze, he can get his BA in just over two years. As a returning student, he's entitled to free tuition and health care—even his books will be paid for.

But on the day he enrolls, the system won't take his social security number. The registry office sends him to talk to the bursar. The lady there tells him his old student loan is delinquent. Until the loan's paid, he can't get financial aid. If he still wants to enroll, he'll have to pay the tuition.

What student loan? Panicked, he asks her to double check the records. There must be some mistake. He hasn't been a student for decades. Okay, *maybe* he took a loan for like, $3,500 back at community college ... but the Farmington lawyer who did his divorce promised *his debts would all go away* when his soon-to-be-ex second wife filed for bankruptcy.

When the woman hands him a print-out he nearly faints when he sees the $21,000 balance. How can this be? *Mr. Garcia, you need to set up a payment plan with your lender.* He has no idea who this lender is, or where to find him. *Once your account is in good standing, you can come back and enroll for your classes.*

Catt reads the bad news on Paul's face when he forces himself to go home a few hours later. She weeps. He can't. She's just paid the checks. How many more obstacles will Paul have to pass before he can live like a regular person? There are almost too many for her, and she is unusually driven. What would it be like to face them alone, with a criminal record and no money or sense of entitlement? Enraged, she calls Hank.

"I need to know what you signed, and with who, and when you signed it," she says when she finally comes out of her office. She looks grave and deliberate, clutching a long legal pad, hair yanked off her face with two chopsticks.

But Paul can't remember.

"Paul this is your life! This is serious."

"Catt, I don't know." He still hasn't told her about crack. "What do you want me to say? I was going to school. This was back in the '80s. And yeah, okay—maybe I *did* take a loan for $3,500." The loan went up in smoke, is that what she's getting at? "I was working full-time at Red Lobster, I just wanted to cut back my hours to study."

She looks at the pad. For the last forty-five minutes, she and Hank have been doing numbers. If Paul opts for payments, that means he *accepts* a principal balance of $21K. For the life of the loan, the interest will continue compounding. If he blows off the loan, she'll have to pay his tuition and he'll never recover his credit. Not a good option ... tuition is $5,135 per semester. He needs six to complete his BA, bringing the total to $30,810. If, on the other hand—as Hank advises—they offer to settle, she can probably get the lender to write off forty percent. At about $14K, they'll break even before the end of the third semester.

"But I never got any $21,000. That's just crazy. I never once in my life had money like that. I would *remember*."

Scanning the print-out, she circles a line dated April 19, 2000. "It says here, you *refinanced* the loan. What about that? Do you remember?"

April 19 more than five years ago ... The past is a blur. But Paul thinks that might be around when he signed the divorce from Moyra. The more he tries to remember, the blacker things get. He was fucked up all the time. But the bankruptcy, that came in through the side, that day at the lawyer's ...

"You have to try and remember."

"Alright. Okay. Here's something. I was with Moyra. We were getting divorced. She said I owed her $1,500, my share of the mortgage, because when we got together I moved into her trailer. But I was broke, I didn't have it. So she and the lawyer set up this thing. He found someone who'd take over the loan and give me back $1,500. But that's still only $5,000!"

"Paul, look at the print-out ..." *The debts of the poor ...* "Loan fees. Documentation. Points, recording, and FedEx ... The balance *started* at $10,380, that's what you signed for. And when you didn't pay, the interest compounded."

Her settlement offer is accepted the next morning. Paul enrolls as a sophomore. Three weeks before classes start, he receives a letter from the school president:

Dear Mr. Garcia,

Your application to attend the University of New Mexico has been referred to our office for further review. Please be advised that in accordance with university policy, your admittance may be rescinded due to your 2003 conviction of Felony 3 under New Mexico statutes. Your application is now under review ...

"Does this mean I can't go to school?"

Catt can't believe it. She calls her old friend, Janine, who's just received tenure in the UNM's Media Studies department. Years ago in New York, she and Janine had passed off $3,800 of forged traveler's checks to finance a Super-8 film. Paul committed a petty, nonviolent felony! *The system is programmed for failure.* Six months after Paul's release from the Farm all the other parolees in his cohort are back in prison for parole violations: failing to report, driving uninsured vehicles, attending gatherings where traces of illegal substances were found in the carpets.

Though she's no longer the wild girl of the past, Janine is outraged. She's ready to take this all the way to the top—the ACLU, the Faculty Senate ...

Paul wishes they would just *stop*. All he wants is to go back to school. He doesn't want this shit to be public.

But before Janine can take further action, Paul gets a second letter announcing *his status is cleared ... decision has been made in his favor*. In the end, he *can* be a student. He just no longer has any feelings about it.

One week before his first day of class, Paul gets off a plane in Manchester, Vermont after midnight. He's never been to Vermont. He's never been on a plane by himself. But the East Fletcher house will be sold in a month. Catt and Michel want him to pick up some papers and books, and drive back to Albuquerque in Catt's Vermont truck, a new white Tacoma.

Flying out here alone feels *different* than being in LA with Catt, and he's apprehensive. Now he's *two thousand miles* out of the county ... What if Romero finds out? He doesn't know anyone here, too many bad things could happen. Catt promised they'd have someone waiting to pick him up when he landed in Manchester, but his eyes nearly pop out of his head when he walks out to baggage and sees an older white guy holding a sign that says Mr. Garcia. He's even wearing one of those caps. Paul wishes he'd brought a camera. If Jerry and Cris could see this ...

When the chauffeur asks *how was your flight*, he says the first thing that pops into his head: *It was uneventful*. He's heard people say this in movies.

And the car is enormous, a black stretch limousine parked out there with the Volvos and beaters. The back seat looks like a room, with a TV, full bar, and little spotlights for reading.

He has no idea where he is. The street lights stop as soon as they leave the airport. Outside, the air is heavy with rain. The dark narrow road cuts through walls of wet trees and branches. He takes out his phone to call Mike, but there's no cell service. The car seems to be heading up into some mountains. And then it stops and the driver gets out. No one around—through the headlights, he sees a big fallen branch blocking the roadway. He gets out and helps the old guy drag it off to the shoulder. The air smells of wet leaves and it's totally silent, as if a dark lid had dropped down on the horizon.

By the time they get to East Fletcher—which, as far as Paul can make out, isn't even a town, just some fields and a few houses—it's nearly two in the morning. The driver carries his bag to the door and then leaves. Paul opens the unlocked front door. The place is beyond spooky ... Who knows what's inside? Anyone could be living here. Fumbling around for the lights, he's actually fucking afraid. The place has been empty for months. It smells damp and musty. *This* is the house his employers are so sentimental for? He doesn't bother exploring all ten dusty rooms. Each of them has an old door, badly hung. He passes out on the first bed he sees.

Waking at daylight, he gathers the books and papers and heads out quickly. He drives west for three days, stopping only for gas and for quick naps at truck stops. Pennsylvania, Virginia ... What if he gets pulled over by some local redneck? The papers are all in Catt's name. They'll think he stole it. His New Mexico license is stamped *Revoked Without Interlock* ... Just driving the truck is a Class 3 misdemeanor. What was he thinking? Romero would not find the "r" joke about "country" amusing. He'd spend the last eighteen months of parole back in prison, maybe with time added on. The whole cross-country road trip, one of his few lifelong dreams, flashes by in wraparound panic.

But nothing bad happens. Three days later, he pulls into the driveway at Dartmouth. When Catt runs out and asks how his trip was, he shrugs and says, *uneventful.*

Classes start in two days. Before leaving Albuquerque, Catt gives Paul the white Tacoma. They pass the red truck on to Joe to use as the maintenance vehicle.

And then he's on his own, and she's back in Los Angeles.

8

CLUTCH

DEAR DR. MULHANEY, Paul wrote to the UNM Psychology Honors Division chair eight months later.

I am interested in Psychology because I want to gain an understanding of the way people's minds work. I am also interested in it because I think that due to my experiences I am in a position to help other people with substance abuse and alcoholism.

I grew up with a mother that was severely mentally ill. She was diagnosed with "manic depressive paranoid schizophrenia." Needless to say, it was a very tough environment to grow up in and as a child there was nothing I could do about it. Now that I am an adult—while there is still nothing I can do about it—I would like to try to understand it better. I think that if I can understand mental illness in its various forms, I can maybe understand me better. I can understand why I feel the way I do inside and why I've had the life I've had. Through this understanding I might be able to help others as well. Growing up was terrible and the only thing that took my mind off of the everyday chaos was alcohol. I started drinking when I was 16 years old.

The other reason I would like to study Psychology is that I would like to become a substance abuse counselor. I am in fact, an alcoholic that has been in recovery for nearly 3 years. Since I was 16 I drank to escape. I drank to get drunk and not have any feelings. Little did I know I was just post-poning my feelings so to speak. I started getting into trouble with the law shortly after that and this began my "colorful" history with it. I got into fights, got DUI's and other non-violent crimes. Finally I ended up going to prison for two years and am now on parole. I am very happy to be in recovery and I think that I can help others to get into recovery. It has been my experience that most people with addiction problems are more ready to listen to someone who's "been there." I realize that there is still plenty to learn and I would like to do that in order to become a counselor to help others.

I am getting ready to turn 40 years old in May and I guess I've done some growing up. I am very serious about getting an excellent education and I feel like I need to do graduate work in order to try for a Phd. I think this would be good for me so that people will take me more seriously when I apply for a job and also when I counsel. I also have hopes of writing, and I think this would help in that area. I am planning on applying to graduate school at UCLA. I am lucky enough to have friends there and my girlfriend is also based in L.A. which makes things easier for me as far as support and a place to live.

My goals for a career are to become a substance abuse therapist and also a writer. I think that since I have a unique history and since I am an alcoholic, I will be able to touch people in a way that perhaps others can't. If by writing, or through therapy, I can change just one person's life, I'll be happy. I will feel like I've accomplished something. I am sorry this application is late. I have no excuse. Thank you for considering me.

Catt was with Stretch in her Chicago guest faculty apartment trying to finish a chapter on Eleanor Marx when Paul phoned to read her the letter. Halfway through the semester, she was leaving for Melbourne next week to speak at a conference. Before leaving, there were two dozen student papers to grade, and a warning had just been slipped under her door to *remove the unauthorized pet* in three days or vacate the premises.

"Oh Paul," she sighed. "You can't send that if you want to get in. He's not your parole officer."

How could someone with these writing skills have gotten all As in his classes? By taking the same multiple choice tests over and over online, until he'd finally punched in all the right answers! In Chicago, Catt's students read and discussed critical theory. Midway through his sophomore year, Paul had not yet had one book assigned or written a paper. His "classes"—PowerPoint outlines of textbook chapters—were taught by grad students and adjuncts. Apparently writing and thinking were not on the curriculum. This was the education he'd fought so hard to receive? An education, as Catt was hardly the first to observe, in the rewards of passive compliance. Consequently, she'd arranged for him to do the summer semester at UCLA and apply to the UNM Honors Program.

"But kitten! *Help me.* I'm at a loss. I don't know what to do here." During the third week of classes, she'd been sick with the flu and Paul had driven all the way up to take care of her. Like most things about him, the letter was touching and sweet. But where do you start? That fall she'd bought him a *New York Times* subscription, and while he was dimly aware of the prestige conferred by the blue plastic wrapper left on his front steps everyday, the only stories he read were about serial killers.

"I'd like you to try and talk like a smart person," Catt often coaxed the shy, sullen girls who signed up for her classes. And everyone laughed, but at least they knew what a smart person sounds like.

"Alright," she'd complied, clearing her desk. "Give me twenty-five minutes, I'll figure it out."

> Dear Dr. Mulhaney,
> In Fall 2005 I entered UNM as a psychology major with the goal of becoming a substance abuse counselor and psychotherapist. Returning to college at age thirty-nine after two decades of alcoholism (which finally led to two years of incarceration) my attitude towards education has drastically changed. While completing the requisite sophomore courses with a 3.8 GPA, I've looked forward to the kind of intellectual challenge, peer exchange, and academic mentoring offered by the Honors Program ...

Etcetera. Catt could write this kind of thing in her sleep.

> ... Eventually I hope to write a PhD based partly on clinical practice that will prepare me to shape new treatment models ...

The acceptance letter from Dr. Mulhaney is still in Paul's brief-case on June 21 when he backs the Z out of the Dartmouth Road driveway. Classes were starting next week at UCLA. He'd spent days deciding which of his things he would need there: a gym bag, his new Samonsite briefcase with all of June's cash rents ($6,300 stacked neatly by denomination), his golf clubs and laptop, a new video camera. A Ralph Lauren jacket, some sports slacks and jeans, his cool gray leather bomber jacket, the AA Big Book and a Bible.

A year ago he'd almost been banned from going to school, and now they were letting him into the Honors Program! "Dear Mr. Garcia," the letter began. (Paul knows it almost by heart.) "Congratulations ... Your outstanding academic performance ... The selection was highly competitive, with more than two hundred applications received for sixteen places." Further proof of what good things can happen when you turn your life over to God! He can't understand why Catt's an atheist, or secular humanist, or whatever she calls it. Without believing in God you cannot be saved.

Still, he knows in his heart whatever success he achieves will always be fraudulent. It's just a matter of time before he's found out. And maybe sooner rather than later: under his name, Dr. Mulhaney had added a note that his acceptance was only *conditional*. He'd have to maintain at least a 3.5 GPA in the UCLA classes, but what if the classes were hard? What if Catt got fed up with his moods and kicked him out of the house? He'd have nowhere to go, he'd have to drop out—good things made him feel queasy. There was always a shadow.

In fact, although she'd researched and paid for Paul's classes, Catt is ambivalent about their plans for the summer. The Chicago visiting job had been pointless and lonely. Now that the East Fletcher house has been sold, she no longer has the long writing days in Vermont to look forward to. If she hadn't promised to stay with Paul in LA, she could be in London, Berlin, or even Campo La Jolla. Her book about nineteenth-century social reformers would be published in London next year. Her career might change for the better if she could find time to think, but since meeting Paul her work has been squeezed into lulls between crises.

Over New Year's she'd gone to Oaxaca to spend three weeks alone with her book. Ten miles from the nearest phone, her concentration was shattered when one of Paul's emails informed her Joe Stillwater had vanished and that he'd hired his cousin Mason to take charge of maintenance. This seemed absurd. Mason already worked full-time at Intel. He had a wife and five kids. When would he find the time to fix leaky faucets? Paying Mason $1,400 a month meant paying double—surely they'd have to find someone else to do the real work when he was busy. At first indignant about Catt's reservations, Paul was soon blind with rage. He'd *promised* the job to his cousin. Did she want him to go back on his word? He was living a life of rigorous honesty. *Yeah, but not on my nickel.* She spent most of the break riding the *micro* ten miles to the Puerto Angel pay phone. Michel and her other friends advised her to "let Paul make his own mistakes," but this seemed crazy. Paul wasn't twelve, she wasn't his teacher. More than once, the thought crossed Catt's mind that their relation was false and unequal.

In Chicago, she'd seen her old friend Terry Stiles at a conference and they'd talked for days. Bracing herself for the summer, Catt asked Terry if she'd like to drive down from San Diego and hang out together at her Campo La Jolla casita for a few days before Paul's arrival.

Backing the Z out of the driveway, Paul sees that the sleazy Dodge van with Michigan plates is still parked in front of the neighbor's. For weeks, the van has been parked in full view of Paul's window, its plaid curtains open just wide enough to see out of. Since it arrived he can never relax, because an old hippie guy—the neighbor says he's an uncle—is apparently *living* inside it, maybe even keeping an eye on him. The street is otherwise full of people with really good jobs, even doctors. Only in Albuquerque.

He is so relieved to be leaving. Last month when he collected the rents, the tenant in number 12 Mescalero was short and offered to give him a blowjob. She was a lap dancer. So much for musicians and artists! The gravel behind the adobe wall Joe stenciled with chevrons was littered with crack vials and condoms; Joe himself disappeared on a bender. Catt should be grateful Mason would even consider working on her apartments! The only good tenants, a lesbian couple from Santa Fe, moved out when the sewer pipes broke and shit backed up in their shower. Even here, the Tacoma's all-weather tires were slashed in the driveway, and by who, another disgruntled tenant? Catt has no idea what he contends with. Paul's never been to UCLA, but he imagines it looks like TV shows set at college.

Every inch of the Z is carefully packed with his belongings. Paul feels good about this. Amazing how organized stuff can be, now that he's sober.

Of course Catt gave him shit about taking the Z. She'd already paid for the LifeSafer to be installed in the Tacoma. *Why meet trouble halfway*, she'd argued. But even though his parole status is Minimum, he still has to take the LifeSafer in once a month to the place where they do the monitoring. Is he supposed to drive back once a month? *No way* can he do this and still pass his classes. Now that Mason is on the company payroll, Paul can ask him to take the truck in as part of his duties. The garage doesn't care, so long as the LifeSafer's clean and they get their one hundred dollars.

Of the many things Paul now owns, the Z is all that remains of his old life in Farmington. He's even been fixing it up: new tires, new starter, new clutch. He imagines taking the tops off and driving up PCH in this killer black car that really *belongs* to him. Hell, maybe he'll even get rid of the Z before he comes back to Albuquerque. He could probably sell it to one of the rich kids at UCLA for $5,000. And isn't the Z like his life? An example of how you can take something bad, and make it better.

Getting onto the freeway, he takes his new black iPod out of his bag and hits shuffle. He has a great new play list, downloaded for him by Mason. First song of the trip: Rob Zombie, "The Scorpion Sleeps." It's pretty mellow for metal, edge without screech. The road's clear, and he passes the county line within minutes. Briefly, he panics—*what is it, what has he forgotten?* But then he summons his rational mind. *You're on a road trip. Relax.*

Catt is jogging with Terry along the beach when Paul's new clutch seizes up an hour later. Seventy-five miles south of Albuquerque, the clutch drops while he's shifting down before a work zone. *He can't slow the car down.* Metallica pummeling his ears while he pumps the brakes and steers onto the shoulder.

Safe, he turns the car off. Somewhere between Belen and Soccoro, the desert's dead flat and the orange cones up ahead look like they're melting. Except for a few workers, the road is empty. And now he's stuck. How can this be happening?

Forcing himself not to panic, he pops the hood open. There's nothing wrong that he can see, no broken parts. Back in the car, he pries the clutch up with his foot. Each time it drops. He has no idea what he should do. He can't call Catt because she's in Baja. The only choices are to get the car towed home or find a mechanic in Soccoro. At least he isn't broke, he has Catt's rents in his briefcase. But either way he'll have to walk miles and lose a whole day of travel. He's already promised to meet Catt and Terry down in Baja. He imagines the long dusty walk into Soccoro ... the desert rat who runs the garage, a redneck obviously, maybe friends with the town police officer ...

Just when Paul thinks he cannot do this, he hits the clutch again. This time it grips! Like magic, twenty minutes later, he's back on the road as if it never happened. For the rest of the trip the clutch will work perfectly.

Jayce Robbins, the only inmate at the Farm Paul considered a friend, paroled out last month. A big bearded hippie guy in his early thirties, Jayce had a wife and kid. During yard, they'd talked endlessly about stuff they'd do—hikes and camping trips—but of course none of this was really on the cards because Jayce lived in Las Cruces. No way was Paul going to take a weekend and drive three hours south to hang out with his old prison buddy. But Jayce's town is on his route, so Paul decides to give his old friend a call, maybe stop in and see him.

Jayce works afternoons tending bar at the local VFW. He tells Paul to come right over. Even without Jayce's detailed directions, the VFW hall would be hard to miss: a Quonset hut with flags and eagles. At three p.m., a few half-comatose old guys are sitting at the bar when Paul walks in. Windows on the hut blacked out, year-round Xmas lights strung over the bar and twinkling. Jayce, even rounder-looking without prison garb, looks up. *Hey, it's Paul Garcia—look at you, man!*

Paul knows he's out of place. He's wearing ripped faded Levis and (another gift from Catt) a Zapatista t-shirt with Sub-Commandante Marcos holding a rifle. Afraid to leave cash in the car, he's carrying the new leather briefcase. He looks part college kid, part businessman, maybe part drug dealer. "Jayce! Any of your buddies here know you're really the Cookie Monster?" Bullshitting in the yard, they'd made up nicknames for each other. Jayce asks him about school. One of Jayce's plans is to go back to school next year and become a screenwriter. Paul looks around the dank hall. "Pretty easy gig you've got here." It's the first time he's been in a bar since getting sober, and maybe Jayce will make it, maybe not—but in the VFW Hall, Paul feels like a walking target. Hideous country and western music grinds through the PA. Is this the music Jayce likes? Is he a redneck? They'd kept themselves amused back at the Farm cracking jokes about the African-American gangster contingent, strictly wannabes in Minimum, who went by stupid handles like Outlaw and Blood ... Maybe his friend Jayce is actually a racist. At the time, it seemed like he was being witty.

Why did he even come here? Of everyone he'd known from Las Lunas to the Farm, Jayce and that creep Frank Harwood are the only two who haven't been reincarcerated. Daryl got revoked for being at a party when cops were called for loud music. Ray Whitebear, his best friend among the Natives, called Paul last month drunk, from the bus station. He'd already blown off parole and needed two hundred bucks to get to Oakland.

Jayce is talking about shutting the bar down, bringing Paul back home to meet his wife and baby. Paul sips his Coke and looks at the clock. "Thanks, man, no. I gotta go. My girlfriend Catt's expecting me in Baja."

While Paul is saying his goodbyes to Jayce, Homeland Security stops a Mexican cargo truck twenty miles east of Tucson. Forty-eight Asian migrants are hidden behind a wall of boxes in the truck's container. They speak no English or Spanish. The Mexican driver insists he had no idea what was behind the crates when he left the warehouse in Chihuahua. The terror alert jumps to red, and the National Guard shuts down I-10 from Tucson to the New Mexico state line in Lordsburg. No one knows if the driver is an independent operator, or if he's one of a convoy, or if the truck is a decoy for some larger contraband or terrorist. None of the National Guard, Border Patrol, or Homeland Security agents posted in Tucson speak Mandarin. The highway is closed until they locate an interpreter.

Later, Paul will replay the day's dissonant string of events and ask himself if there were signs, or maybe causes. What would have happened if the clutch had *not* seized up, if he hadn't stopped at the bar, or if he'd said yes when Jayce asked him to meet his wife and baby?

Just west of Deming, Paul remembers he hasn't eaten all day, so he stops at a truck stop with a Taco Bell drive-thru. The new dash mat is slipping onto the console and he wants the car to be right, so he parks and picks up a package of Velcro. Leaving the plaza, he misses the I-10 on-ramp. Instead of turning around, he takes the service road west towards the next exit. A mile or two on, there's an old country road going north, with the remnant of some little town in the distance. He still hasn't unwrapped the burrito. The ghost town looks like a nice place to eat, so he detours a few hundred yards and pulls into a pumped out gas station and parks under the old Texaco sign.

Stepping out of the Z, there's no one around. Except for the low drone of trucks from I-10, it's deeply quiet. At six thirty, the wraparound desert heat is starting to ease. Wind rattles the branches of a dead cottonwood tree. He sits on the hood and unwraps the burrito. Why not make this the best part of the trip? A few organ pipe cacti rise from the desert floor. Emptiness settles around him.

Paul thinks maybe he'll just drive through the night. If he keeps on without stopping, he'll be at Campo La Jolla by eight. He'll have breakfast with Catt and Terry, then take Stretch to the beach and crash out under a palm tree. For the first time in weeks, he can breathe freely. He puts the Taco Bell wrapper on the floor of the car, and then carefully places the new Velcro strips on the dash mat. At the base of the sky, splashes of pink score the deep golden light on the horizon.

This was the bomb ... for the next hour or two, he'll be heading straight west into the sunset. He's never done this before and Paul thinks maybe he ought to film it. He takes the tops off the Z, and the video camera out of the back.

Holding the camera over the windshield with his right hand, Paul drives back to the freeway. Weaving between dozens of long-haul trucks, he thinks the I-10 is like a huge factory belt spinning everything west. Twenty miles later, the traffic starts to clump up until it comes to a standstill. It's some kind of terror alert—the road up ahead is totally closed—everything's detoured onto County Route 70 for fifty-five miles across the state line. Road guys and National Guardsmen are buzzing around the I-10 shoulder.

So much for making good time ... the whole procession crawls towards the detour. He can *feel* the dusk in the air by the time he turns onto County Route 70. The traffic spaces itself out in a line moving north ... maybe this isn't so bad. Cruising along at thirty or forty, the t-tops still off, the air smells sage-y and pungent.

The road travels north, and then west across the state line into Arizona. It's the second longest day of the year and the sunset is lasting forever, deep crimson laced with black velvet, and Paul's camera is catching it all. iPod Shuffle gives him Pink Floyd and long backlit fingers of clouds reach behind sand and rock mountains for a sunset finale. Now there's nothing to see except tail-lights, cars moving slow through the darkness in front and behind him.

Putting the camera away, Paul is thinking about asking Mason how to transfer his songs off the iPod onto the video soundtrack when a south-bound Chevy Blazer turns and cuts into the small pocket of roadway behind him. He sees the Sheriff's Department shield on the door. Then the Blazer's whole roof rack of red, white, and blue flashing lights switches on. And then the sirens.

Heart pounding, Paul carefully signals his turn and sits with his hands on the wheel, breathing and waiting.

The sheriff's halogen flashlight first in his face, then probing every inch of the open Z car. "You aware you're missing a tail-light?"

"No sir. It must have just gone out—"

"And I clocked you ten miles over the limit. I need your license and car papers."

Forcing himself not to shake, Paul takes them out and the sheriff waddles back to the Blazer. This makes no sense at all. Even if he was over the limit, he was doing the same speed as every other car in line on the detour.

Paul grips the wheel while the Blazer's Fourth of July light show splashes all over the dash mat. He has to stay calm and assess the possible damages. The worst, and also most likely, thing is, the sheriff will see the interlock stamp on his license and then ask Paul to show him the LifeSafer. But it's a *New Mexico* license ... maybe the laws in this state are different? So, alright: worst case, they'll report him to the New Mexico DMV and he'll lose the interlock license. As long as the DMV doesn't talk to parole and Mason brings the truck in to be checked, he's covered. Yeah ... why be so negative? This speed-trap town sheriff probably won't even want to get into that, he'll just write up a ticket. But why was it taking so long, then?

"Mr. Garcia, I'm going to have to ask you to step out of the car please."

What the fuck?

"I'm going to have to ask you to turn around and place your hands on the vehicle."

Paul's knees bend as he puts his palms on the side of the car, his ass tilted up towards the sheriff. The sheriff pats him down. He'd done this dozens of times in the past, but never sober.

"Now turn around please. Slowly. Mr. Garcia, you're under arrest."

This cannot be happening. "But what for?"

"I've just been informed that the Maricopa County Sheriff's Department has a fugitive warrant for your arrest."

"Heh, sir—I'm not a *fugitive.*"

"The database says you've been at large for nine years."

"Officer, please—wait a minute." Paul's mind races forward and back. "This has to be a mistake, some kind of glitch in the system." He would never have gotten parole if there were any outstanding charges. And he'd tried to do the right thing. Before his parole hearing, when the caseworker asked if there was *anything else she should know about,* he'd told her all about Phoenix. And she'd been alright with that. She checked it out on the database and there was nothing. "Looks like you're all clear," she'd said, smiling. So: the warrant cannot be valid, but he can't say that to the sheriff, without bringing parole into the story. The sheriff's department will call parole office and he'll be revoked for being out of the county. He'll go straight back to prison for the rest of parole, or possibly longer, if they file any new charges—

"And the charges are serious. Felony 4, Leaving the Scene of a Fatal or Serious Injury Accident."

"I swear you've got it all wrong! Please: just *look in the computer.*" Paul wishes he'd worn another t-shirt this morning, not the one with Sub-Commandante Marcos holding a rifle.

"I need you to hold your arms out together."

Paul knew he was in a familiar country when he felt the metal cuffs click tightly over his wrists. Cars driving by, everyone seeing this.

"You have the right to remain silent ..."

Cuffed, Paul sits in the back of the Blazer while the sheriff goes through all his belongings: the camera, the golf clubs ... the cop seems especially pleased to find $6,300 cash in the briefcase. Shit, now they'll think he's a drug dealer. Finally, he radios for a tow truck.

They drive to the county jail. Cops all around when the sheriff walks him into the charge room. When they give him his phone call, he tries Catt's cell number, hoping just maybe she'll have service in Baja, but it goes to voicemail. Paul's been in this situation often enough to know he can't leave a message. Once you open your mouth, that's it for your Right to One Phone Call. By now it's nearly midnight. No way are the cops gonna let him call a Mexican landline, so he tries Mason at home. Paul nearly weeps when he answers.

The sheriff was already finished typing the charge sheet. As soon as Paul got off the phone, they locked him up in the drunk tank.

9

9th STEP

ALL NIGHT HE SAT ALONE in the tank. Trying to keep each other awake, two guards down the hall talked until morning, the mechanical sound of their laughs erupting like clockwork. Not that Paul could have slept anyway. Since arriving in Albuquerque he'd felt shadowed, as if a bad thing could happen at any time. But he'd never thought, at least not in his conscious mind, that the bad thing would be Phoenix.

Except for Mike D., he's never told anyone about the event he's come to describe to himself as *the accident*. Parts of it surface sometimes in dreams.

He's lost in a strange city full of wide roads, bigger than anyplace he's ever been.

He's driving a shiny white car. The car isn't his. It's a rental. Outside it's dark. He's drunk, no not really that drunk, trying to find his way back to a freeway.

Cars are moving fast all around but he can't keep his mind on the road because he's thinking about Dylan Combs, his old friend from Albuquerque. He's just seen Dylan Combs, and Dylan's changed. He's sober, he seems really happy. He's living in Scottsdale and dating a girl from the ASU law school and Paul wants to be happy for him but in the restaurant he's ordering whiskeys and beers in rotation while Dylan sips Coke and all he can think is, does Dylan know I'm coming down from a crack binge?

Paul feels like a freak. He's about to turn thirty, he was always the smart one and here he is, not drifting but deep into crack again ... But maybe Dylan was fooled? He's out here for KleanTech about to start a really good job, chief engineer in a microchip factory ... Dylan seems really impressed, and he wants to tell Dylan: This isn't my life—I don't give a shit about microchips, *but he can't because Dylan's already grown up, he's accepted adulthood. The older he gets, the younger the people he finds to party with will be, and this makes him feel old and sleazy. And in the dream, a male voice—maybe his own, maybe God's, maybe Dylan's—starts to say* the future is open. *The voice stuns him. He's thinking about this— does it mean he should get clean, that moving to Phoenix is his chance to start his life over?*

He's thinking so hard about this he misses the ramp. He has to turn the white car around, like his life. Coming up to a big four-point intersection, he veers left and then something blindsides his car out of nowhere. He almost loses control but forces his hands to stay steady.

Easing left he sees a huge Honda bike collapsed on the road all in pieces ... and then up ahead: a man's body. How did the body get there? Did it fly over the roof?

Traffic around him is stopping. The whiskeys and beers are still in his blood. Even without them he shouldn't be in the car because they took his license away after DUI 3.

He has to get out. He floors it.

For nine years, he's been running from this and now they've got him. He'll be three years sober next month, and what was the point? He's on his way back to prison. All night, he keeps feeling like he's been airlifted out of his fraudulent life, back into his real one: a small county jail in the middle of nowhere, and that's just the beginning. He may as well have kept drinking.

The last words out of the sheriff's mouth before the guards brought him down here were *you're being held without bail.* Did that mean forever, or until the arraignment? But he can't be arraigned here, because the warrant was issued in Phoenix. The nice guard told him: *You'll have to sit tight until Maricopa processes your paperwork. They'll send a van.* So far no one has said one word about his parole status. One more thing to look forward to: he'll be revoked and sent back to Las Lunas to finish the Farmington sentence. As soon as that's over they'll send him back here to start serving more time in Arizona.

At this point he'd gladly barter his iPod and briefcase and golf clubs and Ralph Lauren jacket for a drink. None of that shit was really his anyway. What would Catt think? UCLA classes were starting next week. She'd already paid his tuition. If he didn't complete them with a 3.5 GPA he could forget about getting into the Honors Program.

Even though he's alone in the tank, the plastiform bench is too short to sleep on. He sees his new life falling away: his education, the nice house on Dartmouth, his upper-middle-class girlfriend, the trips to LA. If only he'd stayed with his dogs in the Farmington trailer! It was a pretty good life. The cops would have left him alone. He wasn't a criminal.

Each day in prison, he'd tried harder than ever before to lead a good life. He'd gone to chapel, read the whole Bible, done all the step work, earned every Christian Living certificate ... stuff he would have dismissed in the past because it was so cheesy. He really believed his new life with Catt and even Michel had been his reward: fixing up the apartments, collecting the rents, going to UNM lectures. For his birthday this year, Catt's dad had sent him a fat new Oxford dictionary.

The *Shorter Complete*, as her father called it, was still on his desk back at Dartmouth. He'd tricked everyone down to Catt's parents that he was a person. Even himself. And the warrant: *Leaving the Scene of a Fatal or Serious Injury Accident*. He'd forgotten the charge because so much had happened after the accident. *Fatal* or serious? Manslaughter 5? Maybe the sheriff knew something he didn't. Frank Harwood did fourteen years in Las Lunas for hitting that tree, and he had no priors.

You've got to try and put it behind you, Mike D. had said when they worked Step 9. *It was an accident*. According to Mike, the answer was written right there in the step: *You make your amends unless to do so would injure yourself or others*. He had no money to send to the victim anonymously. All he could do was confess, and get sent back to prison. Strictly speaking, the accident wasn't even his fault—the bike shouldn't have been in the intersection, and anyway the guy worked for Sony, he must have had great insurance. *We do not regret the past or wish to shut the door on it because it's brought us to where we are now*, Paul read in the Big Book. He'd done his best. So why was this happening?

Around four, he drifts off to an uneasy sleep despite the guards yammering.

Jogging with Terry and Stretch on the beach near Campo La Jolla, Catt drinks in the fresh summer morning. Shot through with light, the pale blue waves of the bay shimmering like a newborn thing at the edge of the sand bar. Baja is such a reprieve from her life in LA! The rocky mass of an island looms in the distance and pelicans fly in straight lines over the water. In fact, running was never Catt's favorite activity—she'd just as soon sit on the beach watching the birds. But Terry, still rangy and lean, takes her athletic regime very seriously. And now she is sharing it.

The last time she stayed anywhere overnight with Terry was at an ongoing party in the East Hampton house Terry was caretaking one winter in the early '80s ... an amphetamine vortex where day and night crashed into each other outside the windows. Even though they're both sober and twenty years older, they've settled into an easy routine since arriving. A quick cup of coffee, a run on the beach, maybe an afternoon swim and then dinner together. The rest of the time they leave each other alone, as if they'd formed their own writers' retreat.

Four and a half hours south of LA, the beach at Campo La Jolla is practically empty. On the US side of the border the small public beaches are crammed and patrolled, while the rest of the coast has been sliced into luxury beach homes, with no trespassing signs posted all the way to the shore. And yet it's the same sand, the same ocean. *It's like*—Catt calls out to Terry—*what's the name of that film?* Memories of Underdevelopment? The absence of capital leaving the world's beauty intact for whoever wants it.

Two hours south of the border, there is no Fed-Ex, no Wal-Mart, no ATMs, no American flags or lapel pins. No security cameras in stores, or flat screens playing Fox News in public lobbies. Weekends, the beach will fill up with Mexican families. Indian children will sell packs of stale gum from trays hung around their small necks, but not too aggressively. And as the weekend wears on, differences between the Mexicans, the Americans and the Indian vendors will blur, everyone getting beached out together.

Already, Terry and Catt have seen more of each other's lives this weekend than in two decades worth of chance meetings at parties and conferences. To Terry, Catt seems more grounded than in her actress-y days; less subdued than when she and Michel were together. Still, Terry can't understand why Catt's running around doing deals, or why—given the fact that they're both with other people—she and Michel are still married. Catt is impressed by Terry's job—with no more than a BA, she's a tenured professor in San Diego. Using the academy to support her relentlessly uninstitutional work, Terry has created a base for herself and other radical friends. But Terry hates San Diego and is thinking of quitting, even though she's in her mid-fifties with no other real source of income. Catt thinks of Brigittte in Fresno—broke, middle-aged, and trying to pick up a few classes—and wonders if Terry knows what she's doing.

Still, the two friends are aware that they've landed roughly in the same place. This is a source of frustration and pleasure. Unlike most of their contemporaries, they aren't dead, or wildly famous, or living in tract homes in Denver. Their work appeals more to kids than to their so-called peers, but at least they've continued as artists.

Expecting Paul to arrive before dinner, after the run Catt decides to pick up some things at the Wednesday market in Maneadero. Every week *ejido* farmers come down from the inland hills to sell produce and livestock. Figs, lemons, string beans, chickens, parrots, and rabbits. Set up on truck beds and in stalls on a few rutted dirt roads, the Maneadero market was as archaically Mexican as anything she'd seen in Oaxaca.

Most Wednesdays, Catt was the only gringa there, but today as she loads her Trader Joe's bags full of fresh fruit and carrots, she sees two women like her, a butch and femme couple, buying tomatoes. In her mid-thirties, the butch of the pair was strictly Jane Bowles meets Banana Republic, in a beige Tilley hat, a white Oxford shirt, and a slim khaki skirt that covered her knees. Her girlfriend—about seven years younger—sported a floppy straw hat and a floral print sundress, cut low at the back with a cinched puffy skirt. Arm-in-arm, the two looked like they'd stepped out of a period remake—*Far From Heaven? The Talented Mr. Ripley? At least*, Catt thinks, *I'm finished with that*. During the dream years she'd spent with Michel, she'd dressed herself for a different period movie each day. The art directed life reflects its own kind of misery.

Crop dusters swoop over vegetable farms as she drives home along the peninsula. Making one last stop, she picks up an armload of gladioli from a vendor outside Twin Brother's Farm. By the time she gets home, Terry has already started slicing papayas and mangoes for lunch. Paul should arrive any time. And then her cell rings, and it's Mason.

The service is bad. She struggles to hear Paul's cousin's nasally whine. He's telling her that Paul's been arrested—*he's in Arizona, he's in jail in some little town*—and Catt cannot believe this. Lately Paul's been nothing but trouble. She sees the movie unfolding—pulled over for speeding, the cop looks at Paul's license and sees there's no LifeSafer in the Z—the whole thing is so stupid. *Why didn't he take the Tacoma?*

Catt wait—you're not gonna like this—but I think there's some other charge. An outstanding warrant? Because they're not giving him bail—no, I don't know—look I can't talk, I'm at work—you better just call the sheriff—Right babe, stay strong.

Catt flips the phone shut. "Stay strong?" No longer the hostess at a getaway beach house, she's been cast as a pregnant teen or a mother-of-four busted for bartering food stamps. Her Boyfriend's in Jail. Mason, the ignorant sleazebag she's been forced to employ, pities her.

Running back in the house—*Terrrryyyyyy ... You're not gonna believe this ...* Should she weep? No, she can't, that would be even more pathetic. *Paul's in jail, he's been arrested!* Still eating fruit salad, Terry looks up from her book. But now the house and its Ikea brown leather couch, the long talks with Terry seem so immaterial. *That was Mason. Paul tried phoning here last night but couldn't get through. And he's on parole, you know that? Mason can't even say what the charge is, but they're not giving him bail.*

When Catt left this morning with her Trader Joe's bags, Terry was struck by how much she resembled her ex-girlfriend Brianna, a real Connecticut girl, but now she's in a whole other movie. Before the phone rang, they were discussing some Persian poems, whether flowers were used as symbols or metaphors. At the last moment, Terry had brought a new video camera she'd bought to fool around with over the summer. The camera bag's on the floor. She unpacks it.

Catt, meanwhile, has already picked up the landline, dialing the numbers she'd scrawled on her hand while talking to Mason. *This is Catt Dunlop calling for Paul Garcia.* Glancing over at Terry, there's a camera in front of her face—*Terry are you FILMING this?—Yes, sure, I'll hold.*

"In some tiny way, Catt, I thought you of all people would *enjoy* this," Terry cracks. This is hysterically funny. Goaded on, Catt channels her Nice White Lady voice for the sheriff while Terry surveys the room through her viewfinder: the long row of books (Derrida, Poe, *The Three Faces of Fascism*), the sweet ice-blue of the bay faraway through the living room windows, the white flokhati rug where Stretch's long body is sleeping, and back to Catt, standing up at the glass table, on the phone writing things down.

"You see sir, I'm out of the country right now. I'm almost eight hundred miles away. I want to help sort things out, but I can't help unless I know what the charge is."

When she finally hangs up the phone, she pauses. "Terry. Put that *away*." This is too real to be taped. "Well. The sheriff wasn't that horrible. He doesn't know much except what's on the warrant. The jail is in Clifton—or Clifftown?—it's about four hours from Phoenix. So. Apparently. Nine years ago Paul got *arrested* in Phoenix. Now they're holding him there until the Sheriff's Department in Phoenix can come out to get him. But," and now her voice starts to lose it, "Terry, the warrant wasn't just some petty thing. It was for leaving the scene of a fatal or serious injury accident. Do you know what that MEANS? He hit some-one, the guy was just on a *bike*, and drove off without helping him. I mean the guy was hurt, really *hurt*, and he just left him on the side of the road, maybe even unconscious—how could *anyone* do that?"

"Catt, he was probably drunk."

"Do you think that *excuses* it?" Terry's look is opaque. "I know you're in AA but this is totally *heinous*. Someone who'd do something like that must have no conscience, it's just totally wrong. And Paul never told me about any warrant in Phoenix. I never knew he'd even been there. And that's not all. You know how he has to use that LifeSafer thing for drunk driving? Well, I paid to have it installed when I gave him the Tacoma. But he didn't want to drive it. He insisted on taking this old beater from his Farmington days, a Nissan ZX or something, dull black paint, really low slung, the car is a fucking cop magnet. It's completely illegal for him to drive without the LifeSafer, even if he were not on parole, which he is, and one of the conditions of his parole is he's not supposed to leave the *county!*"

"Sounds like he wants to get caught." The wisdom of this sinks into Catt like a stone.

"So what will you do?"

"I don't know." The afternoon air in the house has become hot and still. Until the phone rang, she'd been thinking about maybe taking some distance from Paul Garcia. Yesterday while they were juicing carrots and complaining about their respective careers, Terry had stopped and looked at her obliquely. *Isn't it weird, how nothing coming out now even mentions what's going on?* And Catt *knew.* It was like they'd had to leave the country in order to say it.

At least ten times a day for the past two or three years, Catt's thoughts hit the same wall as Terry's. To speak them out loud was completely uncool, because where would you start? God Bless Our Troops, hanging chads, *Saw 2*, Janet Jackson's wardrobe malfunction? Do not expect truth. *Nazism permeated the flesh and blood of the people through single words, idioms, and sentence structures which were imposed on them in a million repetitions and taken on board mechanically and unconsciously*, wrote Victor Klemperer, the Jew who'd remained in hiding in Berlin throughout the Holocaust. In the summer of 2006, six thousand National Guardsmen were presidentially dispatched to patrol the Arizona/Sonora border. Guantanamo Bay had been closed to journalists, human rights monitors, and the Red Cross after two prisoner suicides that Vice President Cheney described as "acts of asymmetrical warfare." Deprived of even the right to define their own deaths, hundreds of prisoners languished there, chargeless.

And in the US, in Maricopa County, at the very jail to which Paul awaits extradition, chain gangs of juvenile prisoners dig roadside graves for the indigent. Electorally unbeatable, the affable fascist Sheriff Joe Arpaio was indicted again just this month, this time for hawking DVDs of the women's jail toilets on the county website, his 24/7 webcam feeding live from the doorless stalls—an abject form of comic relief from the jail's other tortures: the four point restraint chairs, the hooded suspects detained for drug use and shoplifting, the "Tent City" jail where thousands of petty-crime suspects who could not afford bail were detained while awaiting their trial dates. And even these acts were merely a *screen*. Arpaio's bumptious brutality was a signature riff designed to render less spectacular forms of abuse, occurring throughout the US every day, newly benign and normal.

"Terry. I have to do it. I'm going to get Paul out of jail."

Years in the program have trained Terry to offer no judgment. *We all make our own decisions.* "What else can I do? If I don't, he'll go back to prison, and what good would that do?" Terry says nothing, but Catt feels her understanding. The fact that Paul was her boyfriend is irrelevant now. After all these months of inertia, the chance to alter the outcome of one of thousands of daily acts of injustice has been placed in her path. There's no choice but to take it.

"So. The first thing is to hire a lawyer—in Phoenix, because that's where they're taking him." Her mind already jumping ahead to the next set of moves. "And then I'll drive out to Clifton."

"Good plan."

"Let's do it."

As soon as she says this, the casita is no longer a beach house but HQ for an assault on American justice. There's no time to lose … but still, the whole thing feels deeply hilarious. Terry turns on her camera while Catt wanders between rooms gathering clothes, cash, and makeup.

"One of my former students is in LA now shooting an HBO pilot," Catt calls from the bedroom, tossing shoes in the bag. "My friend Luke Petit is meeting with architects to design a Los Feliz house that will be green and sustainable, and I'm in a Mexican trailer park thinking about *how to get my boyfriend out of jail!*"

"It all comes down to this, doesn't it," Terry drawls, zooming in on the fresh gladioli they'd so recently placed in front of the Virgin of Guadalupe fresco over the mantle.

"Terry, can I catch a ride with you back to San Diego? If only we'd known—I wouldn't have left my car at your place. Sorry to screw up your visit. You can drive back if you want."

Terry zooms in on the yellowed page of the novel she'd picked off the shelf: *Cain's Book*. Terry wonders why she'd never read this.

My study of drugs has led me to reject the social hysteria of which they are a symbol … I demand that these laws be changed … Hah! Talk about cut-ups, this was the Third Mind in action …

"No, I'm going with you!"

"Terry, you mean it?"

"You think I could sit around this nice little beach place while you drive to that hell? We'll take my truck. Tomorrow you can buy me a plane ticket."

"Yes! You use my car till I'm done. Then I'll drive back to San Diego." She gives Terry one of Paul's prison high-five's but her eyes are teary.

They put Stretch and their bags in the truck and leave the peninsula.

Fingerprints, photos, strip search, delousing and shower: a tight grid of fluorescent-lit rooms and hallways. The jail seems pretty small. He's the only one being processed this morning. Compared to San Juan, the procedure is minimal. Stay polite, don't try and be friends with the guards. None of these rooms have windows, so he has no idea yet where he is.

The cell they bring him to is called "the Annex": a 10' x 12' room once used for interrogation, it's been repurposed for jail overflow with two bunks, a steel toilet, and a steel table/bench module bolted onto the wall. Both bunks are occupied, so the guard gives him a "boat" to put on the floor: a thin blue Styrofoam pad, like what you'd use for camping.

The door shuts. It's late morning, but one of the two guys— fat, pale, and slack-jawed—is asleep in the lower bunk. The other one paces. Quietly, Paul looks for a spot to put down his pad. *Don't worry, he's not gonna wake up*, the pacing guy laughs. *They've got him on meds.* Paul's boat takes up room on the floor but Eddie's okay with that. He wants to talk. In five minutes, Paul knows everything about the situation, which will not change. Mike, the one on the bunk, is mentally ill, and Eddie doesn't shut up. At twenty-two, he lives with his grandma in Safford and has acne scars all over his face. Last week the bitch judge stuck him with two and a half years in Short Hills. The time he could handle, but Short Hills? Short Hills is crawling with Mexicans. Any day now the van's gonna show up. He's never been in prison before. Some buddies of his are doing time in Level II in Tucson, they would have looked out for him.

This is what Paul has to face, before things get worse. His whole life is like this. Because—he reflects, while Eddie drones on—you imagine "the worst" as the end, a black hole, almost a reprieve, but it never is. "The worst" is never a blanket of absolute badness, it's more like the desert floor teeming with life on the Discovery Channel. There are always the contours, the details, time broken down into hundreds of new situations. When he'd been homeless, it shocked him how much *effort* it took to live on the street. Homelessness wasn't the stupor he'd longed for and feared. There were more problems to solve on the street than he'd ever handled at KleanTech. His job now is to tune Eddie out. He has no books, no belongings, nothing except the orange jumpsuit they gave him to wear. Which is the same as he'd worn at Las Lunas.

Since turning her grades in, Terry's vague indecision about what to do with the summer has metastasized into a paradigm of how fucked up her life has become since she left New York for San Diego. She does not want to write. She's just finished a novel. Any day, any week, she'll hear back from her agent. Unless she's writing or teaching, there's no reason to stay in the comfortable house that she bought when she started the job, but no one will sublet it over the summer, and she still has to cover the mortgage. In fact, the market has started to slip, and the house that she's so rarely in—because her friends are all in New York, and she's dating a woman in Canada—is worth less than she owes on it. Her Canadian girlfriend wants her to come up and go to a spa for three weeks in July, but she's on the plane at least twice a month every semester, and that just cuts up the summer. Maybe she should go to Provincetown? Her Canadian girlfriend is great, but she's twenty-six—is there really a point to all this commuting? But there's no one to date in San Diego. The only dykes there are her students, or Republicans.

Terry loves driving. Until she flies back to San Diego tomorrow, she won't have to make any decisions.

Catt thinks they should bypass the long border wait at Tijuana by taking an old truck route to Tecate over the hills. The checkpoint is much faster there, and they'll come out just west of Yuma. In their excitement to leave she's forgotten the map, but she knows the route starts behind Ensenada. Instead of taking the highway from the tourist marina, they veer north onto a more local thoroughfare with new glass-fronted banks, street vendors, pruned ficus trees, and crippled beggars: the whole disjunctive third world panorama of wealth and its corollary. Catt finds this thrilling. They buy Cokes and a bag of Doritos from one of the vendors and give an old mariachi two dollars.

The avenue winds into the hills, traversing an endless perimeter of makeshift homes, stray dogs, junkyards, llanteras. Here, the pavement gave out. The sun was behind them. The route seemed much longer than Catt remembered. If either of the two friends had any navigational instinct, they would have looked at the sky and known they were traveling south, but it would be eighty-five miles until they came to a road sign.

"Why *wouldn't* I want to do this," Terry sighs as they pass the last junkyard. The road drawing them deeper into the brown desert hills. "I wish I'd worn my shit-kicker boots. This is the bomb, a real summer road trip." She ripped open the bag of Doritos and turned on the video camera.

As the afternoon heat sank into the hills, Catt felt her excitement ratcheting up towards a state of absolute happiness. She wanted to throw herself into the landscape. She also wanted to share it. "Terry, do you want to ride in the back and look at the sky? I can take over driving." Catt's best-ever birthday had been the night she sniffed heroin and lay out in a truck bed, just the right shade of wasted, while the driver circled Manhattan. It was imperial. Terry complies, although she is dubious.

Pushing the Ranger farther into the hills, Catt feels like she's *giving* the landscape to Terry: outcroppings of rock on the roadside getting increasingly large as they gain elevation. Hot wind blows Terry's hair into tangles. They change places after awhile. By now the rocks have become giant boulders arced into the sand like alien villages. Everything turning to red in the dusk, the few ancient trucks flagging Terry to pass as the road becomes twisty and mountainous.

Catt wonders if she's ever seen anything this monumental. Her phone is way out of range. Instead of thinking about Paul or what will happen in Phoenix tomorrow, she's thinking about the Tarahumaras ... the crystalline boulders Artaud described when he took peyote, both the drug and the heat remaining inside his body. *After several days, the physical hold was still there* ... The gravitas of the chronicle. There's no point, she thinks, going back to teach in Chicago. Chicago isn't her home. She's too old to take these journeyman jobs, Visiting This or Guest That. They're for people who update their CVs and still believe they are progressing somewhere other than death. *Wherever the fuck I'm meant to be, I'm already here*, she thinks gladly.

The temperature drops thirty degrees with the sun. Too cold to stay in the truck bed; they're high in the mountains. "How many more miles," Terry asks, "before the border?" Catt doesn't know. It's after eight and all they've eaten all day is a distant fruit salad and the Doritos. There are no road signs, no city lights … just thousands of stars scattered across the thick night. No billboards, no truck stops—they seem to be in some kind of national park without trailheads or rangers. Catt knows she's fucked up and she's afraid to tell Terry. A ways on they see a small road sign to Pueblo Santa Maria but when they get there, it's just an old chapel, crows flapping around in the dark.

"Are we lost?"

"I'm sorry. But the road's got to come out somewhere."

Two hours later they rejoin the highway, 180 kilometers south of Mexicali. There's still no food anywhere, but at least the trucks passing by are newer and bigger. Tired and hungry and justifiably pissed, Terry doesn't blame Catt for this six-hour detour. Gratitude pours through Catt's body. Yesterday, talking about art world politics, Terry observed how, whenever there's trouble, the boys always close ranks while the girls turn on each other. And here Terry is, standing firm.

Eight miles south of the border, the desolate road comes to life: bustling taco and fruit stands, idling trucks, light bulbs on strings powered by generators. Amazing how *Mexican* every-thing is this close to the border. The air smells of diesel, dirt, chemical fertilizers. They stop at a plywood *loncheria* and order burritos and Fantas in heavy glass bottles. Wearing a hand-woven shawl, the young proprietor works while holding her baby. Terry and Catt are the only gringas around and *lesbianas*, obviously, but the young woman smiles and offers them pickled onions and carrots.

Thousands of cars sit lined up at the border. Confused and exhausted, Terry enters the short line: Restricted Entry. If they don't get out of this line, the guards will turn them around and they'll lose another three hours. Desperate, Catt offers a twenty to a Dodge Ram beside them. The driver puts his foot on the gas and gives them the finger. Just before reaching the cement dividers, Terry braces herself and cuts off a sputtering Datsun.

A tall floodlit fence with narrow openings between metal slats separates the two countries. On Sundays, families gather on both sides to visit. They bring lawn chairs and children and bar-becues; they even pass food through the openings. Those on the US side clearly can't cross because they don't have papers. Why do ICE, INS, and Homeland Security raid meat-packing plants in the Dakotas when they could pick up hundreds of people here every weekend? Another anomaly.

The border guard wants to know what Terry and Catt are bringing back, where they're going and why, and what they were doing in Mexico. If they're really coming from Ensenada, why didn't they cross in Tijuana? "We took a wrong turn," Terry says meekly. The guard glances between their tired faces and photo IDs several times and waves them back into America.

10

SUMMER OF HATE

THE FIRST LAWYER CATT MEETS wears a knotted string tie over a pale blue cowboy shirt. His name is Roy Bucknell. Catt saw his ad in the Phoenix phone book: Felony DUI? Protect Your Rights! A framed photo over his desk shows a much younger Roy wearing similar clothes shaking hands with presidential candidate Ronald Reagan.

Catt and Terry arrived at the West Phoenix Econolodge around four in the morning. Catt slid her credit card through a slot in the bullet-proof glass. They walked three stories up with Stretch in the bag, and turned on the rusty a/c. Too tired to care about the palomino bugs in the bath, Terry crashed on the bed and Catt curled up on the sofa. Too wired to sleep, she browsed the forty-five pages of attorney ads in the Phoenix phone book. At nine, she hit the phone while Terry slept. She tried a dozen small offices first, but couldn't reach a live voice. Moving on to the big firms, the receptionists could not disclose fees: *for an initial hundred-dollar fee you can come in and an attorney will review your case ...* the balance of power established, as if she had no choice. Finally Roy Bucknell had answered the phone. He could not discuss fees, but the consultation was free. She took an appointment for two. Then she booked Terry a noon flight to San Diego.

The temperature hovers at 115 when Catt reaches Roy's storefront office. There's nothing to do with Stretch except leave him locked in the truck. Roy greets her himself—*my girl's not back yet from lunch*—and motions her to sit down in front of the American flags lining his desk top.

"First thing you need to know," he begins, "is my felony fee is $12K and I'd need that *paid in full* before his arraignment." Catt smiles. The number that's been bouncing around in her head was eighteen. "I think you're gonna find that very *reasonable* compared with the other felony/DUI guys here in town who are frankly, you know, taking advantage of the situation." By "situation," Catt guesses Roy means Arpaio. She opens her eyes a bit wider.

"That fee is contingent on us accepting a plea. It'll be another $15K if we take it to trial. But really, Miss uh Dunlop, that's an option you shouldn't discount. Telling your story in front of a jury is a basic American right."

Twenty-seven, she thinks.

"Now that fifteen is a fixed rate for going to trial, it's set in stone. No matter how many depositions I take, I won't bill you another dime. But—you might see some other costs come up along the road. We'll want a PI, find out if the victim's story is straight. Because the warrant you're talking about, it's not a simple DUI thing. It's a serious charge, Felony 4. We'll probably want to retain an accident reconstruction specialist—"

"Accident recon*struct*ion?"

"I know a great one in Salt Lake. Because you can bet your life the DA's gonna be doing the same."

Her heart sinks. She sees the fees adding up. Roy Bucknell is not like any lawyer she's ever met.

"But honey, I'll give you one piece of free advice. Whatever you do, do not discuss the case with your friend while he's in custody. Not if you visit, not on the phone. Because they've got technology, even out in the sticks. And about his parole: he'd better call his PO right away. Give them a chance to be lenient, you know? As soon as you make up your mind, I'll call him in Clifton and he can tell *me* the story on an unmonitored line."

When she leaves Roy's office, she has no idea what to do next. Find a better motel? It's already three. Too late to talk to another attorney, she'll have to wait until Monday. Stretch is hiding under the wheel, nearly dying of heat. Her head hurts. How can she choose the right lawyer when she doesn't know the first thing about the case? And there's no way to find out. Anything Paul says to her will be bugged. The only way to find out is to make a blind leap of faith and pay Roy, or somebody else.

Years later, decoding her death wish, Catt will replay the events of this week as if the crime happened here, and it was hers.

She punches 611 and adds another two thousand minutes to her monthly plan. Then she calls Hank. To her enormous relief, Hank thinks she's done the right thing. "The important thing, Catt, is you're *there*." He doesn't think she should use an attorney at all. "What you need to do now, is take yourself down to the County courthouse. Some of the brightest young people from the top schools start their careers as *public defenders*. In Phoenix, they're probably starved for a little, uhh, intelligent conversation. Go in with the file, explain your situation and get one of them working for you."

Catt's only been in Phoenix twelve hours, but she knows this cannot be true. Charm isn't part of the local currency.

Driving back to West Phoenix through meshes of freeways, she remembers a story she saw in the local paper that morning: a Spanish newspaper reporter forced to apologize to gubernatorial candidate Don Goldwater for using the words "concentration camp" to describe the tent city he promised to build at the border to contain the "illegals" who'd be put to work building a wall. The whole story would have slipped under the (razor, barbed) wire had CNN not repeated the phrase. Courting votes from elderly Jews, soon-to-be-presidential candidate John McCain then denounced Goldwater's remarks as "deeply offensive," to which the former vice president's son then replied: "But John! This kind of program has already been proven effective as well as accepted at our own county jail." Arpaio marched his band of prisoners—pot smokers, drunk drivers—through downtown Phoenix in chains wearing nothing but his trademark hot pink briefs and handcuffs. A medieval pageant of cruelty ... Phoenix was a city of psychos and vipers, not a small civil rights-era town.

She checks into a slightly more comfortable room at a Ramada and goes out to find something to eat. Taco Bell, KFC, Denny's ... Catt wonders if there's even a point in calling any more lawyers. She can't crack the code. Roy Bucknell had warned that Paul's charge could bounce up to Felony 2 because of his priors. But since those convictions occurred after the date of the warrant, weren't they *subsequent*? Did Arizona's *No Bail for Parolees* law apply, since Paul was not on parole in this state? It was like walking in quicksand. The phone rings in her bag—

206 / SUMMER OF HATE

You have a collect call from an offender at the Greenlee County Correctional Facility. For your protection, this call will be recorded and monitored. Press 5 to accept the charges.

"Catt? Catt, where are you?"

Straining to parse the logistics, she hadn't pictured Paul locked up as "an offender."

"Catt, don't cry." Mother*fuck*. The phone is bolted down in the hall, in front of the main cells and the guards. "I'm in Phoenix"—"You are?"—"Talking to lawyers ... But it's really hard."

"Catt, I've been thinking about this since they locked me up. And if you want to break up with me now, I'll understand. You have every right. I know I can handle this shit, I've been through it before. But the thing is, the warrant they have—it's not how it sounds—"

"Paul, stop. How's the weather out there?"

"The warrant was never an issue. I mean, if there was ever an outstanding warrant, they would never have let me out of the Farm."

"Paul, I've been *talking to lawyers.*"

"I know it sounds bad, but I want you to know all the facts," and then his voice disappears underneath static ...

"Paul, it's breaking up—"

"You're breaking up with me?"

"No, the connection. The *phone* ..."

A robot-voice: *You have one minute left ...*

"Paul, I love you—sit tight—I'll be there tomorrow."

Still driving the West Phoenix streets, she sees an old disabled phone outside a Circle K, its receiver cut off from the wire. A guy walks out with a twelve pack. Wherever you look, billboards lining the roads: *God Bless Our Troops, God Bless Our President, God Bless Our Troops and Our President.* Everywhere, heat and pavement. *Pray for Our President. Be Afraid or Be Ready.* But the billboard that bothers her most is the one with a young, pretty brunette holding a textbook: *From Homeless to Harvard—Determination!—Pass it on.* And isn't this the crux of the problem? Couldn't they say, *From Homeless to Community College?* Why do you have to win big, in order to win at all? But she's no de Tocqueville, this isn't her life. Except for Hank, she still hasn't talked to anyone in LA. Maybe Bettina will know what to do. She used to be a reporter. As far as Catt knows, she's still going out with Larry Delgado, the LA city attorney. Surely he'd know what to do. She calls Bettina at work. Bettina tells her to wait. And isn't this like the old saw from Hank's days: *Choose any mistress you want, but marry the woman who knows how to get you released from jail in a foreign country.*

Twenty-five minutes later, Bettina calls back with a name.

Craig Durbin takes Catt's call right away when she says she's a friend of Larry Delgado. He's in the office till six. Does she want to drive out?

Cool mist descends from nozzles under the striped canvas awnings of the café outside the large Scottsdale atrium building. The café sells Orangina and Stella Artois. Across the street, there's a Coach and a Borders.

An Asian receptionist buzzes Catt into a circular waiting room entirely free of Southwestern décor: mid-century black and white leather couches, redwood panels. Craig and the eight other attorneys who work in his firm handle nothing but felonies. The office looks like a place where people who could live anywhere might exile themselves for a decade to become indisputably rich. Like Dubai. If not exactly Catt's taste, at least she knows how to read it.

Shaking Catt's hand, Craig says, *You must be exhausted.* In his mid-thirties, he is tall and athletic, well-dressed. *Larry and I go back to USC undergrad days. You'll have to give him my best.* For the first time since arriving in Phoenix, she can relax. Relieved, she tells him the story: from Mason's call, to the overnight drive, to her heat-exhausted small dog locked in Terry's truck.

Why don't you bring him inside? Asana—Could you get Ms. Dunlop's dog a bowl of water?

When Catt returns with Stretch, Craig is already in the conference room with two bottles of Evian. Good art on the walls: John Baldessari's *Kiss/Panic*, the same handgun positioned against different backdrops in twelve black-and-white frames. *Edgy*, as they used to say in the '90s. Like Weegee, but with the corpse replaced by the weapon.

"As I'm sure you're aware," Craig begins, "Larry would not recommend us if we weren't the most capable criminal firm in the state. Your friend is about to be extradited to the most shithole jail in the US. And—you've read the charge—he's facing some serious stuff. We don't even yet know if the victim *died*. After we got off the phone I looked up the case. They've got him down for Failure to Appear back in '98. Which makes it a fugitive warrant."

"And he's still on parole!"

"*Exac*tly. We'll want to keep that out of the mix."

"You don't think he should call his parole officer?"

"No way. But—you say he's a student? Driving out to take summer classes at UCLA?"

"They're starting on Monday. But if he withdraws now, we could still get the tuition refunded."

"Bad idea. When I tell the prosecutor he's a UCLA student, she'll see he's completely reformed, not the criminal type. Then I'll ask for low bail."

"That is *so* good."

"Okay! Our felony retainer is $35K. That's a flat fee, whether we get the charge dropped or go straight through to trial."

"Mmm." Thirty-five thousand dollars was nearly twice what she earned in Chicago, but somewhat less than her rents. Her head spins. Which standard applies? Roy Bucknell was talking about twenty-seven but he's clearly inept—why pay if you're not going to win? "Yes. I'd like you to handle the case."

"Good decision. Angie—she's the office manager—will take care of the details. And then we'll get moving."

Angie, an ex-ATV racer with spiked hair and tattoos, talks non-stop while running the card. Catt's never made an impulse purchase above $200 in her life, so she interrupts. "Angie, listen—I'll sign. But I still haven't seen Paul. Could you wait until Monday to put the charge through?"

Outside the temperature's dropped to a cool ninety-eight. Trim, middle-aged people jog along sidewalks with heart monitors strapped to their wrists. Modernist houses crouch behind thoughtful cactus displays. Hard to believe that Scottsdale and Phoenix are in the same city. Scottsdale was Whole Foods and Humane Borders and SMoCA, the best contemporary art museum in the Southwest. It was also the headquarters of Taser

International Corporation, world leader in the design and production of electro-torture devices. Still, Scottsdale was a haven for people wealthy enough to pursue ideals beyond money. How could they live in a county where jail inmates are routinely tortured? To the people of Scottsdale, Arpaio's tent city was "regrettable" in the same way as African genocide.

Driving back to the Ramada, Catt tries to make sense of the day's events. Craig's fee was three times higher than Bucknell's, unless Bucknell took it to trial, which he gave every indication of wanting to do. If Craig's fee was inclusive, surely it was in his best interest *not* to take it to trial? Which meant, *it all comes down to the plea.* Part of these $35K retainers must go toward political contributions ... he wasn't spending it all on good art and Evian. Some of her money would go towards the reelection of Sheriff Joe Arpaio. Glimpsing the nauseating architecture of the status quo, she pleads with herself: in a corrupt world, wasn't enlisting corruption in your favor the right thing to do?

The whole train of thought was exhausting. For the rest of the evening, she hides out in the motel.

When Paul calls at nine she's already asleep. This time he has it together. *What did you have for dinner? Catt, did you remember to eat?* Helpless in jail, he wants to turn things around, be her protector. She remembers the things he told her about prison. How you have to stay strong, maintain respect ... a protocol observed by those who are debased and treated like shit.

Paul can hardly believe she's coming to see him. Visiting hours are from three to five. He has nothing, no commissary— can she bring him some stuff? He's allowed three pairs of boxers, three t-shirts, three pairs of socks. Everything has to be white. Each set needs to be factory-sealed in clear plastic. The robot voice interrupts before he can explain the rules about tooth-paste. *You have one minute left—goodbye.*

At the Globe Wal-Mart the next day she gets confused looking at underwear packages. The white boxers came only in family-sized four packs, all the singles were patterned or colored, but the limit was *three*. Stupefied by this dilemma, she stands alone in the aisle and then finally goes with the four pack.

Catt is still wearing the same sleeveless dress she put on before leaving Campo La Jolla. She browses the children's department and chooses a plain cotton skirt in fat-girl's 16—same size as a women's 6, but ten dollars less—and an organic cotton Save the Whales t-shirt. She needs her hair off her face, but the ponytail bands come only on maxi-sized cards, $5.99, so she slips one onto her wrist. Back in the truck, she changes her clothes and puts on lip gloss.

Set at the end of I-60, Globe is a bereft desert town. Even the Wal-Mart is too small: it's a rebranded K-Mart or Ames, its parking lot only twice the size of the store. Twisting her damp hair into a knot, Catt wonders who gave the town this Eliza-bethan name. Were they thinking of celestial orbs? Or Shakespeare's Globe Theatre?

Not even ten a.m. and the temperature outside the car is 104. Catt starts the truck and searches for NPR … sixty miles east of Scottsdale, *All Things Considered* can barely be heard over *Bible Talk* at the 89.5 spot on the dial. *I'm Melissa Black. And I'm Robert Segal.* This Saturday morning, Melissa and Bob are engaged in a semantic debate about how to describe the freakishly hot month of June spread across the US in 2006. Is it a heat wave, or heat storm? Sold out of air conditioners, Home Depots in Oregon await new shipments of fans. In California, bodies of the elderly poor are being removed from sweltering single-wide trailers. *Robert, a heat wave is a prolonged period of hot weather accompanied by high humidity. The longest heat wave was recorded in Western Australia in 1923 when temperatures exceeded a hundred degrees for 160 consecutive days—That's right, Melissa, but a heat* storm *is characterized by continuous heat, temperatures remaining high overnight—*

"Heat wave"—the phrase used by Fox News on the flat screen in the Ramada lobby—conjured ice cream and childhood beach days, whereas "heat storm" was more troubling, evoking the end of the world or plague portents. The difference between the two words was similar to the difference between "abuse" and "torture" … the simplest words subject to endless redefinition, each debate spiraling further away from the thing these words referred to. George W. Bush didn't need the Supreme Court to stop the electoral recount in 2000. He'd already won when Melissa and Robert started chattering about chads. *And Robert, what is a chad? Well, Melissa, a chad is the impression made on a cardboard ballot by a voting machine. It can be hanging, or pregnant, or even dimpled …*

Catt remembers how, on the TV talk shows from her childhood, the really smart people like would leap in and say: *I disagree with the question.* The content hadn't been binarized yet to multiple-choice. *Click here to learn more. For your protection, this call is being recorded and monitored.* Disagreement is not on the menu. It's no longer a choice.

Chris Kraus / 213

Except for his cellmates, Paul finds the Clifton jail nice and quiet, compared to others he's been in. The place is too small to serve institutional food. Twice a day, an old Mexican lady brings them delicious homemade burritos and stews. It's like the Twilight Zone here. From the concrete pad they go to for yard, he can see palm trees through the fence, and an old metal bridge over a river.

Still, there's plenty of time for Paul to think about what he is feeling: guilt, sometimes, but mostly boredom. He'd been so smooth, disclosing his "colorful past" that day in the park. Now he was dragging Catt down to the same shitty place he'd come from. What will she think when she sees him in jail? Counting the night in the tank, he's been here three days ... days they'll subtract from his new prison sentence—but he can't let his thoughts move that way. He looks like a beast. They have not let him shave. He has to be careful, not say anything wrong, when Catt comes to visit. She'll be gone before he can think of taking it back. But if the visit goes well, that's even worse. After that, there's nothing else to look forward to. The person is gone, and you're still behind bars.

Classes are starting on Monday and there's not *one thing* he can do except wait. Still, he'd better chill out because from here things will only get worse.

The young white guard doesn't respond to Catt's joke about dithering over the underwear packs. *Place your items here on the desk.* Funny how everyone now says "items" instead of just "things." *Items, incident, stated* ... it's the language of the police, turning the subject into a *suspect.* Titus and Sharon fully embraced it: the deadbeat tenant "stated" she'd mailed her rent check, leaving "various personal items" behind when she skipped out. The underclass mantra: My Life Sucks and So Should Yours. The guard rips open the family pack of white boxers and throws the fourth pair in the trash. He won't accept the Freud case study book she bought for Paul at the Scottsdale Borders, but he accepts Zora Neale Hurston's *Their Eyes Were Watching God*, perhaps because of the title. Then he tells her to wait.

In the lobby, the brown and orange tiled walls are covered with sheriff's department memorabilia: Fourth of July picnics, retirement dinners, a 1980 Arizona Association of Architects Merit Award. Built with federal funds, the jail was the newest building in town. Despite its small size, it has satellite towers, stadium lights, surveillance equipment, an electrified twenty-foot fence, and a fleet of new sheriff's department SUV Blazers. Landscaping consisted of a giant American flag on a fifty-foot pole. Catt feels dirty and shamed here.

A second guard walks her through metal-check and into the room with the visiting booths. He opens Booth 5, and she sits on a chair in front of a bulletproof screen. After awhile, another guard opens the door on the opposite side. Standing out in the hall, Paul holds his cuffed hands in front of his chest. The guard removes the restraints without looking at Paul and locks him into the booth. She had not pictured this. Paul gestures for Catt to pick up the handset.

"Kitten, don't cry."

The booth is the same thing she's seen on TV hundreds of times, but it's worse than she'd ever imagined. Paul was already in jail. Why did they have to bring him into the booth wearing handcuffs? She feels suspect and tainted even though she's on the free side of the wall. And the orange jumpsuit! Hard to match the person she knows with the inmate on the other side of the glass.

"How was the drive?"

"Uneventful." She cracks half a smile.

She's sniffling, still. Paul can't read her face. "Catt. Listen to me. I know you don't want me to talk about why I got arrested. You probably got that from Hank. But I need you to know: the warrant they have? It wasn't supposed to exist. It was supposed to be over. If I thought there was even a one-percent chance it would ever come up, I would have told you." This is awful. He's dragged everyone down with his shit.

"So that's it. I won't say anything else about it. But what's amazing to me is, you're *here*. 'Cause I've been thinking about this. You know how they say *being in jail gives you time to think*? For a long time, I promised myself I wouldn't trust anyone. Even after we met. But that's changed. What you've done for me is amazing. No matter what happens now, for the first time in my life, I can *trust* someone."

Catt feels like she's in the wrong movie. How did she get here? A jailhouse declaration of love ... and maybe it's all part of Paul's hustle, but in her heart, she doesn't think so. Really, she's touched.

"How's little Stretch?"

"He's a trouper. He's holding up."

Paul puts his palms on the glass. She places hers next to his and emits a sad laugh. "Paul, this is so *cliché*!" But, also, real.

"I've been talking to lawyers. I think I've found someone good—a friend of a friend of Bettina's. But it's going to be really expensive—he wants $35,000 as a retainer."

"That's *outrageous*. No. Find someone cheaper."

"Paul they *all* charge a flat rate ..." Why is she telling him this? Paul is so naïve. Even Hank doesn't know what to do.

"It's not right, Catt, just forget it. I'll go with the public defender."

"Don't do anything yet. You need to sit tight—"

The guard opens Paul's door. *Another five minutes.* For the rest of the time they lean their heads against the glass. Then the guard returns, and Paul stands up to hold out his arms for the cuffs.

Craig Durbin calls just as Catt's pulling into the Rode Inn Motel. He wants to know if she's made a decision. While he reprises his pitch, Catt paces the lot. *We'll start off keeping things cool ... fast extradition, low bail ...* Since watching the guard cuff Paul's hands, it's like she's crossed into another country. He was compliant, nonviolent ... the gesture was so gratuitous, also so cold, as if Paul were a thing. She's read all the books about symbolic violence, soft forms of control, she's even taught them—but observing this small routine humiliation made her feel the same way as looking at Holocaust photos when she was twelve. As if she'd crossed a line. She could no longer look at another person without thinking, *I know this, you don't.* But how, and to who, could she ever explain this? When Craig finally stops, she says yes. Like her, he's someone freely walking around who knows what goes on, on the other side of the glass.

"That's great, Ms. Dunlop—can I call you Catt?—I think you'll find you've made the right decision. And while previous litigation does not guarantee future results—"

"Yes, I know."

"I can almost guarantee getting him out on low bail. But first things first: someone from my office will be phoning Clifton at least three times a day to find out when he's going to be moved. We'll find out before the DA, and we'll be waiting. I'm going to try and fix things so he's arraigned as soon as he gets off the van, because believe me, Catt, you would not want him spending even one night in that shithole."

Still pacing the lot, her grief already channeled into proactive steps, Catt wonders if one can maintain a visceral knowledge of horror and combat it at the same time? Because they require such different energies.

"So this evening, I'll phone Mr. Garcia. And then there's the, uh, '81 Nissan? It's been impounded."

"Oh right. The *car*."

"You might want to see about getting it out, because they have also his seized his effects. A laptop, a briefcase with $6,300 cash—"

"Those were my rents."

"So you'll be wanting that back. I talked to the assistant DA, she's all over the fugitive warrant thing, but she does not seem to have the first clue that he's on parole. So that's good. Another plus is, this happened *nine years ago*. With any luck, the evidence has been destroyed. I'll need to talk to the victim of course, but that's no sweat—he's right here in town."

"So he's alive!" Just yesterday, before she'd paid, Craig implied that the victim had died.

"Believe me, they wouldn't have let the warrant sit around all these years if it was fatal. He was injured, how bad yet, I don't know, we'll subpoena the medical records."

Okay, Craig conned her; that was part of his job. But she's shocked that the only relief she feels about the victim's survival is, *this gives us a better chance at beating the charges.*

Doug's Impound & Tow—a junkyard and trailer-home two miles from Safford—isn't easy to find. But when Catt finally meets Doug the next day, she's relieved: compared to the guards at the jail, he's so friendly.

"You're the lady here for the ZX? It's been here since late Tuesday night. Not a bad little car."

Doug gives her some papers to sign and looks at the plates on her truck.

"Out here from California? You've come a long way."

"Yeah. It wasn't exactly planned." And then she tells him about Paul's arrest, the extradition, no bail, the borrowed truck, she'll take Paul's effects but *please*, can he just hold on to the car?

"Yeah, no sweat. I've got plenty of room here in the yard. Damned if I know why they're holding your friend. It's not like he's dangerous. He seems like a regular guy."

"And he's supposed to be going to school!"

"I tell you one thing, the warden's been thinking about letting him go. I've got friends working over there at the jail, and from what I've heard, nobody here wants to keep him that long. Maricopa's the one with the warrant. It's happened before. Greenlee picks somebody up, and then Maricopa just takes its time about sending the van. Meanwhile who foots the bill? Taxpayers here. What I hear is, if Phoenix can't get its act together soon, the warden just might cut him loose. Right to a speedy trial, it's the American way. Costs five hundred a day keeping somebody here."

She lets herself hope.

After that, there was a hot springs, and also a restaurant. "The first thing that stood out was the palms," she'd written that day. "Tall sensuous palms fed by a spring, behind the motel and in some of the yards around town. The palm trees felt like a gift." There were also Australian ferns. Back in NPR range, President Bush tells a sweltering nation, "I have my own plan for global warming." In the restaurant she ordered a salad, but the waitress would not let her eat it outside. Somewhere that day, she lost the blue notebook. Another six thousand National Guardsmen dispatched to the Mexican border instead of Iraq.

Years later, decoding her death wish, Catt will research the town. She'll discover that Clifton had been the scene of a bloody copper-mine strike two decades before. When its unionized workers voted to strike, Phelps-Dodge shut down the mines and hired replacements, once known as "scabs." State riot police marched over the hills. When someone yelled, "Get the fuck out of my town," the police opened fire. It would still be another few years before the Supreme Court overturned the Right to Strike law, but as one historian wrote, "American labor history ended on the desolate highway to Clifton in 1984." When she reads this quote to Paul, he'll be perplexed. "Why shouldn't a company have the right to hire whoever it wants?" He doesn't know what a trade union is. She'll try to connect this to the events around Paul's arrest, but she'll fail. The words are too heavy because they refer to things that no longer exist.

Driving back on I-10 outside of Tucson, this evening's orange terror alert is really an ICE Special Op. They're rounding up more illegal crossers. Armed Border Patrol and National Guardsmen line the freeway with searchlights and speakers. Their white trucks are the same as the ones used by Animal Control, but instead of small cages they have one tiny door at the back. *I'm Melissa Bloch. And I'm Robert Segal, and this is All Things Considered.* Slowing down in the westbound lane, Catt watches five National Guardsmen flushing a terrified man out from behind desert rocks.

11

SAFE

BACK IN LA, CATT finds herself walking on eggshells, as if she were the one who'd been let out of jail. It's too hot to work in her office; it's too hot to stay in the house. She spends most of her days sitting under an overgrown thicket of trees behind a friend's Elysian Park house. Her life in LA seems like a parallel world. When friends try to pull her back in she tries to respond in appropriate ways but their words hang in the air as if she'd suffered a stroke.

Years later, the Mar Vista analyst will ask her to *look for the link between Paul's experience and your own* and she'll be stumped. Abjection implies a descent. In order to suffer this degradation, doesn't the subject first have to *exist*? Sitting under the trees, she eats chocolate chip cookies, tries to read Rilke, and watches small tribes of white cabbage moths flit around in the dust.

Dearest Catt, Paul writes from Clifton …

I hope this letter finds you doing all right. The pen that they give you to write with here is bendable and flexable. It is hard to get a good grip because it's so thin so if my writing seems kinda weird, that's why. I was hesitant to write a letter because it kinda makes things real; me being here, that is. It gives it some weight and makes me feel like I really am here. But I know you would like it. I know I can't talk about the case on the phone so it's safe to assume I shouldn't write about it.

I will say, though, that this was definitely supposed to have been a non-issue, long ago, or I would have been much more concerned and told you about everything. Everything. So this is like a kick to the groin. I can just imagine what it's doing to you. I am so sorry that you are having to go through all of this. If I could I would take it all away quickly. Right now my nosey little cellmate has gotten out of bed and is watching me so I'll write more later—

Alright I'm back. So it's Monday now and of course I'm anxious for it to be Tuesday morning so I can call you and maybe get a better idea of things. It's such a bummer in here. No one to talk to. Here's an example of the intellect in here: Eddie my cellmate just produced a loud fart. He said: "If it starts can I ride it?" And then: "Ohhh that's a blowhorn." But you brought me that book by Zora Neale Hurston and I'm about halfway through it. Oh Catt, oh. You are amazing. The other guy Mikey is on so much medication he literally sleeps eighteen to twenty hours a day. He said that he's had two doctors over the time he's been here (since February) giving him two different combinations of meds. One would raise them, and then the other would double his perscriptions to match. Now its like triple what it was when they started. I guess he's mentally ill. And Eddie just won't shut up, he just keeps talking even if no one's listening. He says he wrote, or is writing, a book about a serial killer. I wish they'd medicate him, laughing hysterically at his own meaningless jokes.

All right enough about these guys. I'm happy about the trust thing. I can't believe it, but you have succeeded in gaining my trust. I told myself a long time ago that I'd never trust anyone again. But you know what? It feels very good. I can't wait for the day when I can be with you again. I can't wait to go camping and hiking with you and Stretch. I was really looking forward to being with you this summer. Hopefully we can figure out a way to still be together. You're my favorite person. Well, I'm gonna try to keep my chin up on this end and you do the same on that end, 'k? It's about ten right now and I'll be talking to you in a couple of hours. I love you. I love you a lot.

Paul

On Friday, January 27, 1995, Detective Dave Yennie of the Phoenix Police Department wrote:

On 01-26-95 at approximately 2104 hours I responded to assist in the investigation of an injury hit and run collision that had occurred on McClintock and Curry.

Tempe Traffic Supervisor TOM STUBBS advised me that a motorcyclist had been traveling in a southbound direction when a vehicle attempted to make a left hand turn from northbound McClintock to westbound Curry Road, failing to yield to the motorcyclist, causing the two vehicles to collide. After the collision occurred, the vehicle which was attempting its left turn left the scene. The driver of the motorcycle was identified as JUDD MASON PLATZ.

I was contacted by SERGEANT STUBBS of the Tempe Police Department and learned that the injuries MR. PLATZ received in the collision were a broken right arm, broken right leg, and a broken pelvis. MR. PLATZ also had a laceration on his forehead.

There were several witnesses including one SCOTT J. CARBONE. MR. CARBONE witnessed the collision and had, in fact, followed the suspect vehicle, a Dodge Intrepid, New Mexico license plate 340 GRP ...

As soon as Paul put his foot on the gas, it's like the channel has switched. The crash is close at his back, like a killer or ghost. Streetlights arc overhead. He has to get out of there fast, he has to get rid of the car. He pulls into a gym thinking he'll ditch it there in the lot, but two guys standing outside watch him get out of the car. He's already been seen. He changes his mind and drives on. And how will he get back to the hotel once he ditches the car? He has to call Bill ... Bill Hernandez works with him at KleanTech and they're sharing a room at the Wyndham. Pulling into a Circle K to get change for the phone, he sees the smashed front of the Dodge, streaked with red paint or blood. He pushes a dangling headlight back in. What if somebody sees? He gets back in the car and drives another half mile to an apartment complex set back from the road.

Whispering Palms ... He parks head-in at the edge of the lot and knocks on one of the doors. By now he's pretty shook up. The woman inside cracks it an inch and asks: *Who is it? What's wrong?* The only thing he can think of to say is, *Someone's just stolen my car.* The woman is so sympathetic he continues the story when Bill answers the phone. He was at the Circle K, he left the key in the car, someone got in and drove off. But he can't stay in the apartment so he tells Bill he'll wait at the Circle K.

Walking back on the side of the busy road, Paul is amazed he's still free. But the first thing Bill asks when he arrives is, *Did you call the police?* Now he has to call 911. When the dispatcher asks, *Are you calling to report a life-threatening emergency?* he remembers the crash, doesn't know what to answer. Calmly, Bill takes the phone and reports the theft. Thirty minutes later, the cops still haven't arrived. Tired of waiting, they decide to go back to the room. Bill goes to sleep, but Paul knows the cops might show up any time. For insurance, he drinks a quart of Jim Beam. If the cops find him smashed, they won't link him with the crash, because he was too drunk to drive.

Meanwhile, the Tempe police have traced the Intrepid to the Thrifty Rent-a-Car office where it was leased by Paul's employer. They've found the wrecked, blood-streaked car outside the Whispering Palms. They've learned from Paul's boss that he's at the Wyndham and written a warrant. At three-thirty a.m., eight cops show up at the door. Still drunk, Paul has the presence of mind to give nothing except his identification.

At the station they let him call Dylan before he's locked in a cell.

Three days pass. The prints that the Tempe police took from the headlight—the only hard evidence linking Paul to the crash—were misplaced. Without them the DA cannot build a case. The file remained open, but they released him.

Sober, Paul found himself in the street. He couldn't go back to the job but he had $2,500 left in the bank. At first, he crashed with Dylan. When Dylan asked him to leave, he bought a used 250cc Honda bike and rented a room in a house with some people he didn't know. He still had enough left to buy food, beer, and drugs.

At the new house, everyone was on meth and soon things got strange. One day, coming down, one of the girls unzipped his jeans and started sucking his cock. After he came she expected him to fuck, but he couldn't, so she called 911 and reported a rape. Two cops showed up but the girl was so wrecked they didn't want to file charges. There was semen all over his jeans but they didn't even ask for ID. "Just tell us you were just jerking off," they pleaded.

Paul understood that as a sign to leave town. Back in Albuquerque, his parents were getting divorced. Off her meds and sick with diabetic gangrene, his mom was alone in the old family house. Someone had to take care of her now. Since Paul was the only one of his siblings who didn't have kids, he moved in. The weeks of her final illness gave him a peaceful respite. His mom was too weak to give him much shit. Cashing her SSI checks, he settled into an easy routine of clinic appointments and pharmacy trips and fixing meals. He drank whatever was left. His life was so mellow now, he rarely used crack. Thus settled, he gave his address to the DA in Phoenix.

The first summons arrived in mid-March. His 250cc had long since been sold, so he caught the bus. In court, they told him the case was postponed, so he took the bus back.

In April, he was summoned again. This time he borrowed a suit, hoping the case would finally be closed. The bus trip took eleven hours each way. But the case was postponed because Tempe still hadn't located the prints.

The third summons found him in worse shape, with barely enough for the bus. Still no prints: the case was postponed once again. This time he slept in the park, because he was no longer welcome at Dylan's.

When Paul's mother died, the SSI checks stopped. She had no assets except for the house, which Pam and Joey—the most functional of her six offspring—decided to fix up and sell. Providing Paul worked on the house, they'd let him stay until it sold. This was a jolt. Who'd been feeding their mom, who'd been cleaning her shit all these months? Now they were throwing him out like a dog.

Paul was broke when a summons arrived on August 18. Given their treatment of him, he couldn't ask Joey or Pam for a loan, so this time, he did not go to Phoenix.

Sometime after that, the federal marshals arrived with a warrant while he was building a fence. The judge gave him two days to post $25,000 bail.

This time he had to call Joey and Pam. If he didn't post bail, he'd be sent back to Maricopa, for who knows how long? But none of his siblings had that kind of cash. Pam was in school. His mom's house still hadn't sold, and they were only expecting $18,000 to split when it did. Pam—who felt guilty about leaving Paul to care for their mom—begged Joey to sign over his house for the bond.

Released with $5.65, Paul couldn't pay for a cab. So he bought a pint of Jim Beam and he walked. Things continued that way until his mother's house sold. And then they got worse, because he had nowhere to go.

He didn't take anything with him. He just walked. By now it was fall. Nights were cold. He slept mostly in parks. During the day, he walked around looking for work. Sometimes he'd make twenty dollars, which he would use to buy beer. Chinese buffets and Chuck E. Cheese were good places for scavenging food, although he sometimes resorted to dumpsters. He tried to keep to himself, but there were always other people around.

After a few weeks, his blisters filled up with pus and he couldn't walk anymore.

His aunt Jane took him in. Catching up on the family news, he learned Joey's house had been released from the bond, so he assumed that the case had been dropped. When his foot healed, he got a fast-food job and moved to a trailer outside of town. He bought a used Corolla. He was more or less clean. Summonses arrived at his mother's old house, and the new owners threw them away or sent them back.

After a while he drifted back into crack and took $200 from the night's close at the restaurant. The next day the manager told him they wouldn't need him any more. Days, maybe weeks, passed, but one afternoon driving home with his dogs, he saw a sheriff's car outside his trailer. He never went back.

Farmington was the only place Paul could think to go because his sister Renee was living there. Renee would not take him in, so he slept with the dogs in the car.

Fast-food jobs were easy to find in Farmington, because everyone worked in the fields. Soon he had three. In a few weeks he'd saved up enough to rent an old single-wide in a small country park. He had no phone, no ID. No one knew he was there. The only loose thread was the car, which, since he'd stopped making payments, was technically hot. One night he ditched the car in the hills and took off the plates. Now he was clear. He almost relaxed.

Two years after the crash, the Tempe police located Paul's prints. Finally the case was ready for trial. A flurry of registered letters went to Paul's old address. A fugitive warrant was filed when they came back unanswered.

In Clifton, Mike is pacing the cell like an autistic child because somebody mixed up his meds. Each time he reaches the door, he bangs his head on the glass and screams, *I want the judge!* Eddie drumrolls with his fists, braying with laughter.

The cell is like a locked ward. When the guard, Madera, brings lunch he gives Paul a complicit look. Paul knows not to talk to the guards but this seems like a chance. Very polite, he asks if there's any place to buy stamps. *Sure bro, I'll take you down there.* They do the thing with the cuffs, but then Madera catches Paul's eye and says, *You know, the warden's been thinking he might let you go.* Paul's heart leaps. He keeps his voice flat: *Oh yeah?* Madera gives him a smile. *Yeah man. I heard him today on the phone. If Maricopa don't send up the van soon, he just might cut you loose.*

For the rest of the day Paul keeps his eyes on the door. Someone comes in with new meds for Mike, then another guard takes them to yard. Paul keeps his mouth shut when Madera brings in the dinner at five, but he's all friendly again. *Garcia, what's up? You still in this joint? Ya know, tomorrow might be the day. Hang tight.*

The next day—the second day of classes at UCLA—Paul is too anxious to read. No sign of Madera—maybe he's off. Whenever the warden walks past the door he wants to shout, *Look! I'm still here! Taking up valuable room.*

By Wednesday Paul thinks his heart will explode. He's been here a week. How long can they keep him like this? But as long as the van doesn't come, there's still some small hope of being released. Madera's on duty that night and Paul wants to ask him for news but the guard's face is blank.

Craig Durbin calls Catt that night in LA at six, just as she's walking into a Chinatown opening. He's just found out that Paul will be moving to Maricopa. "No, it's good news," Craig insists. "We've got it covered. I know for a fact the judge working that shift is going to be *very* receptive to our request for low bail. Now, he's going to have to go through the motions, stipulate that Paul stay in the county until trial. But as soon as he grants the request, I'll hand him a second petition, which he'll move to the top of the list. We'll put Paul in a hotel overnight, he'll see the judge Friday morning, then he'll fly back to LA."

Craig asks permission to put another $5K on her card. "Bail and hotel, Angie will book him a room. Court clothes, some incidentals. When he gets out of that hole, he might be in pretty bad shape."

At two thirty a.m. the cell lights snap on. *Garcia Get Up, Get Dressed, You're Moving.* Half blind, Paul gropes around for his glasses and staggers up in his shorts. *Do It Now.* Eddie's awake and watching all this. Paul's hands are shaking so much he can hardly get into the suit, but the guard is waving the cuffs. *That's Right. Step Forward. Arms Up.* The guard leads him out of the cell and into a room he hasn't been in before. No windows, some lockers, a bench, and another guard—it's Madera—undoing a set of restraints. *Arms Out,* Madera barks, as if he's never seen Paul before. The white guard holds Paul in place while Madera loops a twenty-pound belly chain around his waist. The lights are too bright. He blinks. Already he wishes he were back in the cell. The white guard cuffs his legs. Madera adds weights and then places a black metal bar in between them. *Palms Flat. Open*

Wide. They're rigging some chains to a new set of cuffs on his arms and then Madera locks a black metal box between his hands. His elbows are bent. The black box is twelve inches wide. Now he can't move his fingers or even his wrists. The guards say *Move* and for a moment he can't. Arms straight ahead, he stumbles between the two guards with his legs weighted.

Outside: a van and two other guards with Tasers in front of their guns. The four guards have to practically lift Paul onto the seat, where there's one other guy, really a kid, wearing the same black box, same rig. For the next two hours, until they unload him outside a vast prison, the kid talks nonstop. He doesn't shut up. Since they left Clifton, Paul had been hoping for this, but now that it's quiet all he can feel is the bright tingle of pain coursing between his hands. Outside it's dark ... and then hazy. Then light.

At the Fourth Avenue Jail in downtown Phoenix, the van drives underground. *Opened in 2005, this state-of-the-art facility is considered one of the most secure and technologically advanced in the nation.* Unloaded, he's led through an electronic door into a hallway. More buzzers and beeps, and a second door opens to Processing 1: an 8' x 8' windowless room, no bench, eight or nine guys who've also been up all night leaning up against walls. *Designed with the interest of public safety, the Fourth Avenue Jail has a capacity of 2,064 beds, of which 288 are specifically designed to house the highest-security level inmate.* The door slides shut behind him. Finally the guards remove his restraints, and there's even a spot on the wall for him to lean on, but the room starts filling up fast. Soon all the standing-up spaces are taken. The newer guys sit on the floor and the air is so heavy and close he starts to measure his breaths. He's not sure if he can stand this, but the next time the door opens the guard says, *Remove All Your Clothes.* And then everyone's banging around, peeling off jumpsuits and shorts until they're all standing naked. By the time the uniform trolley arrives, Paul is almost relieved to put on a pair of pink boxers, a pair of striped black and white pants, and a tunic that's stenciled *Property of Sheriff Joe Arpaio* on both sides. After all the high-tech, the sight of everyone stepping into these clothes seems almost funny, except he can't breathe. Also, there's no toilet here and he needs to pee.

Before the last guy is even dressed, a new guard steps in and calls, *Garcia!* Fuck this is weird, why are they calling him now? He was the tenth to arrive. *Arms out.* The cuffs match the shorts—bright fuschia pink—and he's led to a door labeled Processing 5. This room has a clock. Fingerprints, retinal scan, number assigned. After the photos the guards bring him to Holding, another windowless room, slightly bigger than Processing 1 but inside it there's forty-five guys. He sits on the floor. Everyone's talking, some are filling him in: no meals until they're assigned to a cell. A few of the guys have been here two days … who knows how long that will be? When a guard calls his name, Paul looks for *another* Garcia—he was the last to arrive, it can't be him—but no one steps forward.

In Classification, they chain him to a bench in front of a desk. A long list of questions. *Prior Incarcerations?* Paul answers yes. They assign him to Maximum Security, Ward 6-B … a long walk through a series of ramps, halls, and electronic doors ends at a room stacked with cages and ramps.

Paul's cage has four bunks. Two black guys and one Mexican kid on a top bunk—Paul guesses the black guys are running things here. One of the black guys is crashed out facedown on his bunk, either high or on heavy meds. The older guy, Horace, welcomes Paul to the cell and points to the empty top bunk. The guy's nice, but nosey. He wants to know where Paul is from, if he's been to court yet. He wants to know what Paul needs. Paul hasn't figured the system out yet, but he knows this isn't good. Before Paul can stop him, Horace reaches under his bunk and hands Paul a bar of green soap: *I think you're gonna want this later on—No man, I'm cool—No, you'd better take it.* Fuck. He's only been here ten minutes and he already *owes* Horace, for what? A thirty-three cent bar of soap?

Paul is still wondering how this will play out when a guard calls his name. *Garcia Get Down. You're Being Arraigned.*

Court is another windowless room, with sixty guys cuffed to steel benches in front of a judge. The old white guy in robes holding a gavel looks like he's been airlifted in from another channel, talking to a tall good-looking guy in a suit. Before the guards can lock him down on the bench, the suit-guy gives them a nod, and the guards walk him straight to the judge's desk. *Bail Is Granted.* The guy in the suit—Craig Durbin—shakes his hand. Paul's too confused to ask questions, but he guesses this means he can leave. Instead, the guards walk him back to 6-B.

Hunnnngh, Horace howls, *Sounds like they've misplaced your file. Now what did you do to piss those guards off? Unless that smart lawyer of yours gets on the phone, you're gonna be here another forty-eight hours.*

Around five, the guards empty the cells on their tier for dinner. Long lines of guys file down the ramps to a big room, like a school cafeteria, with tables divided by race. Guards line the walls. Paul doesn't know what to do … there are no Others here. Horace sits with the blacks. Finally one of the Mexicans sees his nametag and says, *follow me*. Latinos take up more than two-thirds of the room. When the meal's over, they bang the table five times with their fists and stand up as one.

Processed out the next morning, the guards give Paul a big FedEx box—"from your lawyer"—with a beige linen suit, a white shirt, a wrapped cigar, a hotel reservation, an envelope full of cash, and Craig Durbin's card. Wearing the new clothes, he steps out into the blinding daylight and gets in a cab. He hands the driver the print-out of his reservation in Scottsdale, the Gainey Suites Inn. The fare is eighty-five dollars. Paul adds a large tip. Set at the end of a long circular drive, the Gainey Suites Inn is known for its eco-friendly design and excellent golf course. It attracts old-school Republicans, people who might not have necessarily voted for GWB in '04.

Solar-powered glass doors open onto reception. The girl at desk gives Paul a key card. The door to his room opens onto a kitchen, and beyond it, a huge king-sized bed with down pillows arranged like a puzzle. The white duvet is soft. Paul steps into the marble-tiled bath. The shower is hot. Sharp sluices of water massage his skin. He puts on a white terry robe. Vertiginous with a sense of complete reversibility, he steps onto the balcony, lights the cigar, and looks down to the black-bottomed pool.

12

ERASE

PAUL LEAVES PHOENIX just in time to start classes at UCLA.

For the rest of July, Catt forces herself to go to her office and work on a catalogue essay about postmodern architecture. Looking up definitions for terms like fenestration (rhymes with menstruation, and when's the last time she had a full period?) she cannot stop thinking about how obscenely rich she and everyone she knows in LA actually is. Fenestration: window in English; *fenêtre* in French; *finistri*, Italian. Irina (a role she once played) in Chekhov's *Three Sisters*—"Where is it? Where has it all gone? I can't even remember the Italian for window!" She writes:

In B.'s radical revisioning of site, fenestration, dimensionality, and texture combine to create an illusion of continuous space.

She checks and rechecks her email. An artist whose work she's reviewing wants to be sure she has it right:

I wanted to send you a couple of thoughts I had after you left the gallery. My project is of course rooted in language but it is also founded in the idea of codes. Specifically coded language. I have been thinking about this from the position of abstraction as a form of representation.

Paul quickly forgets the nightmare from which he's been saved. His anxiety shifts to the late August trial date and his UCLA grades. Whenever he talks about Phoenix, it's with contempt for Craig Durbin, the victim, and the DA. "It was an *accident* ... I was supposed to have put this shit behind me ... I've been sober three years!" Alone in her interiority, Catt wonders if ethics and Twelve-Step behaviorism aren't mutually exclusive. Contained as they are within a structural solipsism, aren't the concepts "addiction" and "recovery" falsely opposed?

At the end of the month, she flies out to Albuquerque to pick up the white truck. She finds the Dartmouth Road house littered with condoms and candles. Paul's cousin Mason has been using the place for afternoon trysts with his married girlfriend Janine. Meanwhile, half her tenants have moved out or stopped paying rent. In despair, she begs Paul to fire Mason— *Where do you think the money comes from to pay your tuition and lawyers? From renting apartments!*—but Paul refuses to do it. *He's my cousin! You're lucky he's willing to even deal with your shitholes. If you want Mason gone then tell him yourself.* But in order to do this she'd have to stay on in Albuquerque. Instead, she offers Janine fifteen dollars an hour to do Mason's job until she can think of a better solution.

All summer, the Arizona Border Patrol and National Guard target illegal crossers, arresting as many as two thousand a day. Catt's whole body tenses each time she hears someone using that word. *Why don't you call them what they are*, she has to stop herself shouting. *Economic refugees!* If it weren't for Monsanto and NAFTA, the migrants would still be at home growing coffee and maize.

The UCLA campus is larger than Paul imagined. He doesn't explore it. He's afraid to get lost. Each day he walks from his car to his classes with a ghost hanging over his shoulder. Will he be sent back to prison? That's the most likely outcome. So why is he wasting his time doing all of this work? All Catt wants to talk about is Arizona, Arpaio, the border. She's told all her friends about his arrest, which is embarrassing. At least when he's in school, no one asks any questions. It's not really that different here than at UNM. People show up, disperse for the breaks, and leave straight after their classes. Catt keeps asking if he's "made any friends," as if this were some hippy art school. He doesn't want to share homework or go out for coffee or whatever they do.

All summer, Catt writes down her dreams.

I'm with a serial killer. He's also a poet. He's decided to kill me after we've read a few poems. But he postpones. I try and talk my way out: If You Don't Kill Me Now We Could Read Another Bernadette Mayer Poem in the Morning. We argue. He tells me to go to bed and set my watch back an hour. I comply. In bed, I realize I could escape through the bathroom window—he's in the other room—but it's easier to lie in bed than to try climbing out. I realize I'm waiting for him to kill me.

At the end of July, Janine's husband, who is also Mason's best friend, discovers their Dartmouth Road meetings and fucks up her face. Now she can no longer show the apartments. Catt flies back out to hire a replacement. At Tulane, one of the tenants has skipped out and abandoned his dog and two cats. Three starving animals howl inside the now-empty apartment. Smells of urine and excrement waft through the vents. Catt wants them out, but Mason won't give her the keys: *Don't you know it's illegal to dispose of abandoned property? It's my ass on the line, my liability.* Instead, he calls the police.

Three squad cars arrive and six officers storm into the complex, their guns drawn and aimed at the door of Apartment 8-B.

This is the Albuquerque Police ... We are securing the scene ... You have ten seconds to exit the premises ... Arms raised over your head ...

Children gather to watch. When they break down the door, the dog barks, defending her ground, but the cats flee.

Paul finishes his classes in early August with a 3.8 GPA. He and Catt leave for a week to go camping in Baja. Even though he's now on bail as well as parole, they have no fear about crossing the border. On the beach they watch pelicans, dolphins, and whales cavort in the bay. For the first time all summer, Paul relaxes. Catt is happy. They write songs for the birds. Once the trial is behind him, Catt thinks, this is how it will be.

Summoned to court on August 18, Paul flies to Phoenix with Catt. They rent a car at the airport and check into the Gainey. The court date this month is not for a trial but for a "pre-trial conference," but it isn't even a conference because the DA is on leave. "All you need to do is show up," Craig advises.

Driving from Scottsdale to Phoenix, Catt stops counting American flags when she reaches a hundred. There are flag decals on trucks, flag buntings on buildings, flags over car lots and self-storage units, flags suspended from porches, flag poles in the yards of the small stucco houses. Paul is wearing a silk tie with his new Hugo Boss suit.

Waiting in the gallery, Catt studies the court's mise-en-scène. Far stage right: the detained defendants, chained to two benches. Stage right: their two public defenders. Both of these lawyers are frumpy and white. The straggled-haired woman wears J.C. Penney, her colleague—a morbidly obese man in his thirties—wears a brown jacket mismatched with brown pants. Because their caseloads are too heavy for briefcases, they use enormous wheeled trolleys to transport their files. Center stage left—a few feet nearer the judge than the public attorneys—the assistant DA sits with a colleague. The DA is almost shockingly butch, with cropped hair, a black pants suit, and a white button-down shirt. Upstage center left, Judge Sherry Levine presides over the scene. The judge is surprisingly pleasant, soft-spoken and intelligent, wearing a chiffon floral dress under her robe.

The detainees, of course, are miserable. Twelve men and a woman wearing striped black-and-white tunics, *Property of Sheriff Joe Arpaio*. Their hands are cuffed, their legs are connected by chains locked to the benches. They've been up and unfed since before dawn, being processed, prepared, and transported. Each suspect holds a beige folder of "paperwork" —charge sheets, police reports—between two cuffed hands. Still, the handcuffs permit movement and one teenaged inmate has used a jail pencil to color both sides of his folder with flowers and doves around a huge heart: *Miguel Loves Alicia*. Grinning, he occasionally raises the folder towards the blushing young woman in the first row of the gallery who must be Alicia. Everyone else stares at the floor. Paul is the only defendant this morning who sits in the gallery; the only one who's made bail.

As each new case is called, Catt observes that the leg unshackling-and-reshackling procedure takes only slightly less time than the hearings. While a bailiff reads out the charges— possession of crack cocaine, grand theft auto, receipt of stolen property, criminal mischief, dishonored checks—each prisoner stands in front of the judge, eyes looking down toward cuffed hands. Why are the prisoners cuffed? Catt remembers a *TV Guide* cover she'd seen as a child, a court drawing of Black Panther Bobby Seale shackled and chained to a chair in front of Judge Julius Hoffman. At the time, this was widely deemed *shocking*. Of course Seale was on *trial* in front of a jury, and these are just hearings. None of the inmates in Judge Sherry's court will ever be going to trial ... Instead, imprisoned but not yet convicted, they'll receive continuance after continuance until the DA finally arrives at a plea.

Paul doesn't look at the guys in the dock. He has to *stay positive*. Their sorry-ass plight reminds him how much he owes Catt. Blinking back tears she wonders, *can anyone locate the point where this present begins?* Before Abu Ghraib, before Guantanamo Bay... Was it the soft bans on public assembly? The laws against second-hand smoke, the DUI limit lowered to one glass of wine? Parks allowed to degrade until everyone wanted them closed, the defunding of public transportation, bottles of water that cost more than half the hourly minimum wage? *For quality and training purposes, this call is being recorded and monitored ...* the first clause now mostly eliminated because it is no longer necessary. Or did it begin with Over-Eaters or Co-Dependents or Debtors Anonymous? Imprisoned by credit-card debt while the banks raked in billions, those who weren't incarcerated Made a Decision to Turn Their Lives Over to God. Or what about, "Save Trees—Eliminate Paper"? But the questions lead nowhere, they just make her feel old.

Paul stands upright in front of Judge Sherry when his case is called. Craig speaks for a moment. The assistant DA asks for continuance. The judge hits her gavel and then they go home.

Enrolled in the Honors Program, Paul waits for the day he'll be exposed as a fraud or be sent back to prison. The classes are actually hard, and the case will not go away. Each month he's summoned for Trial Status, Postponement, Trial Management conferences—postponements, he thinks, of some darker fate. He flies out to Phoenix from Albuquerque and Catt joins him there from LA. That fall his friend Jayce goes back to prison when he's pulled over for speeding and the officer finds a half ounce of weed in the glovebox.

When Catt's short book on the Bloomsbury social reformers is published, she goes out on tour. Instead of a collar, she carries *The History of Western Philosophy* so she can help Paul with his homework and essays. Standing behind lecterns, she describes the utopian impulse: the personal cost of pursuing ideals that will always be flawed.

Paul phones her in Toronto, San Francisco, New York, and London to talk about Hobbes, Locke, and Hume, but she's at home in LA when he calls to talk about Amber.

Amber Reiss: twenty-seven, married with two little children, looks like a geek with her long braids and striped stockings, but she's totally cool. By far the most brilliant of the Honors students, Amber reminds Paul of Catt. Of course she's not as sophisticated, but on one of their study dates (Amber's been coming over to help Paul with Statistics) she threw down her books and said, *I can't do this, I can't think about math anymore because I'm so attracted to you!* Paul's, of course, flattered, but also confused. What does Catt think he should do?

Almost since they met, Catt has been waiting for this: not with dread, but with bright anticipation. Her project, if you could call it that, has been to encourage Paul's education so that, eventually, they would be equals. Except for Catt, Paul hasn't dated a woman when he wasn't fucked up on crack. Catt found her freedom when she moved to LA and abandoned her search for romance (i.e., her female masochism) for sexual friendships. Paul has no confidence, no experience, not even close friends—he's younger than her, and so dependent. If Amber's as smart as Paul says and she *intends to stay married*, who could it hurt if their friendship became sexual?

Catt meets Amber for lunch at an off-campus restaurant during her next trip to Albuquerque. Devoted to her two little girls, Amber would *never* do anything to jeopardize her marriage, or even think about coming between Paul and Catt. In her thrift-store print dress and furry cardigan sweater, Amber reminds Catt of herself in her late twenties. Although, with her two children and plans to do graduate study at Berkeley, Amber is much more advanced. Catt thinks about Susan Sontag and Mary McCarthy—great minds and young mothers. Maybe female accomplishment just skipped a few generations?

On their next court date in Phoenix, Paul gives Catt a beautiful ring. They vow to remain Permanent Boyfriend and Girlfriend but things change after that.

Amber and Paul discover they are twin souls.

Pregnant and married at 18, Amber's husband took her to live in Tel Aviv with his Orthodox family. At home all day while her husband studied software engineering, Amber realized she loathed him. When they returned to Albuquerque, she decided to leave but got pregnant again before her plans fell into place. She knows *exactly* how Paul felt being in prison: she's been in prison her entire adult life! Before meeting Paul, the only person Amber had ever slept with was her jailer, her creepy spouse. But now, during their afternoon meetings at the Dartmouth Road house, she experiences an Awakening, like the book they've been reading in Feminist Lit. Trapped in an ugly tract home with an insensitive mate, Amber needs Paul and Paul needs to be needed.

On the morning of Catt's next arrival in Albuquerque, Amber falls on the library steps. She can't reach her husband at work, she can't move her left wrist, and there's no one except Paul to take her to the hospital. Trusted to deal with this emergency, he can't meet Catt's plane and cannot understand why she's being so selfish and pissy about taking a cab. Is she too cheap to spend thirty bucks? She's rich. Grudgingly he turns off his cell for the rest of the weekend, but he's haunted by thoughts about Amber's wrist. Is she in pain? Is she trying to reach him?

This is going too far, Catt realizes when she changes her flight to slink home a day early. As soon as he drops Catt at the airport, Paul turns on his phone. His mailbox is full. When Amber arrives they fall into bed and she admits that she's literally dying of heartbreak. For her own self-respect, she needs to break up with Paul unless he ends things with Catt, but to do this would mean the end of her, Amber's, life.

Paul knows she means it. The skin under Amber's striped stockings and sweaters is crosshatched with scars. Paul has no idea how he'll stay in his house or pay for his lawyers, but his own survival is a less imminent crisis. *Alright*, he concedes, *I'll end it with Catt*.

But each time he gets ready to do it, he loses his nerve. He can't do it over the phone. *Yeh, yeh, it's cool*, he assures Amber when she asks him how Catt took the news.

In November, Catt books a stopover in Albuquerque for three days on her way home from a conference in France. This, to Amber, seems strange. Why would Catt choose to visit if she's really been dumped? Accidentally-on-purpose, she forgets her laptop is open to one of Paul's most passionate emails when her husband gets home from work. He throws her out of the house when he reads it. Alone in the street with just thirty-eight dollars, Amber calls Paul. He says she can stay at his house. One day before Catt's arrival, Amber's still there. There's no way he can tell Catt what happened so he gives Amber $1,200 to find her own apartment.

This time Paul looks at Catt with fresh eyes when he picks her up from the airport. Jetlagged and wearing an Agnes B jacket, she seems ruthless and brittle. She's just been to *France*—a country he's never been in, the birthplace of her ex, who was attending the *same conference*. For all he knows they slept in the same bed, and she acts as if nothing is *strange*? Amber won't even speak to her husband. She's ready to die for their love.

When Catt offers her face for a kiss he can't do it. Stunned by Paul's distance, she tries not to show it. She jabbers on about France, how gorgeous it is, how they'll go there together this summer when parole is finished. He tells her he's got a lot on his mind, the case hanging over his head, tons of schoolwork. He's taking things One Day at a Time.

Accustomed by now to his moods, Catt doesn't pursue it but when she goes into the bathroom at Dartmouth she shrivels as if she's been punched when she sees Amber's eye-glitter, face cream, and lip-gloss. *Is there something you'd like to say*, she asks when she finally emerges. *I don't know what you mean!* he shouts back. They go on like this until he's exhausted. "Catt. Little Kitten." He is Living a Life of Rigorous Honesty: "I can't lie to you any more. I don't know what to do because I like you so much, you'll always be my best friend. But I think I'm in love with Amber."

Why hadn't she known this? Catt's been so busy touring her book and thinking about Paul and his case that she's missed the most obvious fact. She wants to throw herself on the floor but how can she? She knew all along that Paul was not an adult. Paul is managing thirty-six units. She's about to begin the Midwest leg of her tour, there's no way she can stay here in Albuquerque. "Then I guess you'll have to decide. I mean it seems really shitty. But when we got together, I promised I'd keep the business stuff separate. And I'm not going back on it. So long as you do your job, you can keep working for me even if you start a new life with Amber."

To Paul, this is terrifying. He cannot imagine no longer being Catt's partner and mate, but her *employee*. "No Catt, that's wrong. I'll tell Amber it's over."

Each time he tries to give Amber the news, the conversation is preempted by crisis: custody threats, a dead cat, Amber's two wailing children. Until the divorce, Amber's husband won't give her a cent. She can't even buy groceries.

When Catt joins Paul in Phoenix for his next court date, she can't understand why he hasn't brought flowers or chocolate. It's Valentine's Day! Last year in Chicago, she'd practically wept when the deluxe bouquet assortment (a stuffed bear, a dozen red roses, a mug) arrived at her doorstep. When she complains, his protests turn vicious.

The next day in court, she's too stunned to notice the abject sight of the prisoners. Craig does his thing, bluffing to take it to trial when the DA offers them Felony 2 with up to a year of jail time. The judge sets a trial date. Jury selection will start May 19.

Until then, they'll return once a month for Trial Management Conferences.

I already told you: we broke up! Paul snarls whenever Catt asks about Amber. *And you made me do it!*

He's angry whenever they speak. She is bereft, but her days are crammed with new duties, commuting to Berkeley one day a week to teach a guest seminar. Paul is no longer the person she met. She's created a monster. But the chain of events set into motion when she hired Craig Durbin won't stop until the May trial date. There is nothing to do but *hang on and wait*. In a half-hearted effort to use this time wisely, she enters analysis. She still hopes the situation with Paul will improve after the trial. And if it doesn't, she's free. She considers possible ways to be old. Maybe rent an apartment in Paris? But until the case is resolved, there's no way to address it.

The only times she sees Paul for the rest of the year are in Phoenix for court dates. They stay in motels because she can no longer afford to pay for the Gainey. Paul remains sullen.

On these last trips, having given up knowing Paul, she tries to understand something about Phoenix: the fastest-growing American city, in the first years of the 21st century it eclipses LA as a futurist metaphor. She becomes obsessed with the accident victim, Judd Mason Platz, convinced there must be a *message*, a secret knowledge about American culture and class embedded within the visceral fact of their collision. She searches the files for his address: 10285 Sycamore Lane, Chandler.

On the night before the last Trial Management Conference, she leaves the motel alone to drive past it.

Incorporated in 1912, Chandler has effectively been absorbed within Phoenix's South Arizona Road business corridor. The

2001 construction of a 1.3 million foot mall spawned the construction of numerous housing developments. One of
these—the one where Judd Mason Platz purchased a home in
2003—is called Spanish Springs. Built by Lennair, the gated
community consists exclusively of stucco single-family resi-
dences ranging in size from two to three thousand square feet
and painted in neutral earth tones. Seventy-five percent white,
Spanish Springs's average household income is $100,000, thirty-
three percent higher than Chandler's overall median.

When Catt drives past Judd Mason Platz's house, she sees a
single patio light in the backyard behind the fence of the empty
driveway. Not counting its attached three-car garage, the house
looked to be about 2400 square feet. Its facade was sand-colored
stucco. Sycamore Lane ended in a circular cul-de-sac several
houses away, which were already dark at eleven on this
Wednesday night in mid-April. The accident must have changed
the lives of the residents of 10285 Sycamore Lane forever, but
there were no clues here as to how. The neighborhood felt like
a whisper.

"There's no way this case is going to trial," Judge Sherry
announced the first morning of jury selection. Since the state
passed a new bill making the use of false ID an unbailable
felony, the calendar's been backed up for a year. The state didn't
have enough translators. Bound to pass sentence on streams of
bewildered migrants, she'd applied for a transfer to family court
and was just holding her breath to get out of here.

"You," she told the DA, a tough blonde in her thirties, "are
going to have to work this out with the attorney. And you,"

turning to Craig, "are not going to waste this court's time anymore. That's not gonna play."

The DA is crushed. Twelve years after the accident, she's assembled the evidence. The victim Judd Mason Platz is here, and Detective Dave Yennie has been summoned from his Sun City retirement residence. She has paint chips and x-rays and two hundred pages of medical records. Large full-color charts, drawn to scale, depicting the moment of impact have been prepared by an accident reconstruction specialist.

Craig and the DA retreat to Judge Sherry's chambers. A few minutes later he returns with the DA's new improved plea: one year of unsupervised probation, no jail time; $5,000 restitution to the victim and they'll downgrade the charge to a misdemeanor.

"Five thousand dollars," Paul snarls in the hallway. "How am I supposed to come up with that? I thought the guy had insurance." Craig and Catt exchange troubled looks. Paul is talking about someone he left on the road with three broken bones in his legs, cracked ribs, and a fractured pelvis. Even Craig is appalled: "Mr. Garcia, if you don't take this plea now, I'm walking. You'll have to find someone else." But Catt sees that Paul's anger is really animal terror. Holding onto his arm, they walk down the hallway. "Paul. Don't you see? This is very good news. We *won*. In a few minutes all this will be over."

Paul doesn't feel like a winner, but he follows Craig and Catt into the courtroom to sign all the papers. Judge Sherry reads out the plea.

Do you understand what I have just said to you?
Do you agree to this charge?
Is there anything else you would like to say to this court?

Paul stands very straight. Judd Mason Platz, a fifty-six-year-old man wearing beige Costco slacks, overweight, not very athletic, sits between the DA and Detective Yennie. Everyone's looking at Paul, and he can't see Judd Mason's face, but he knows he's ashamed: ashamed to be back in court, ashamed of his life to this point, and of his new Ralph Lauren jacket.

"Your Honor, may I say something to the victim?"

"You may."

He finds himself holding back tears. Turning away from Judge Sherry, he looks straight at Judd Mason Platz, forcing himself not to see the DA or Yennie. "Mr. Platz. I'm very sorry. And I know this doesn't matter, after what you've been through it doesn't change anything, but I've thought about this every day for twelve years and I'm sorry. What I did was wrong. I have no excuses."

With the judge's permission, Judd Mason stands. "Mr. Garcia, I accept your apology. You know, for a long time I was out from work after the accident. I couldn't walk. I stayed home for three months, and about the only thing that kept me going then was thinking about how they were going to catch you. I still have a steel plate in my knee and, frankly, sometimes it gives me trouble. I came here expecting revenge. I wanted to see you behind bars. But if what your attorney says about you is true, if you've really reformed—well, that's rare. I hope you can keep it up. I wish you a good life in the future."

This is too much. Paul's eyes tear up and he lets out a sob. "Dismissed," Judge Sherry says, pounding her gavel, and everyone feels a weight lift. Never a fan of catharsis, Catt takes a last look at the detainees chained to the bench before leaving the room.

They put the full restitution on Catt's credit card and Paul registers for probation. Then they get in her car and drive back to Los Angeles.

As soon as they cross the state line, Catt's spirits lift. It's the beginning of summer. Her classes are over, and in a few days they'll drive down to Baja. By this time next year Paul will have his BA. They'll hire someone to manage the buildings in Albuquerque and he'll move to LA, sign up for grad school. Two or three years after that he'll be a therapist, maybe have his own private practice. They'll travel together. They'll reclaim her house from the tenants. She'll rip out the Himalayan bamboo and replant hibiscus. Now that the case is no longer hanging over his head, Paul will become sweet and attentive. They'll sing cowboy ballads again and sit on the beach watching the dolphins.

A black cloud follows Paul west. He does not want to stop. He wishes this could be over.

When they arrive at the compound, Catt's tenants are sitting outside drinking mimosas in front of a wall of white oleanders. Light streams into the kitchen of Catt's little house as she bustles around making iced tea with fresh mint. Paul is even more sullen. Each time she asks him what's wrong, a new set of muscles clenches. She moves towards his lap and he pushes her off.

"Catt, NO. There's something I've got to tell you. Shit, this is awful. I feel like I need a drink. You're such a good person. But if I want to stay sober, I can't keep on lying. Can't you see this isn't working? I like you a lot but I'm not in love. We need to break up. I just don't feel it."

"Are you back with Amber?"

"It never stopped."

Catt drives Paul to the airport. At first she's enraged, and then stunned. And then, finally, empty. She knows she won't trust anyone this way again. In the coming weeks, she will question her judgment and motives. She'll wear out her friends. She'll force herself to sit through a half-dozen Al-Anon meetings. When she finally stops weeping, she'll realize she no longer has to search for a killer. She's already been killed. But she isn't dead.

When Paul arrives back in Albuquerque, he'll move in with Amber. She'll be jealous whenever he leaves the house. There will be suicide threats, pills and razors all over the bedroom. He'll wonder, *what was I thinking?* They'll buy their groceries with food stamps. Three months later, he'll get in his truck to escape from the vortex.

Sponsor Mike lets him sleep on the couch and Mike is nice, but Farmington isn't his place any more, he's outgrown it. Determined not to go back to Amber, he waits several more days. Then he calls Catt. He still has her number.

Acknowledgments

I'm grateful to many friends who read this book in its early stages, and especially to Tamar Brott, Fred Dewey, Veronica Gonzalez, Fanny Howe, and Michael Tolkin for their detailed and helpful suggestions. Thanks to Robert Dewhurst for researching political events that have already receded into distant memory, to Sylvère Lotringer for his insight and continued support, and to my editor, Hedi El Kholti, for our ongoing collaboration. I'm grateful to Donna Leone Hamm and James Hamm for spending two days in Phoenix introducing me to their modest, heroic work with Middle Ground Prison Reform, an organization devoted to upholding the few legal rights of the incarcerated; and especially to Philip Valdez, my consultant and partner.

Partial proceeds from this book will be donated to Middle Ground Prison Reform.

About the Author

Chris Kraus is the author of the novels *Aliens and Anorexia, I Love Dick,* and *Torpor,* as well as *Video Green: Los Angeles Art and the Triumph of Nothingness* and *Where Art Belongs,* all published by Semiotext(e). A Professor of Writing at European Graduate School, she writes for various magazines and lives in Los Angeles.